TRIP OF FOOLS

MARTIN MAYER

Paperback ISBN: 978-1-61929-511-7
Hardback ISBN: 978-1-61929-513-1

Flashpoint Publications First Edition: July 1, 2023

Printed in the United States of America.

Cover design by TreeHouse Studio

www.flashpointpublications.com

Epigraph

"It's not what you look at that matters.
It's what you see."

–Henry David Thoreau

Chapter One

Get Out Of Town

"Don't worry about Ponce while you're gone. His routine won't be interrupted," Chuck Adams said, reassuring his partner.

"I know." Carl Minton kneeled, squeezed the dog's paw, and kissed him loudly on the dry part of his nose. "Goodbye, Poncie boy."

"I suppose I'll get a pat on the head," Chuck said with a grin.

The cab sounded its horn in the driveway. Carl stood, patted Chuck on the head, grabbed his suitcase, and left the house. He turned around and went back in. He hesitated, leaned over and kissed Chuck on the bridge of his nose.

A few minutes later, Carl's cab arrived in the parking lot of the Bovina Health Center, the health center where he sold most of his tour offerings. He paid the driver and stood back to look at the passengers milling about the bus.

The bus cast an enormous shadow in the early sunrise, looming huge like a skyscraper, dwarfing the waiting passengers. Something caught Carl's eye. He walked up to the bus and fingered the duct tape on the rear-most compartment. The bus looked like an old, retired battleship. Something had obviously hit the bus, and judging by the dirt fill along the scrape, the accident happened some time ago and had never been repaired. Shaking his head in dismay, Carl strolled over to greet each of his clients as they boarded the bus.

"Why are y'all late?" Sally Duran said as she greeted him.

"I'm not late. I told all y'all that the bus wouldn't arrive until seven thirty. It's only seven twenty-five. The bus is early, Sally."

"Well, you should be here just for security for the people who come early. You know we get here early so we can get the best seats."

"We're only going as far as New Orleans."

"So what? It's practically dark out. You should be here to make sure it's safe."

"What time would you suggest? Maybe I should bring a tent and sleep here in case somebody's really early."

"You don't have to get sarcastic with me. You know sarcasm is the last resort of the weak."

"No, I didn't know that. Where did you hear that one?"

"Never you mind. I'm standing here flappin' my jaws with you and my favorite seat's probably gone."

"Okay, up you go." Carl gently pushed the diminutive Sally onto the first step.

The next passenger, smiling, looked more chipper and friendly. "You know I've never flown before," Holly Saunders said as she approached the open doorway. At forty-nine years old, Holly was probably the youngest passenger on this tour.

"That's exciting, Holly," Carl said as he placed his arm on Holly's elbow to move her along into the bus. "There aren't any crashes or hijackings scheduled in the next few days," he muttered.

"What?" She turned toward Carl, eyes wide, looking down from the bus's steps.

"Nothing. Just try to relax and get some sleep on the flight so you feel good when we get to Rome tomorrow morning."

He turned to the next client. "Hello, Ann. Are you ready for this?"

"Of course, I'm ready," Ann Anderson answered gruffly. "I told you I've been to every country in the world. I've taken cruises to every country in the world. I told you that."

"How many countries are there, exactly?"

"Well, it's at least thirty."

"I would say so. And how did you get to the ones that are landbound?"

"What are you talking about?" Ann squished up her face as if Carl had asked the most incomprehensible question she'd ever heard. "We go to all the ports, of course. They all have ports. You're not so smart for a tour guide, are you?"

"I'm not your tour guide, Ann. The tour guide will meet us once we land in Rome. I'm just here to make sure everything goes smoothly. And I'm a passenger, just like you, here to enjoy myself…and your company."

"I don't know how you're going to make things smooth when you don't even know where the rest of the world is."

Carl rolled his eyes but put his hand under Ann's forearm to help her to the first step of the bus. When she looked into the bus, her eyes widened as if she had momentarily forgotten where she was.

Slapping Carl's hand away, Ann growled at him. "I don't need your help. Get your paws off me. I'm perfectly capable of taking care of myself or I wouldn't go on your damn trip."

"Okay. Enjoy yourself," Carl said as he turned to the next passenger. "Well, Briana. We made it."

Briana Johnson's's big hair would never last the trip. Dyed black curls hung down the sides of her face and the rest of her hair, lacquered, stood precariously on top of her head, reminiscent of a country-western singer of the nineteen fifties. She wore a granny dress with cowboy boots. Not a style she'd likely find in Rome.

"I'm so ex-cited. I nevah been more than forty miles from ho-ome! Birmingham. That's the farthest. Maybe that's a little more than forty miles. Maybe Birmingham's more like seventy miles," Briana said, in one of the most pronounced Southern accents possible. Many of the words had more than the prescribed number of syllables in her Southern dialect. Briana's eyes rolled upward as if performing the calculation. "Even the Nawleans airport is farther than I've been. And then flying. Hoo-wee, this is so ex-citin'. Are you sure all my things are okay under the bus? Ah am not so su-ure mah things ah so se-cure."

A line had formed behind Briana as other passengers impatiently awaited getting good seats.

"Everything's locked up safe and sound," Carl reassured her as he ushered Briana into the bus.

Cory Evans and her friend Helen Davis waited next in line to go on board, both pushing walkers. Ida Sue Williams followed close behind, like a retainer for the hesitant Cory and Helen. "Are you sure we can take these things all the way?" Cory asked, indicating the walkers.

"Sure. They have to be checked as luggage and you won't claim them until we arrive in Rome, but they'll be there."

Helen looked perturbed, shaking her head. "But I need mine in the airport and when we change planes in Amsterdam."

Carl calmed her fears. "We asked for wheelchair assistance all the way through. It will be a wheelchair or one of those big electric carts, or something like that."

Helen continued to shake her head as she mounted the steps. Carl motioned to the driver to store the walkers in the storage compartment closest to the door.

Ida Sue stood back while the older two boarded the bus. "I bet you're all excited. I know I am," she said.

"This will be a wonderful tour," Carl agreed.

"I just miss my Mickie. That's my cat. Don't you miss Ponce? Isn't that your dog's name? And what about Chuck? Isn't he your partner?"

Carl hesitated a moment. "I'll sure miss Ponce a bit. Chuck I'm not so sure about." He chuckled.

"Oh, come on. You'll miss them both, I'm sure." Ida Sue gave Carl a big, exaggerated, knowing wink, and stepped into the bus.

Fred and Martha Singer, both retired police officers, approached next. Fred greeted Carl with a handshake. "Now, you know if you need any help, you can rely on me."

"I know that, but I'm hoping we can both relax the whole time."

"I don't know if I can get used to that. I'm used to doing something. Anybody needs help, just let me know. It'd give me somethin' to do."

"Okay. I'll remember, Fred. Just try to relax."

Just then a late model Ford SUV pulled up and Owen Clark, perhaps the oldest of the passengers, slowly emerged with difficulty from the passenger door. His middle-aged son, driving the car, unloaded Owen's luggage and came over to shake hands. "Thanks for taking my dad on this tour. It means a lot to him, especially that you're willing to share a room and look out for him."

"It's a shame you couldn't join us," Carl said.

"I really can't get off work for more than a couple of days at a time. At least not right now. Since Mom died two years ago, Dad has mostly been on his own. She used to look after him on tours but even without her he still wants to go. Maybe next year I can get away if Dad's still traveling."

Owen wandered onto the bus, completely oblivious of his luggage or saying goodbye to his son or even hello to Carl. His son just shook his head. "Do you mind giving this to dad? It has his medications in it." He handed Carl a small backpack.

Carl's vision suddenly darkened from the large shadows cast by the three sisters who merged into his peripheral vision. These three black women had worked in education before retiring, so they were exceptionally well educated and somewhat more worldly and well-traveled than most of Carl's clients. Mahalia Harris had been principal of a local high school and sisters Latrisha Martinez and Eugenia Wilson had served as department chairs in other high schools. They all went on every one of Carl's tours and were probably his most loyal, but not necessarily most cooperative, clients.

"Hello, ladies. You all ready?"

"I can only speak for myself," Latrisha said. "I'm ready but you should see the load of junk Mahalia is taking with her. She can't even lift her suitcase and I told her I can't do it. I hope you have a strong back, Carl."

"Don't worry, ladies. We'll have porters. I'm sure it isn't anything out of the ordinary for them."

Carl guided the three sisters up the steps, a painstakingly slow process.

Ava Jean Moore approached, carrying a big box-like suitcase that looked like an old-fashioned makeup case.

"Morning, Ava Jean. I don't know if that suitcase is going to fit in the overhead compartment on the bus."

"Well, it better. It's all my makeup. It's the most important thing."

"It will be safe under the bus. Here, let me give it to the driver to stash."

"Nothin' doing. I'll hold it on my lap if I have to."

Ava Jean barely managed to maneuver the case up the bus steps.

Sophia Randall followed closely carrying what looked like a stack of empty, folded shopping bags.

"Welcome, Sophia. What're those for?"

"Shopping. There better be good shopping on this trip. These will all be full by the end of the tour."

"How will you get all the stuff home? You can't check a full shopping bag as if it were luggage, Sophia."

"I'll find someplace to buy another suitcase. One suitcase for the new stuff, and one for my old stuff."

"Wow. That's dedication. You must be my number one prize shopper!" He offered his hand for her first step onto the bus.

Meanwhile, Victor Lewis locked his chipped, rust infested car and ambled over, carrying only a small backpack.

"Is that all you're bringing, Victor?"

"You wouldn't believe how much stuff I can fit in here. Besides, I'm not like these crazy women you have here who have to change their clothes three times a day."

"But still…"

"And do you know if I got a roommate yet? Remember I signed up single share? I hope I get a room by myself, but I'm willing to share with just about anybody. You know I can get along with just about anybody."

"I hope so. No, World Tours didn't tell me about the rooming situation," Carl answered. "You'll find out when we get to the hotel in Rome."

After the final passenger boarded, Carl climbed the several steps into the bus and grabbed the microphone next to the front seat.

"Welcome, everybody. We're going to have a terrific time in Italy. The scenery, the food…all spectacular. I need you to do one thing before we start off for the Louis Armstrong airport in New Orleans. Please. Take out your passport and make sure you have it. Then put it back into a place that is very safe."

Ann's hand went up. "I don't have my airline ticket. I don't think you ever gave me an airline ticket."

"There's no such thing as an airline ticket. They're electronic. Your tickets are all in the computer at the airport. I saw a list and I know every ticket is there. Don't worry about tickets, worry about your passport. Don't put it in the pocket of something that you could accidentally leave on the bus. This is the most important thing you have with you. Your passport is more important than clean underwear."

There was laughter and a few guffaws from the passengers before Carl continued. "You can always buy new underwear, but if you lose your passport, I guarantee you, it will ruin your trip worse than if you ruin your underwear. You'll be delayed coming home and that will cost you another airline ticket. I had a friend do that once and the ticket home cost seven thousand dollars because the only ticket available was first class. You don't want that to happen to you. So, make sure your passport is safe and that you know where it is at any given time."

A hand shot up near the back of the bus.

"Yes. A question in the back?"

The extended hand waggled its fingers to come closer. "Okay, just a minute," Carl said as he put the microphone back in its holder and headed toward the back of the bus. A hand reached out from every other seat, vying for his attention, and trying to ask questions. Carl motioned, shushing with his open hand, indicating that he would take additional questions later.

As he reached Cory, the owner of the waggling fingers, she motioned to bring Carl closer, as if intending to impart a secret.

"I'm so embarrassed," Cory whispered.

The entire bus fell silent so most passengers, at least in her vicinity, could hear the whispers.

"What's wrong?" Carl whispered back.

Chapter Two

The Big Delay

"Cory forgot her dern passport is what's wrong!" Ida Sue, sitting next to Cory, spoke for her, loud enough for the entire bus to hear.

Cory turned to shush Ida Sue.

"Don't shush me!"

"Cory. Tell me this is not true. Tell me we are both having the same bad dream."

"No, Carl. I'm so sorry. Can't I go get it? Won't you wait for me? You won't make me drive all the way to New Orleans by myself, will you?"

Carl stared up at the ceiling. He looked at his watch and at the other passengers who stared at him, anticipating his decision.

"I'll drive her home to get it," Ida Sue offered. "I can drive faster than her."

"I don't want anyone driving fast and having an accident," Carl warned. "Where exactly do you live?"

"Piney Woods, just south of Jackson. It's about a half hour."

"I can do it in twenty minutes," Ida Sue offered.

"Are you sure you know where the passport is? You don't have to tear the house apart looking for it?" Carl sounded skeptical.

"I know I put it on the table right next to the front door so that I wouldn't forget it on the way out. I know it's there. I can just picture it."

"Well, that plan didn't work very well since the passport's still there and you're here. Okay, you two. Go get it. Don't speed and remember to be careful."

Cory and Ida Sue made their way up the aisle and off the bus. Moments later a screech of tires issued from the parking lot. Carl put a hand on either side of his head and squeezed, looking upward as if to heaven for guidance. He picked up the microphone. "We are going to be here another forty minutes since Cory forgot her passport at home."

"I don't want to be late for the flight," Sally shouted, even though she occupied the seat behind Carl.

"Don't worry. We planned to be there three hours early. That's too much time anyway. Since it's almost a three-hour drive to New Orleans, I suggest everyone go into the fitness club and use the bathrooms. If we have time, we'll stop at the Louisiana welcome center. But you have forty minutes to wait for Cory and Ida Sue, so I recommend you use the time to pee."

"I don't see why we just don't leave them. They're inconveniencing the whole group, maybe even ruining the trip if we end up having traffic or an accident pile up on the interstate," Sally complained.

Several mumblings of agreement rumbled through the bus.

"I'll leave everyone behind who wants to complain," Carl said in a low voice, without turning on the microphone, Then with the microphone on, he spoke again. "We're waiting this time, but it doesn't set a good example. The tour guides won't wait, and once we're in Italy, I'm not in charge anymore so my overwhelming kindness will have no effect."

Carl's effort at humor failed to get even a chuckle.

"The tour guides have to run things on time," he continued. "And they never wait more than about ten minutes. Don't push your luck with those guys."

Two figures appeared in the doorway of the bus, Georgia Mae Miller and Joseph Hall.

"Georgia Mae! Joseph! Nice of you to join us," Carl said.

"Are we late?"

"About twenty minutes late," Carl admonished, but he blushed beet red.

"We won't do it again. I swear we won't do it again." Georgia Mae sounded genuinely penitent.

"You almost got left behind," Carl said.

Sally, who didn't miss a trick when it came to discovering

opportunities for criticism, spoke quietly so only Carl could hear. "You forgot to count. Shame on you. You didn't even know they were missing, did you?"

Carl ignored the comment and allowed Georgia Mae and Joseph to find seats. Almost forty minutes to the second, Ida Sue and Cory returned, with another screech of tires as Ida Sue applied the brakes. Cory practically ran onto the bus clutching the forgotten passport in front of her face with both hands, apparently having forgotten that, an hour before, she had depended on a walker for mobility.

"Now, for God's sake, Cory, put it somewhere safe. Do not let it stray from your person." Cory looked at Carl as if he spoke Greek.

"Don't worry, Carl. I'll make sure she minds her passport," Ida Sue said as she pushed Cory toward their seat near the back of the bus.

An hour later, nearing the Louisiana state line, a clatter came from the back of the bus and a red light flashed on the dashboard. The driver gently pulled onto the shoulder of the interstate.

"What's wrong?" Carl leaned over in the front seat, trying to see what the red light meant. "We don't have time to break down. We've lost so much time already."

"Don't get your knickers all in a wad, buddy. It's just that last door popped open. I got to go out and tape it shut again."

Carl leaned toward the driver and lowered his voice. "We didn't lose any luggage, did we?"

"No. It's the engine compartment. Nothing to worry about." The driver grabbed an enormous roll of duct tape and lumbered his considerable hulk out of the bus, like a graceless walrus slipping from the rocks into the ocean.

Within minutes they resumed the journey.

"If that's the worst thing that happens…" Carl said to the driver.

Chapter Three

Arrival For Departure

The international terminal, the latest addition to the Louis Armstrong Airport, a great glass and steel structure, loomed out of the fog. The motorcoach pulled up to the international departures entrance, and it looked like a futuristic Hollywood ghost town set. No porters, no airline representatives, no other passengers. Rumor had it that the port authority built the terminal but didn't consider how many new employees it required, leaving it chronically short-handed.

"Either there are so many porters that your luggage is in danger of disappearing in several directions simultaneously, or there is no one, like now," Carl said to the driver.

Carl picked up the bus microphone. "You can all leave the bus and get your luggage from the driver. I'll go inside and try to find porters. Wait on the sidewalk until I get back."

"What do we do if our luggage isn't there?" Briana asked.

"Did you see your luggage get put on the bus in Jackson?"

"Yeah."

"Briana, did we stop and unload anywhere?"

"There was that breakdown," Briana reminded Carl.

"That was the engine compartment. Where could your luggage be, except inside the bus?"

"I don't know, but I know things get lost faster than you can spit and say howdy! I had some loose shoes down there."

"Loose shoes?" Carl sounded incredulous. "Loose shoes?" he repeated.

"Well, they were in a shopping bag, but with all the jostling, I'm sure they could have fallen out."

"I don't believe it," Carl mumbled to himself as he made his way to the door of the bus.

"Don't worry. You'll find your shoes," he shouted back to Briana.

Cory interrupted as Carl tried to make his way off the bus. "Don't forget my wheelchair. I can't walk through the whole terminal."

"Me too," Helen added.

"I have two requests for wheelchair assistance. Everyone else has to walk."

Carl scurried off the bus, like a rat leaving a burning ship, into the eerie quiet of the nearly empty airport terminal. He took a deep breath of the cold, stale, air-conditioned air, full of paint and sheetrock dust. It was a vastness of air not breathed by other human beings for at least several hours. Carl asked a ticketing counter agent to call for porters and two wheelchairs.

"Do you want to handle my whole group in a single line, since we're all going to the same place?" Carl asked. "There are forty-five of us."

"No. Since it isn't busy, it will be faster if you spread out to all lines."

A sound like a rain of nuts and bolts drew Carl's attention to the entrance. The sound came from fifty squeaky-wheeled suitcases dragging alongside two porters making their way across the hard terrazzo floor, the sound echoing off the glass walls. He turned to the entrance only to see his wards already entering the terminal, some walking off in the wrong direction. Sally approached ahead of the crowd.

"Sally, where are y'all going?" Carl asked.

"Some have to use the restrooms, and some are going to look for something to eat."

"Jesus, you're not even checked in yet. There's no food on this level of the airport."

"You can't control everything, Carl, even though I know you want to," Sally warned as she just continued walking in the opposite direction, seemingly admiring the ceiling a full four stories above her head.

Carl walked back to the check in lines. "They want you to spread out to all lines," he directed in a voice made louder by cupping his mouth with his hands to create a bullhorn.

"Can we stay together?" Helen asked.

She and Cory had apparently decided to push their walkers to the ticket counter rather than wait for wheelchairs.

"You can stay with whomever you want. Just get on the shortest line."

"Sometimes the shortest line doesn't move the fastest, so how can you tell?" Ann seemed serious in her concern.

"Any line will do," Carl said, distractedly, as he pushed Ann along with a hand on her shoulder.

Carl joined what appeared to be the longest line, from which vantage point he could watch his clients up ahead. Briana came down his line with two pregnant looking shopping bags, bulging as in their third trimester. She seemed to be stopping at each passenger in line, handing something from the shopping bags to some of them. Others refused with a wave of the hand. Some just ignored Briana.

"Briana, what are you doing?" Carl asked, as she approached.

Chapter Four

Well Heeled

"The ticket lady told me I can't take two shopping bags of shoes. I tried to fit them into my luggage like she said, but these won't fit. I'm askin' other people to take 'em for me. Some people I don't even know. I think some fell out of the bag and got left under the bus 'cause I know I had more shoes than this. Guess it's too late now, but could you call the driver and ask? Meanwhile I have ta ask people to carry these for me."

"Good solution, Briana, except for one thing."

"Whadda ya mean?"

"All these people on the ticket line are probably going to different places. Your shoes will go all over the world."

Briana squinted and wrinkled her brow. "Whadda ya mean all over the world? I thought we was goin' to Italy." She unscrunched her face and continued. "I don't care. I have to get rid of them or I can't fly."

"Why did you bring so many shoes, Briana? Didn't you read the traveling instructions? Didn't they say one or two comfortable pair and one for dress up?"

"But I wanted to be able to change my shoes at least a couple a times a day."

Briana continued down the line past Carl like a street hawker in a third world country, handing shoes to whomever would take them.

By the time Carl checked in, only a few of his passengers remained at the counter. As he left the check-in area and headed for security, he saw some of the stragglers who had gone to try to find food or a restroom. On the last line another three of his people waited, the three sisters who always traveled together.

Mahalia was talking angrily to the baggage check-in agent. "Wadda ya mean, it's too big. It's just a suitcase." Mahalia sounded outraged, voice rising.

Carl strode up to the three women.

Mahalia turned to Carl. "My sisters had no trouble checking their luggage."

"Maybe theirs wasn't the size of a refrigerator," Carl said as he turned to the brown canvas case, surely the size of an average European home refrigerator. It was so large and so stuffed that the steel superstructure could be seen embossed in the canvas, like some sort of industrial-strength tent. A rare suitcase, indeed. Like an old-fashioned steamer trunk, except made of steel reinforced canvas.

The counter agent chimed in. "I didn't say she couldn't take the thing, I just said we had to weigh it and she'll have to pay extra for anything more than forty pounds."

"Mahalia, I thought we talked in the pre-travel meeting about traveling light."

"That's easy for you to say. What do you need except shirts and a couple of pairs of pants? I can't get away with that."

Carl stared at the enormous suitcase and finally sighed. "So, you don't have any choice but to weigh the damn thing and find out what amount of money the agent is talking about."

"That's easy for you to say," Mahalia said, sounding like a broken record. "I can't lift that thing, and neither can my sisters."

"Ma'am, you are going to have to be able to handle your own luggage. I don't lift customer's luggage." The ticket counter agent folded her arms in finality.

"Okay, I'll help you." Carl hesitated, his right hand checking himself for a hernia. Then by tipping the refrigerator suitcase over onto the scale he wiggled it into place without lifting it.

"Okay, ma'am, you are thirty pounds overweight. That will be one hundred eighty-five dollars."

"What!" Mahalia shrieked like the wicked witch of the west.

"Calm down, Mahalia." One of her sisters put a hand on Mahalia's shoulder. "You have plenty of money. Just pay the girl and let's get going."

"No," the agent said. "Oversized and overweight luggage has to go to counter one on the other side of the ticketing hall. I can't accept payment. You'll have to go over there to counter one, weigh in, and pay with a credit card there, get a receipt, and bring the receipt and the suitcase back to me or any one of these counters to check in and get a boarding pass. You better hurry. You still have to get through security." She smirked at the suitcase. "And that flight will start boarding in fifteen minutes."

"Can I at least leave the suitcase here?"

"No, like I said, they are going to have to weigh it at counter one, you pay, and then bring it back here or to one of the other check-in lines with the receipt."

"You're shittin' me!"

"No, ma'am. And it won't help to get profane with me."

Mahalia leaned over to get into the agent's face as much as she could with the counter between them, probably the way she intimidated her students at school.

"Come on, Mahalia." Eugenia tugged her arm to get her away.

Carl slid the behemoth suitcase off the scale and Mahalia grabbed the handle and took off, rolling the titanic-sized suitcase, rumbling like a tank, a distant thunder, across the lobby, Mahalia tugging at it like a stone meant for the great pyramid.

Carl did not follow. He went on to see what kind of havoc his clients were causing at the security check.

Carl passed through security with no problem and then came upon a quarrel raised at the last security counter. Ava Jean, arms akimbo, raged at the security officer.

Chapter Five

Cosmetic Improvement

"There's nothing dangerous. I swear there's nothing dangerous. It's my makeup. All of it. Stop calling it non-essentials!"

The handsome security officer, eyes closed, face averted to heaven, spoke calmly. "I don't care if it's holy water, you can't take these larger liquids on the flight with you."

"You don't seem to understand." Ava Jean paced a tight circle like a lion tamer and came to rest with her hands on her hips, getting even closer to the security officer, aiming her ample bust at him like two mortars about to fire rounds. He had to take a step back or get poked in the chest. Ava Jean continued in rapid fire. "There's more than six hundred dollars-worth of makeup in that case and I'm not leaving it."

"Why don't you just leave these big bottles? The ones more than three ounces? The rest is okay."

"Those big bottles just happen to be my hair conditioner and that one is my body wash. I have dry skin and can't just use any crummy old hotel soap."

"Sorry, lady, but the rules are the rules. You can throw the liquids out or leave this area. But you are not boarding the plane with all this stuff."

"It's not just stuff! It's very expensive stuff!"

Carl sidled closer to where he could observe the disturbance more closely. Ava Jean's problem seemed to have turned into a stalemate. The young security officer was particularly good-looking, so Carl walked into the fray.

Ava Jean and the security officer just stood there looking in her half-empty cosmetic case. "Suppose I trade these three little ones for this one big one," she suggested as she lifted three small bottles out of the case and tried to put one of the large ones back in.

The officer reached in and took the large one out again. "I'm sorry, lady, there's no bargaining with the feds."

Carl spoke up. "Ava Jean, what seems to be the problem?"

Ava Jean turned to Carl and swiped her tear-stained cheek with the back of her hand. "This jerk won't let me take my makeup."

"Lady, if you start calling me names, you'll end up on the no fly list."

"Well, if you didn't act like a jerk, I wouldn't have to call you a jerk," Ava Jean replied, with well-formed, methodical sobs.

"Are you related to this lady?" the handsome security officer queried.

"God, no. She's a client, part of a group I'm taking to Italy." Carl peered into the sea-blue eyes of the young security officer.

"Can you explain to her why we're stopping her?" The officer broke eye contact first, but not without smiling at Carl. He looked down at the mess on his counter.

"Ava Jean, there's a rule about liquids. No containers more than three ounces. A bunch of these are bigger than three ounces."

"The FAA is afraid of people bringing liquid explosives on board the aircraft," the security officer added, attempting to be helpful.

Carl turned to the agent. "I bet if you mixed all this shit together it would explode."

The officer smiled again and gave Carl a subtle friendly shove with his hand. Carl nearly fell over.

Ava Jean put her hands on her hips and raised her voice. "You two are going to fool around with one another when I'm in crisis here." She raised her voice even more as Carl slid behind the security officer. "I'm in a crisis here!" Carl looked past the agent's shoulder at the mess on the counter as Ava Jean turned red, flapped her arms, and looked around as if purposely trying to attract attention.

Meanwhile a second security officer, much older and more portly, joined the scene. Both security officers stood recalcitrant, with their arms folded against their chests, as if they were guarding someone in a witness protection program. Carl directed a question to the original, handsome officer. "Suppose she goes back out and checks the makeup instead of carrying it?"

The young officer looked to the older one who answered the question for him. "I guess your wife can do that. That's up to you if you have enough time before the flight. But if you go out and then come through security again, the second time this morning, it's going to flag a problem and there will be more checks."

"Please. She's not my wife. I'm a tour organizer and she's one of my clients. What do you think, Ava Jean?"

"How much is it going to cost to check another bag?"

Carl turned to the older officer who responded. "It always depends on the weight. I think the minimum is thirty-five dollars. From what I can tell it's not more than thirty-five dollars."

"Is it worth it, Ava Jean?"

"Of course, it's worth it, you moron. I just told you it's more than six hundred dollars-worth of makeup."

"Why would you take that much with you? Couldn't you just have thrown a few things in a suitcase like everyone else?"

"You just don't understand. Like everyone else in our group. They look like sacks of potatoes. No. Cabbages. Your clients look like a bunch of cooked cabbages with no makeup. Get out of my way so I can go check in again."

Chapter Six

Watch Out

Carl found the assigned gate and took a seat, closing his eyes, putting off the inevitability of the body count long enough to make sure everyone found the gate. He had a moment's rest, barely. Sure enough, a voice shattered the quiet like breaking glass, like chalk or a fingernail on a blackboard. "Carl!"

Carl opened his eyes partially. The diminutive yet somehow majestic form of Sally stood in front of him, finger pointed.

"Sally!"

"How dare you leave me alone standing at the ticket counter!"

"You were hardly alone. Wasn't the ticket agent with you?"

"That's the problem. I was overweight and they wanted money."

"Your diet is really none of my business." Carl closed his eyes again.

"Don't be a wise guy. The luggage."

"The instructions said forty pounds maximum. That's a lot of stuff, Sally."

"You're a man and wouldn't understand."

"That's right, Sally. I wear the same clothes every day. Even the same underwear. When they start to get sticky, I throw them out and buy a new pair, or not…just go without. It makes travel easy, and I feel so… free."

"That's disgusting. And don't get smart with me, Mr. Know It All. She wanted money."

"Who wanted money?"

"That nagging harpy at the ticket counter."

"That's the deal, isn't it, Sally? They charge for overweight luggage."

"You are so incompetent. Wouldn't you know, my wallet with my charge cards was in my luggage and they had already thrown it onto the conveyor belt. It was gone. Don't you see? You left me stuck there! If you ever do that again I will never travel with you, ever."

"Well, you're here now, so you must have solved the problem. You should feel good that you solved your own problem."

"I had to give them half of all my euros, is what I had to do. You owe me fifty-five euros."

"How do you figure I owe that?"

"Because if you stayed with me, they never would have asked for the money."

"Wrong, Sally. If your luggage is overweight, you pay. It wouldn't matter if Jesus, Mary, and Joseph stood next to you, you'd be expected to pay."

"Don't you go using the name of the lord-thy-God in vain."

"Sorry, Sally, but you shouldn't have put a wallet with credit cards and money into your suitcase. Once in a while a suitcase gets lost. Sometimes a custom agent opens them. Stuff goes missing. It says that in your travel book."

"I have trouble like this and all you can say is travel book? That's it. That does it. I won't be traveling with you again."

"Promises, promises," Carl replied, as if to himself.

"What did you say?"

"Sorry, sorry," Carl said a little louder.

Sally just stood there, her mouth drawn into a rictus, so Carl got up and walked to a different part of the waiting area where he overheard a conversation between two of his passengers.

"And you should have seen the hotel he had us stay at on the way to the Grand Canyon," Sophia said to Ida Sue. "There were even spots on the carpet. I don't know what they were, but they were suspicious. And I swear there was mold in the shower. The whole place smelled like a wet goat. A dirty wet goat."

"Yeah, I heard that they're not always the best hotels. But it's for one night on the way, isn't it?"

"When you get where you're going it's no better. And then there's the restaurant we ate at the first night."

"What was wrong with that? I didn't hear anyone complain about the food."

"It was supposed to be an all-you-can-eat buffet, but every time I got up for seconds or thirds, everything was run out. It was one sorry all-you-can-eat buffet."

"I better think twice about going to Maine with him in the fall. I signed up but I'm not really committed. After hearing what you say…"

Carl interrupted. "Hey, ladies. Couldn't help but overhear. So, you didn't like the Grand Canyon trip, Sophia? Wasn't that about the tenth trip you went on with me?"

"Yeah. So what? I'm sure you wouldn't give me my money back if it's bad."

"I'm surprised you think they're so bad if you keep signing up for them."

"There's nothing else to do around Jackson."

"I'd appreciate if you would keep quiet. This is my business. Most of these are inexpensive trips. It's less than a hundred dollars a day including the hotels, meals, transportation, admissions. What do you think you can get for that? The Ritz? You want to stay at the Ritz? You go find a group that's going to stay at the Ritz and instead of six hundred dollars, your trip is going to cost you three thousand, if you can find such a trip. I'll tell you if you keep it up, trying to ruin my business, you're going to find yourself being shoved out a window when this plane is above the Atlantic Ocean."

"Hardy har har. All talk. That's what you are. All talk."

Chapter Seven

Credit Check

Ruth Ann Swenson, red-faced and flushed with perspiration, pushed between Carl and Sophia. "Carl, what am I going to do? You have to help me."

"What's wrong, Ruth Ann?" Carl jokingly stuck an index finger in each ear as to not hear the latest travesty.

"Listen to me." Ruth Ann reached over, grabbing Carl's hands to pull the fingers out of his ears. "I left my credit cards home. I took them out to call the banks to say I was traveling, and I left them all on my desk. What am I going to do?"

"Did you bring euros? How many euros do you have?"

"I have five hundred euros only."

"Ruth Ann, five hundred euros is a lot of euros. All you have to buy on this tour is your lunch every day. Surely in seven days lunch won't cost five hundred euros."

"But you don't understand."

It had to be the hundredth time today a client uttered that phrase, like a mantra.

"I have to buy gifts for people. I have to buy things. I need my credit cards."

"Call your credit card company and find out how long it takes to get new ones and we can figure out what hotel we'll be in on that day and have them delivered there."

"That won't really work, will it, Carl?"

"It depends how long it will take to replace the cards."

"Suppose I call my neighbor who has a key to the house and ask her to mail them."

"Give her the list of hotels and dates you'll be there and let the post office decide where to send them. Remember we are in hotels mostly for one night only and at best three nights. I think it would be safer for you to choose the three-night hotel in Venice."

"Alright, but I need those cards."

"I understand, Ruth Ann, but it won't be the end of the world if you can't shop."

"Yes, it will."

"Okay. I get it. Let's see your tour book."

Ruth Ann rifled through her carry-on bag and after several minutes of nervous searching, dropping things to the floor and muttering southern invectives, such as *dern* and *gosh*, extracted the crumpled, and in several places, torn and perforated tour book. She handed it to Carl by the cover as if it were a dead rodent she had found among her belongings.

Carl accepted the booklet hesitatingly and turned to the hotel list. "Here, Ruth Ann. On the fourth day we arrive in Venice and stay there for three nights."

He took out a pen and circled the Venice hotel with its address. "If your neighbor does next day air or whatever is available, it should be there when we arrive or while we're there. I'll tell our tour guide about this and he can call ahead."

"What if they get stolen?"

"I can't control everything, Ruth Ann. Maybe you should insure them or require a signature. There's tracking from the post office so it should be safe."

"I don't know why I let you talk me into these things, Carl. I wish I had stayed at home."

"Me, too," Carl responded, under his breath.

"What?"

"You'll be just fine. You have plenty of money for the first three days."

Chapter Eight

To Pee Or Not To Pee, That Is The Question

In Amsterdam the group needed to change planes.

During the flight, Carl checked with the head flight attendant to make sure two wheelchairs would be available to help with changing gates and that the airline had the correct names, as often other passengers absconded with the wheelchairs. With only a half-hour left in the seven-hour flight, Carl walked up the aisles to find the two passengers and give them their wheelchair instructions—to remain on the plane until the regular passengers got off.

Holly grabbed his arm as he walked past.

Carl stopped and waited for Holly to speak. She wagged her finger for Carl to get closer, as if about to impart a juicy bit of gossip. Carl bent toward Holly. "You know she has not gotten up out of her seat once during the whole flight." Holly pointed to an enormous woman, not one of Carl's clients, in the next row.

"God bless her. What's the significance of that?"

"Seven hours, Carl. She's been in that seat for seven hours. What'd you have to do in the last seven hours?"

It only took a moment for Carl to comprehend Holly's meaning. "You don't suppose she…you don't think the seat is…wet? Now?"

"I'm just saying. I'm not saying anything. But seven hours? Maybe you should tell the crew. Someone's going to have to sit there on the next flight."

Carl righted himself with some difficulty due to the stiffness of having sat for so long, looked at the heavy woman, and seemed to be considering the situation. "What, do you think I'm in charge of the world? Why would I tell the crew?"

Holly shrugged her shoulders and Carl returned to his seat. He stood in the aisle, hesitating. His seatmate looked up as if wondering why Carl stood in the aisle.

"Did anyone sit in my seat while I was gone?" Carl asked.

The seatmate tightened his facial muscles as if forced to answer the most stupid question he'd ever heard and spoke in a clearly British accent. "Why, for fuck's sake, would anyone sit in your seat while you were gone?"

Carl replied apologetically. "I guess that's an answer." He gingerly felt the bottom seat cushion with a single, easily cleanable fingertip. Finding it dry he took his seat for landing.

The seatmate put down his magazine and stared at Carl.

• • • •

Contrary to the inefficiency of American airports, their European counterparts run like clockwork. Attendants with wheelchairs met Carl's two passengers on the jetway and the other forty-two passengers milled about in the terminal waiting area. Only then did Carl find out that the flight to Rome would leave from a gate farthest from their arrival gate. A challenge for even the able-bodied, of which he hadn't many in his crowd.

"Pardon, madame. Some of my passengers will have difficulty getting to gate A110," Carl said, turning to the gate attendant. "Can we have transport take them?"

"Certainly, sir. It will take time, however. I see your flight leaves in an hour. It will start boarding in a few minutes. I will call ahead and say that your group has landed and that you are on your way. Better if you take as many as can walk. Gate A110 will know you are coming."

"Thank you." Carl looked relieved and his shoulders relaxed a little. He explained to the group, in his best bullhorn voice, that those who felt they could walk, follow him, and the remainder should wait for mobile transports. His group seemed to have diminished somewhat and remaining clients tried to explain that so-and-so went shopping, or to a rest room, or to find something to eat.

As he started off, about ten people followed him. The remaining passengers looked at one another, mumbling, and then, not wishing to be left behind, followed until no one waited for the transport. Carl led a crowd that looked like a gaggle of forty some, odd wobbly ducks, or more like a slow-moving herd of sheep or cows, bouncing onto one another and clogging the passageway. Even those who wandered off earlier managed to catch up.

Carl, in terrific physical condition, pushed ahead, but with this crowd of complaining, gimpy, tripping passengers, the walk took forever. And then, as only in Amsterdam, a full security check blocked their way to the departure gate. They found the check point empty, however, as all passengers had already boarded.

"You are late, sir. Your whole group is late," an officious and unpleasant security official informed Carl.

"I did the best I could. They're old."

"The only reason the flight was delayed is that your clients represented a large portion of the passengers on the flight, and the airline does not want to reschedule forty-five people."

"We appreciate that."

"If any of them purchased anything, ask them to take the first line, the rest to spread out to lines two through six."

"Did you hear that, everyone?" The bullhorn voice again. "If you've already bought something here in Amsterdam, get in the first line. Everyone else spread out. Lines two through six. Please hurry. We're late. First line if you bought anything."

Almost the entire crowd got on the first line. The humorless security official approached Carl with his hands raised, palms open in hopeless surrender. Carl shrugged his shoulders and stifled a laugh.

"What exactly did you people buy?" Carl queried.

Everyone spoke at once. "Bubble gum." "Candy bar." "T-Shirt."

Carl looked at the security officer who was turning beet red, his head starting to twitch in a frightening way. "Just tell them to spread out. Forget gum and candy bars. Just get on damn plane please." The security guard was loud enough for the passengers to obey the orders without Carl repeating them.

As Carl's passengers moved through the security check and onto the jetway, Fred and his wife Martha sidled up to Carl.

"Hi. Fred. Martha. I really didn't get to say much to you so far on this trip. I'm glad you're with us. You might be the only two sane ones."

"Just thought you might want to know…" Fred started.

"Don't bring me no bad news."

Fred chuckled and shook his head. "Just thought you might like to know about Victor."

"What should I know about Victor?"

Martha answered. "You know we're both retired police officers. One of only two married couples on the police force in Jackson, although I was patrol and Fred was in the detective force, but still…"

"I guess I knew that. That's great. This must be a well-deserved retirement celebration for you."

"I guess," Fred said. "But it's hard to get that detective work out of my system. For instance, I was watching Victor."

"Our Victor?"

"Our Victor is a big-time shoplifter," Fred said.

"As my grandmother used to say," Martha added. "He'd steal your stove and come back for the smoke."

Fred and Carl laughed.

"While we were waiting for the transport and before you decided to walk it," Fred continued. "He went into that variety store near the last gate. I watched him. He picked up candy bars, pretended to be reading the labels, and then, suddenly like that, they'd disappear. He dropped them into his open backpack. Then he went to the souvenir counter. Same thing. He's going to get arrested."

"Wow. Did you say anything to him? Maybe if he knew that someone was on to him, he'd stop it."

"I wanted to tell you first. See what you say."

"Okay. Next time you grab me, and we'll watch together. I don't mind saying something to him. All we need is someone on our tour to get arrested. I'll tell you, I'm not bailing him out."

"I don't blame you. What a jerk," Martha concluded.

Carl and his passengers made the flight a full half-hour late, unheard of in European airports that tended to run on strict schedules. As they entered the cabin and made their long way to the rear of the economy section, waiting passengers whispered, frowned, and shook their heads.

Carl began by smiling at the already seated passengers but gave up when he received scowls in return. The flight to Rome was thankfully short.

Chapter Nine

Rome

In Rome's Fiumicino Airport, as in Amsterdam, debarkation and the two wheelchair assistances went smoothly. After Carl ascertained everyone had their luggage, he conducted them to the customs line. The signs instructed for all EU passengers to go to the right and all other passengers to the left. He stood at the entrance to the customs lobby and conducted everyone to the left. Or so he thought. A half-hour later, when his turn came to present his passport to the agent, he heard a commotion to his right. Several women's voices, crying and shrieking, sounded like a cage of hyaenas. He closed his eyes as if blotting out the whole scene. The sound persisted. He turned his head in the direction of the noise before he forced his eyes to open. Mary Maples and Briana had gotten on the EU line and were arguing loudly with the customs agent.

Carl turned back to his own agent. "Can you help me get to those noisy women?" He pointed. "They are my travel clients, and they are in the wrong line."

"Stupid Americans." The agent seemed to be dismissing the situation, looking down at Carl's passport.

"I'm aware of that, sir. But to not hold up that line, can you help me get them here where they belong?"

The agent looked up at Carl, then smiled. "Just for you I do."

He pushed a button, and an enormous, muscular, serious-looking security guard came to his door immediately. After a conversation in rapid-fire Italian, ending in chuckles and slaps on the shoulders, the big security guard spoke to Carl. "You follow me, no?"

Carl and the security guard cut across the front of the EU lines to the desk where Mary wept and Briana was emptying her purse, things rolling and skittering to the edges of the counter.

The customs agent calmly collected the items and pushed them back to Briana.

"Mary. Briana. What in the world is going on? Why are you in the EU line?"

"I didn't hear you say the other line. Sorry." Briana blubbered like a six-year-old.

"I can't understand a word he said. Why can't they speak in some known language?" Mary spoke louder than necessary, as if her words might benefit everyone else in the customs line.

"I speak English for you, lady. You no listen, you talk. Always the talk. You talk all time, so you not understand." The customs agent adopted a combative tone, hands gripping the counter in front of him.

Carl, with the huge security guard at his side, interrupted. "My apologies, sir. These two are my travel clients. May I bring them back to the other side, the other passport line where they belong?"

The frustrated agent looked at Carl, then raised his eyes to the enormous security guard at his side. "No, *Dottore*. If you responsible for two, I process right here. I should not do, but for you, *Dottore*, I process, and you get two ladies to leave. Then we have peace in customs."

"I'm afraid we might have peace in customs, but as long as my groups are traveling the world, there will be no world peace."

"I think you make joke, but I get you through anyway."

The security guard stood close, his arms at either side, as if ready to grab all three Americans and squeeze them together like pizza dough before heaving them out. He finally spoke, in sub-bass. "You not need me no more, *Dottore*?"

"That is correct, sir," Carl responded. "Thank you for helping us."

"How did he know you are a doctor?" Mary asked, as the three passed the custom agent's counter. "Wasn't he calling you doctor, or dot-tore? See, I'm learning Italian already."

"No. He has no idea that I'm a doctor. In Italy the title *Dottore* is a sign of great respect. They never say sir or ma'am like in the states. *Dottore* is a sign of respect. He would have called me *Commandatore* if he thought I was really something special."

"So, what kind of doctor are you?" Briana asked. "Mary, I didn't know he was a doctor."

"I'm a psychologist, but I only practiced a couple of years. I quit to travel. To travel with you. Isn't that nice?"

Briana took a step sideways away from Carl and looked at him skeptically. "I guess we better be careful about what we say around you."

"I'm off duty."

. . . .

Carl, Mary, and Briana arrived in the luggage claim area and by some miracle the rest of the group stood aside waiting, all having collected their luggage. A few looked around nervously.

"What happened to you this time?" Sally asked belligerently.

"Some of us had a little difficulty in the wrong customs line."

"You'd think by now you could get in the right line, Carl. Shame on you. And making us all wait like this."

Carl opened his mouth, about to explain, but held back. "You're lucky I didn't push you out of the plane above the Atlantic," he whispered.

"What?"

"I hope you enjoyed the flight, and that the rest of your trip will be fantastic." He forced a big toothy smile.

Carl's clients moved like a giant iceberg through the crowd at the luggage carousels. Their rolling suitcases once again threatened small children, a few small dogs, and upended the incidental piece of luggage left unattended. Finally, in the arrivals hall, Carl headed toward a man holding a World Tours sign and his countenance changed. He patted his hair into place, straightened his jacket lapels, and tucked in his shirttails. He broke into the first genuine smile of the day and made his eyes as wide and bright as possible.

"Hello there. I'm Carl Minton. This is a group of forty-five persons, I think you were expecting us."

"Yes. Dr. Minton. I am François. I will be your tour manager while you are in Italy. Welcome." François offered his hand and displayed no less than thirty-two perfectly straight, white teeth.

"You sound French, rather than Italian."

"I assure you I speak fluent Italian. But I am French. I am from Tours."

"I wasn't being critical, François. I love France. I'm sure we'll get along just fine." Carl cooed.

François was slightly taller than Carl, maybe five foot ten, strongly built in a wiry sort of way, a beautifully sculpted, swarthy face, and raven black hair cut short but stylishly as French men do. He appeared to be of African, possibly Arabic extraction.

Ida Sue sidled up to Carl. "He sure is easy on the eyes." She watched Carl as he studied François. "Remember Chuck's waiting for you at home." Carl frowned at Ida Sue, who receded into the crowd.

"Are we just going to stand here or what?" Sally broke Carl's doe-eyed reverie.

"If you have everyone, we go. First, we go to Victor Emmanuel Monument, and we have lunch with you there. Too early for hotel check in. Meanwhile your luggage goes to hotel so when you get there you can rest for tonight. You got all people?"

"That's the hard part. Trying to count forty-five people when they are all moving around and in a crowd," Carl said to François.

"Once we get settle, I do counting and you relax," François said, squeezing Carl's bicep. Carl's knees buckled slightly.

Fred was standing nearby. "Donna and Leona went to the restroom. We have to wait for them. If they don't hurry, I'm going to have to go, too."

"Do we have time to let everyone who has to go, go here before we head to lunch?" Carl asked François.

"We have to do quickly. Our driver cannot stay at street too long."

"Okay, everyone. Go pee. But hurry." Carl turned to François. "Now I'll have to count again."

"Don't worry, all your troubles soon be over." This time François squeezed Carl's wrist, but Carl seemed prepared and kept a relaxed posture as he stared at François's profile. François watched the wandering group.

When the group reassembled, François led them to the waiting bus, which was parked what seemed like a mile from the exit.

"You told us this trip wouldn't be much walking," Sophia complained.

"This is the only walking you'll have to do. Unfortunately, the airport is very crowded today," Carl responded.

The driver acted surly toward François, waving him away as François attempted to approach. He handled the suitcases roughly. Then he started loading with the wheels down on the floor of the luggage compartment so that he didn't have to get into the luggage compartment with them. He just pushed, and they rolled to the far side, slamming into one another.

"Shouldn't the suitcases be lying flat, François?" Carl asked. "He could break the wheels that way, and if he goes around a fast turn, those suitcases are going to go flying."

"I think you right, *Dottore*. I not know for sure. I not motorcoach expert. But I think you right."

"I don't know for sure either, but it makes sense."

François addressed the driver in Italian but between his Italian and the hand gestures, the gist of the communication was plain. "Giulio. Hey, Giulio. You lay suitcases down flat it better? No wheels break? No suitcase slide when drive. Hills. Left turn. Right turn?" François swayed back and forth, like an unbalanced bus.

Giulio stopped, straightened out, made himself tall, as tall as his five-foot three-inch stature would allow, bending back so he could look up into François' face. Giulio said something to François, giving the universal sign of a prominent middle finger. Not to be outdone, François turned his butt toward Giulio while still facing him, which meant something like, kiss my ass. "Just keep working," he said.

The driver turned the luggage on its side and begrudgingly did his job correctly.

"He will not be our driver on tour, you be sure. Just get us to hotel. Different driver for tour in plan," François assured Carl quietly so that the driver couldn't hear.

"That was scary," Carl said.

"You no worry," François said, seeming to enjoy squeezing Carl's arm again.

• • • •

The bus headed into town and circled the architecturally over-the-top Victor Emmanuel Monument, lovingly but sometimes derisively known as the wedding cake. Giulio dropped off the passengers, who seemed disoriented, many of them having had little or no sleep during the flights.

"You have nice day. You sit on benches. You walk around monument. You not go too far," François instructed them.

François turned to Carl. "I send motorcoach to sort luggage at hotel. It all in room when we get there. Motorcoach come back for us two o'clock. Give hour and a half."

François turned to the group. "I take you pick up sandwich take out and then walk to top of monument. You see all Rome up there. You see Vatican, you see Forum, you see Colosseum, you see hills. I show you. If you not come with me, you be back right here at two o'clock. You maybe cross street, but you go no more. Much better see view here than in little hotel lobby waiting for check-in time. You bored and fall asleep on chair and hurt neck. Two o'clock. You remember."

"What about food? I need food," Mary whined.

"Yes. Food easy. I just tell you. You see just across street. Sandwich shop. If you not want to climb stairs to monument, you see Pompey's Porch. A little expensive. Place where Caesar killed. Take time. Not to kill Caesar. Kill Caesar faster than ordering meal at Pompey's Porch."

"What about normal food?" Georgia Mae asked.

"It all normal food," François answered, but grinned at his own facetiousness.

"No. Good American food. Like McDonalds," Georgia Mae insisted.

"You no have no such thing as McDonald in Italy. You eat real food when here."

Audible groans issued from the group. "No McDonalds, who wanted to come here anyway? I'm not going to be able to stand this…"

"François only tease. You go right around corner there you find McDonald. Nowhere in world without McDonald. You eat all junk you want. Right around corner. You get fast junk food then join us on stairs of monument."

"Thank God for McDonalds," Georgia Mae commented, as she grabbed Joseph by the arm and dragged him across the street.

"*Andiamo*," François said as he also stepped out into traffic that swarmed like wasps, and with a raised hand, stopped cars and scooters. He ushered the group across the street to the sandwich shop and to McDonalds.

François led Carl and most of the group to the sandwich shop. The shop offered a selection of dozens of cheeses, a few processed meats like prosciutto, but many, many different types of bread.

"This is fantastic," Carl gushed. "Much different than an American deli."

"Happy you like," François commented. They each ordered a sandwich, a small bottle of white wine and a bottle of water, avoiding the small selection of soda products, and headed back across the street to the magnificent white marble steps of the Victor Emmanuel Monument. They sat on the steps about half-way up, where the view started to become dramatic.

"You not first time Rome, *Dottore*?"

"Oh, no. I don't even know how many times. I've been coming here since, I think I was fourteen years old."

"How you come only fourteen? You come with family?"

"No. It was a school tour. Our Latin class came for a week to Rome and Sorrento."

"Must be rich class to do Europe trip."

"I guess."

"Then where you come next time you come Italy?"

"When I was in college. It used to be a tradition to come to Europe during the summer of your second, or sophomore, year of college. It was once called a grand tour, and you got a train pass that allowed you to go everywhere."

"So, where you go on grand tour?"

"A friend and me, we started in Amsterdam, then took the Orient Express to Munich to visit friends studying there. Then Austria and Switzerland, down to Venice, across to Milan, then Florence and then Rome. We took the train to Nice and Monte Carlo, then Paris before a couple of weeks in London. My friend went home, and I stayed in London longer and then went back to Paris before going home to the U.S.."

"Big trip."

"Yes, very big trip."

"Must cost lots of American dollar for a college boy."

"We traveled very cheaply back then. The train pass didn't cost much, and I think we found plenty of hotel rooms for twenty-five dollars each night, even less, something like that."

"Something tell me you one rich American."

"No, I work for a living, just like you."

"You fine fellow. Legs like runner," he said and squeezed Carl's knee. The one that was closest to him.

"I do okay."

Ann interrupted the conversation, trudging up to them. "What time do we sail this afternoon."

"No sail. We stay in hotel tonight. Soon we get to hotel and you rest." François's wrinkled brow conveyed his concerned about this passenger's disorientation.

"I guess we sail in the morning, then," Ann offered.

"No. We have full day in Rome tomorrow. You like."

"Oh, I've been here already. I'm just waiting on the steps because I've already been in this church before. I'm sick of churches. Churches and castles. They all look alike after a while."

Carl and François looked at one another. Carl shrugged his shoulders. They accompanied Ann back down the steps to the waiting bus, totally unprepared for the events of the evening.

• • • •

Carl's groups had never stayed at Cielo Borgia, the hotel World Tours had chosen for this tour. World upheld a decent standard, even in their least expensive tours. The inexpensive tours Carl chose for these local Jackson groups, however, used tourist or first-class hotels, not luxury ones by any stretch of the imagination. The little time groups spent in hotels didn't justify the extra cost for a higher-grade. World Tours kept groups busy from breakfast to often eight or nine o'clock at night. It would be different if one planned to hang out and use a spa, but for the purpose of these groups, the hotel served as a place to sleep.

Hotel Cielo Borgia turned out to be a boutique sort of hotel. A small but adequate lobby greeted guests with careworn but elegant gold-leaf furniture, the requisite white and black marble floor, and crystal chandeliers, patinaed with dust, making them somehow more venerable and costly looking. A restaurant occupied the far right-hand part of the lobby, accessed by a couple of broad, white marble stairs. Carl remained in the lobby, watching his clients check in, and the aftermath, the inevitable litany of complaints.

Carl sidled up to the handsome François where he would have a ringside seat to the after-check-in traumas. "This hotel was a nice choice for World Tours. Lots of, how we say, character…."

Just then, Clarice Strain exploded out of the elevator before the door even fully opened, a rush like trapped sea water. She came straight at Carl.

Chapter Ten

Checking Out At Check-In

"I can't believe this. I can't stay in that room," Clarice cried out.

"What to be problem, *Signora*?" François asked, with genuine concern written on his face.

"The lamp shades are tipped, leaning crooked, and I have Meniere's disease, so my balance is off, and the lamp shades are making me sick to my stomach."

Carl looked at her dumbly, mouth agape.

François took over. "We fix lamps right away. I have hotel staff there right away. You go have a drink at bar and I have lamps fixed."

He snapped his finger at a porter while, with the other hand, he directed Clarice to the small, starkly modern—compared to the rest of the décor— Formica and mirrored bar at the far end of the lobby, along the left-hand wall of the restaurant.

"I don't drink. I want to change my clothes and lay down."

"Have a soda and we fix your problem."

Just then Sally pushed Clarice out of the way. Carl quickly drew closer to François, practically joining him like a Siamese twin.

"This is entirely unacceptable. There is a spot on the carpet in my room. It is a very suspicious spot," Sally said.

"I will have housekeeping right away. What room is it."

"Two thirteen. But I don't think it will come out. It is very suspicious."

"Sally, I've been to your house and there are spots in the carpet there and they don't even have the advantage of being suspicious. Spots beyond reasonable doubt." Carl turned to François. "Cats."

François's nose wrinkled and he motioned for Carl to be quiet.

"Can't I have a different room? Louise has already taken all the dresser drawers and most of the closet. I don't think she's going to be a good roommate. I should have my own room. I usually get upgraded because I travel so much. I want an upgrade."

"The hotel is full. You must fix your problems with roommate. If she is trouble you tell me, and I speak with her."

Carl looked at François, seeking some sign of a rift in his cool reserve. François remained stoic, a real professional.

Clarice still stood there, wavering to demonstrate her ruined balance, and Sally had her hands stubbornly on her hips, not willing to go anywhere until receiving an assurance of spotlessness. Suddenly Joseph, of the tardy Joseph and Georgia Mae duo, appeared.

"I hate to bother you, François, but my wife, Georgia Mae, says the room is too hot. I think it's okay, but she is going to whine and complain and drive me…and you… crazy if they can't turn on the air conditioner. She's used to air conditioning. She always worked in air conditioning, and she keeps the house like a meat locker. I go around in a winter coat in the summer, but she says it's comfortable." He made air quotes.

"*Signore*, it fifty degrees Fahrenheit outside. It is April. The hotel not turn air conditioning on until July. It need more than eighty degrees outside for air condition. The windows open. Open window please. Have a fresh air."

"I told her that. She said it makes her nervous. Security and all that."

"You on third floor, *Signore*. What to happen in open window on the third floor? A bird? Is she afraid of the bird?"

"No need to get snippy with me." Joseph turned and headed toward the elevator.

Out of the elevator lumbered Mahalia of refrigerator suitcase fame, who headed right toward Carl. He slipped behind François but not quickly enough.

"I see you hidin' back there. Hey, you know I have a mobility problem and so does my sister, Latrisha. Any chance we get a room on the first floor?"

François answered, "There are no guest rooms on first floor, what you call first floor. All hotel rooms start on first floor, which you Americans call second floor but here is first floor where you stand already."

"Cut the double-talk, buster. What I wanted was a ground floor room."

Carl, peeking around François's shoulder, spoke up. "I requested that you and your sisters' room should be near the elevator. That will help with the mobility issues."

"It sure is near the elevator. Right next to the elevator. You know how noisy that's going to be tonight?"

"It not be so bad. This no entertainment hotel. Most people come to sleep so it quiet by twenty-two o'clock."

Mahalia looked alarmed. "When the hell is twenty-two o'clock? Are we on Jupiter or what?"

"It's ten o'clock in American, Mahalia. Not too late," Carl added.

"I don't care what time it is in America. I plan to sit in that bar until I'm good and tired and wasted, and then I want to be able to go to my room and sleep. No bullshit."

"It be fine," promised François, patting Mahalia's forearm. "No noise for you to sleep."

· · · ·

All the tables in the dining room were set for four people so Carl took one in the back, leaving room for François to join him for the first dinner in Rome. Instead, Mahalia and the two sisters, Latrisha and Eugenia, sidled to his table and sat down.

"You don't mind if we sit with you, do you?" Mahalia asked.

"Not at all. Be my guest." Carl hid disappointment well, behind a smile.

"She thinks that you get better food than the rest of us 'cause you're the boss," Eugenia said, pointing at Mahalia.

"That's not true. No matter where we go, I get the same as everybody else. And since I usually travel alone, except for this tour where I got Owen as a roommate, I get a much smaller room than anyone else."

"I don't believe you. Are you going to at least buy us drinks?" Mahalia asked.

"Dinner tonight comes with a glass of wine," Carl said, placatingly.

François entered the dining room from the lobby and a member of the waitstaff ushered him into what looked like a small, private, and elegant looking dining room next to the larger one where the group assembled.

"I want a real drink," Latrisha, the until-now quiet sister, clarified. "Wine is for sissies. I'm going to have me some scotch or whisky or whatever these I-talians got here."

"Tell you what. I'll buy you all your first drink and then you're on your own."

The wine had, by this time, been poured at each place setting and Mahalia raised her glass. "To Carl and scotch." The two others, Latrisha and Eugenia, raised their glasses in solidarity.

Meanwhile, Sally, at the very next table, who might have claimed diminished capacities in every sense except the auditory required for eavesdropping, started a murmuring that fluttered around the room. Everyone's eyes turned to the table of Carl and the three sisters. Briana stood up and approached Carl.

"They say y'all are buying everyone at your table drinks. Sally said she heard that. If you do that you should buy everybody a drink. That's only fair."

Carl turned pale. He remained silent for more than a moment, a worried look coming across his face.

"Okay," he said gingerly. "But just one on me. The rest you pay for yourself."

The room erupted into applause so enthusiastic that it sounded as if they were splitting a winning lottery ticket. François stood in the doorway and when he saw what happened with the free drinks, broke into a broad grin, and brought his hands together as if in prayer. Happy passengers had the makings of a big tip for him at the end of the tour.

As dinner wound down, François came out of the private dining room and banged a spoon on a waterglass. "Let's have little business meeting then I know you want to get good sleep night before long day tomorrow. Tomorrow morning orientation tour, then you have afternoon free for lunch and shopping near Spanish Steps. Then afternoon at Vatican and stay in hotel for dinner. After dinner we take quick drive in motorcoach and go light show at Augustus Forum. You will never see any so magnifique as Rome at night. Light show be like Rome in ancient times. One thing I caution you. Are you listen?"

At least half of the tables had devolved into chatter. Carl banged his knife on a waterglass. "Come on, people. Give your attention to François for just a few more minutes."

Most people stopped talking but some scowled at Carl for interrupting their important conversations. François nodded his thanks to Carl and continued.

"Italy very interesting place. Rome interesting place. There no crime here." The audience grumbled their disbelief. "I don't mean no crime, but no violent crime. You walk streets here, even at night, even a woman walking at night, by herself, even street walker, and she won't get how you say mooged."

Sally corrected François. "Mugged, the word is mugged."

"Mugged. You not get mugged. You won't get the knife. You no get hit on head. You not get with the gunned. No body Italy has gun. Not even police have the gun. Only Mafia have gun." He waited for laughter which came grudgingly, only after the audience realized he was kidding.

"No. François just tease with you. No Mafia anymore. Only in movies. You not have afraid walk alone any time. You be afraid of pickpocket. Please listen me good. Pickpocket never hurt you, but they take all your money, and you won't know except you look. Then you know. They get everything you not pay attention. I not supposed to say but I say anyway. They say it socially unconscious to say it."

"I think he means social conscience," Sally said, as if she'd become François's official translator.

"Yes. I mean not socially conscience to say Gypsy, but it be Gypsy that pick the pocket. I mean it. You are careful. I know you lady like to carry purse, some men too, pocketbook, what you call it. Gypsy, they grab it. Men you have wallet sticking out of back pocket like a tumor on the butt. They grab that. Tumor gone faster than medical operation. You leave passport and money you don't need in suitcase in room. Room safe. Nobody except maid go in room. Maid never steal nothing. Maid steal something maid never work again in life. No steal. You take only money you need and put in inside pocket with zip or button. Put money in shoe. Wherever Gypsy can no get. You know why called Gypsy?" François looked at his dull audience, only a few of whom seemed to listen.

"'Cause they gyp you?" Briana offered.

"No. 'Cause they from Egypt. At least history think come from

Egypt from Persia then Romania. Everywhere there Gypsy. Even good old USA have the Gypsy."

"I don't think so," Georgia Mae said skeptically. "You're supposed to have your passport with you at all times. The travel book says that."

"You no need passport when shop and have lunch and travel in motorcoach. You need passport when you leave Italy next week. You not have passport in week if you carry it with you every day. You bet my words. Passport get lost."

"What about the safe in the room?" Georgia Mae asked.

"Yes. I say passport safe in room."

"That's not what I mean. I mean there is a safe or a safe deposit box in the room usually. Can we use that to put passport and money?"

"That okay if you remember to empty when we leave for next hotel. I no say how many the tourists leave thing in safe box. Jewelry, watches, car keys, passports, money, eyeglasses, hearing aids, telephones…you get picture? I see it all. Somehow you remember to empty safe before you go. We come back on last night, but you not have stuff if you leave in Rome. Am I make sense?"

Several grumblings of approval came from around the room.

"I say one more thing. Carl, your generous tour organizer, said you can allow some extra people from outside join your group. We have two from Canada and three from Australia and I hope you become friend. Allen, there, from Australia. I hope you be friends. He roommate with Victor. Where Victor?"

Victor waved his hand from a table across the dining room, his fat face white, like a big blooming cauliflower of dissatisfaction with the prospect of sharing hotel rooms.

"Four other come in late tonight and you meet at breakfast here in this room tomorrow morning eight o'clock. Breakfast start eight o'clock. Important you be here eight o'clock for breakfast. We leave nine o'clock you have breakfast or no. Now have good night sleep."

Everyone got up and proceeded to the lobby where they'd wait for the elevator. Notably, the three sisters remained at the table. "Aren't you going to get some sleep?" Carl asked, but it sounded more like a suggestion.

"Not before havin' a few more highballs," retorted Latrisha.

"Okay. I'll leave you to it."

Carl stepped outside the hotel onto the sidewalk. The air seemed fresh and cool compared to the stuffy hotel restaurant. He took in a deep breath and stretched his back, raising his arms in a yoga sun salutation.

"Do you care about walk?" François leaned against the building, watching Carl.

"Sure. I was hoping to do that before going to bed."

"I show you nice place a few block near." François guided Carl with a hand on his shoulder as if old friends. Carl sidled a little closer to François.

François led them to a little square, not much bigger than the center of an intersection of two streets. A small marble fountain stood in the middle of the square with spigots on all sides. A woman filled a jug from one of the spigots. Other than that, the square was practically empty.

"They don't drink that stuff?"

"They do. Water all across Rome to drink. Water fountain from springs. Clean. Cleaner than house water. You try?" François started to get up.

"No. I think I'll skip it. So, you live in Rome, François?"

"No. I Français. Paris home. When I do Italy tour, I do Italy tour all season. That April to October. I live in small furniture apartment near. Only for day off between tour. Sometime no day off between tour. After you tour same day, another tour start and no day off. Not go home to furniture apartment. Maybe go home to change clothes in suitcase on night in furniture apartment."

"I think it's called a furnished apartment."

"You correct. I get noun and adjective mixed in English. Much better Italian. Much, much better in French. Grew up France. I am France. I mean I am French I think you say English."

"Yes. You are French."

"Furnished apartment enough for François. François not have much things. Some clothes. Not how you say materially."

"I think the word you're looking for is materialistic. You're not materialistic. I wish I could be that way."

"I can tell. Watch give it away."

"My watch?" Carl looked at his watch.

"Longines very thin, real gold, real expensive. *Dottore* not like cheap stuff. I tell. Not buy convenient store watch."

"No, I didn't buy this in a convenience store." He emphasized convenience rather than make an outright correction.

"I can tell *Dottore* like fine things. I not like things. Things start to own you. You worry where you keep all things, so you buy house or big apartment. Then you worry to keep house or apartment. Then you work hard you don't want to. You work for things you not really want. You buy more things. You take care of house. Need fix hot water heat, need this, need fix that, you work and buy more. You cut lawn. You pull the weed. You make self crazy instead you enjoy the freedom, the friends, the company."

"You forgot weed eating."

"You eat the weed? François feel sorry on you!"

"No, it's a yard chore that I hate. Noisy. Dirty. But I'm not that bad about collecting things. Someone has to do it, though."

"No, *Dottore*. Lots live like François and have only what one need and spend all time enjoying world. Enjoy the travel. Enjoy the people, the food, the music, the architect. Not have the weed eat to worry."

"But if people didn't collect things, enjoy things, and keep things, there'd be no museums, no collections. Almost everything in great museums had to be collected by people at some point in time. Then there would be no artists because someone has to buy their things, their art."

"The great collectors buy things with wages not paid fairly the workers. Like stealing from poor to give to rich. Buy stuff and make rich even richer."

"Maybe some of them," Carl conceded.

François sat silently for a moment with a slightly furrowed brow. "Maybe *Dottore* right," François finally said. "Maybe different between art and junk. Tourist mostly buy junk not art. Not help artist much. Still think it not so good for people with so much junk."

"It's not really my expertise, François, but I think your European economy would crash if people stopped buying all the crap."

"The crap seller disappear for sure. Find something else to do. Work for environment instead of make crap. I not know either." Both fell silent.

"It a lonely life the tour director." François looked down at his feet.

"But you're always meeting new people. Hundreds of people in a season. Some of them must be fun, or at least nice."

"Most like your client. Pain in ass."

"I've heard from World Tours that my clients are considered a problem here."

"Yes, World Tours warn me about Carl Minton groups. Other tour directors say, stay away from Carl Minton groups, but they also say you person nice and that you helpful and François going to like Carl who handsome like American movie star."

François turned and gave Carl an impish smile. Carl's face flushed even though he'd had only a single glass of wine.

"François, compared to you, I look like a dog, but I hate having that reputation…I mean about my clients being assholes."

"Maybe you make up for it?" François sat back up and put his arm around Carl's shoulder again.

Carl settled into François's arm. "So, do you have a family? A girlfriend? Wife? Significant other?"

"Too difficult when in travel business. Sometimes meet person I like. Then gone. Only in place most a few days. Then gone. Then relationship over. I like meet someone who I see more. Enough about me. What for you?"

"I don't travel as much as you, but it is every month. So, it's difficult to have a relationship." Carl paused as if considering how much he wanted to divulge. "I had a relationship with a man before I started the travel business. Now I'm gone at least once a month and it doesn't work."

"What you do before travel business?"

"I was a psychologist. Since I graduated from college, I was a musician for a few years then I became a psychologist. Ten years was enough. I got sick of listening to people's problems. All the time. Nobody ever came to see me unless they had some sort of godawful problem. It wore me out. Then I had the opportunity to take a group to England and I thought, I can do this, so gradually I started doing more travel and less psychology, but you know what?"

"No, what?"

"Now all I do is listen to people's problems anyway. You heard them in the hotel. They'll make stuff up just to have something to complain about. They don't have it so nice at home, but they'll complain about everything on a trip."

"Yeah. You group have reputation. Some tour director say not want Minton group. You have ninety people on one Italy tour once?"

Carl chuckled. "It was ninety-three to be exact. I could never forget it."

"Those ninety-three they ruin Italy. They at least ruin tour directors.

Three tour directors no more want Minton group." François turned to face Carl and spoke in an imitation of the Frankenstein monster's gruff voice. "World Tours good, Minton bad."

They both laughed and jabbed at one another. "Do you think it's my fault?" Carl asked.

"No. I see them different. Americans difficult to travel. Too spoilt. But yours different. Maybe more than a little spoilt."

They sat silently, François with his hand rubbing Carl's knee.

"I know all the group organizers complain about a few of their clients," Carl said finally. "Plenty of them are really nice people, but there are a bunch of them in every group that make me want to quit."

"So, you think about quit the travel?"

"I think about it. But there's a lot of places I still want to see."

"You need the money travel business? Not so bad. You put up with asshole, but you see world. Money good?"

"The money's not important. I have plenty." Carl looked away and gritted his teeth as if he wished he hadn't said that.

"Then you just travel. You go on own. No cares."

"I don't know. I like traveling with people. It makes it interesting. If you go by yourself, you don't really meet people, you do a lot of things by yourself. It's not the same. On every trip I usually find some group to join…or someone like you who's interesting to talk to."

"Thank you." François leaned and gave Carl the briefest kiss on the top of his head as he stood up. It almost wasn't noticeable, it was so fast, but Carl stared at François.

"You mind if François friendly? You bored and François too friendly. François try to see he make you happy in Italy. We see. But you nice man and François knows to make happy, and you make François happy, and trip be one what you remember. You remember François sure."

"That's nice, François. I'm looking forward to it."

"Lot to look forward to," François said and seemed to briefly smooth the front of his pants, suggestively. Carl looked away, as if embarrassed.

"But you haven't told me much about you, François." Carl also stood.

"Like what you want to know? I'm here and you here."

"Like where did you grow up? What did you study in school? What jobs did you have? Are you married or in a relationship?"

"I study art history and what you call hospitality in Tours in university. Hotel and tour management. Then I start right away for tour director. Want to be special art tour director. Maybe come soon."

"So, you grew up in Tours? It's a genuinely nice city. I've never seen a flower market like the one in Tours, all the way down the main street."

"I grew up in Tours. Some other country, too. Father foreign service in Algiers. Mother from Algiers. Mother African and Arab. Sometime stay with father in Algiers. Some other places in Africa. Make François like travel."

"We better start back to the hotel. Tomorrow is a long day of sightseeing in Rome, and I don't want my clients to see me all worn out."

"We go to hotel. We not wear out tonight. Plenty night for wear out," François laughed and gave Carl a quick pat on his behind before taking off, slowly, for the hotel.

Carl and François entered the lobby a little after eleven o'clock. The lobby looked empty, but the three sisters remained at their table in the restaurant. Fresh, sweaty-looking glasses of whiskey with ice perched in front of all three.

"Hey, Carl. Hey, Francis or whatever your name is. Come here and have a nightcap with us."

"No, ladies. It's time for bed."

"You're a party poop!" Mahalia slurred. The three sisters stood up, each with a drink in hand, unbalanced, as if on a ship's deck in a storm. They clearly had not moved since dinner and didn't realize how drunk they had gotten. Latrisha moved toward Carl in the lobby, holding her glass of whiskey, not seeing the step down to the lobby. She missed the step and lost her balance and footing.

Chapter Eleven

Wreckage

Latrisha reached out for the object nearest her, a plexiglass podium, the *maître d'* station holding menus, a podium not secured to the floor or anything else. As Latrisha grabbed the podium for balance, it tipped precariously toward the neighboring grand piano in the corner of the lobby. She did not relinquish the glass of whiskey. Whiskey, sister, plexiglass podium, and the menus thereon, toppled to the floor and slid under the piano with the sound of shattering glass and moaning, followed by a shocked silence. It looked like the scene following a tornado.

Carl and François rushed to the piano. The porter on duty pressed his palms into his cheeks in dismay, frightened into inactivity. The manager ran back and forth on the keyboard side of the piano, ducking, once in a while, to see the extent of the damage below.

"*Cosa problema, qui problema*," he moaned and pointed to François and threw his hands up helplessly.

François ran to the left side of the piano, along the wall, and Carl ran to the curved side, facing the restaurant. They looked dumbstruck.

"Should we push her toward you or pull her toward me?" Carl asked.

François shrugged his shoulders. Carl squatted on the floor and tried to extricate the jumbled mass of sister, broken podium, and shattered whiskey glass by pulling the podium toward himself. Latrisha, fully conscious although inebriated, contributed no movement forward toward François, nor backward toward Carl at her feet. She struggled momentarily against Carl's efforts to pull her out. Carl reached gingerly to pull her out by her shoes, which came off in his hands. He then grabbed the base of the podium, upon which she had affixed herself and slid it slowly toward him. Latrisha rode the overturned podium out from under the piano like a shipwreck survivor trying to ride a half-submerged lifeboat. François came around the piano to help Carl. He squatted up against Carl and helped slide the considerable weight toward them.

"Oh, my God. Now I'll have a client in the hospital," Carl said to François, quietly. "It won't be the first time. But for sure this one is going to blame the hotel, blame me, sue me, sue World Tours."

The hotel manager interrupted Carl's nightmarish soliloquy by bending down to Latrisha, somewhat ahead of Carl and François in the compassion department. "*Signora*, are you hurt? Do you think you can come up?"

The manager looked to the porter who still had his hands on either side of his face and was pacing in a tight circle like a Doberman acting as a watchdog. The porter not being any help, the manager turned to François. "Don't just sit there on floor. Get chair for *Signora*."

Latrisha started extricating herself from the podium, which seemed to have broken into several pieces.

"I think you should call a doctor," Carl suggested to the manager.

The porter still had his hands pressed to his cheeks and mouth agape in helpless horror, although he stopped pacing and just watched, frozen in place like a victim of Vesuvius.

"No. I don't want a doctor. I'm fine. See, I'm fine." Latrisha took a wobbly step toward the bar.

"Madame, there is a doctor on call at all times. It is not problem. You should see doctor to yourself."

"I see to myself just fine." Latrisha turned around and seemed disoriented. Her sisters, Eugenia and Mahalia, for the first time, came to her assistance, one on either side, supporting her arms. Miraculously, Latrisha seemed barely injured. A little blood but apparently no broken bones.

"So, can I get you something?"The manager asked, having struck out with his offer of a doctor.

"I want to go to my room. Bring me another scotch," Latrisha demanded.

"Are you sure you not want help. You want doctor?" One could see the worry in the manager's eyes and the nervous shaking of his extended hands.

"I said I want a scotch. dammit. Whadda ya all gone deaf? Bring my sisters scotch. too. We're going to our room."

The manager walked behind the bar and grabbed a bottle of Chivas Regal from behind the counter, opened it, and handed it to Mahalia.

"That should do for a few hours." Latrisha looked at the expensive bottle and nodded approval to the manager.

"She won't feel a thing tomorrow. She probably won't even remember," Mahalia assured the manager.

The three sisters, arm in arm, waddled toward the elevator. The manager shrugged his shoulders and turned toward the reception desk, ignoring the porter who stood there rubbing his eyes as if he had dreamed the whole thing.

François and Carl still stood next to the piano, a little breathless from their exertion and fright.

"*Dottore*, I never see anything like it ever on the worse tour," François said.

"I don't think you'd ever see anything like it anywhere on earth." Carl took a deep breath.

"I hope she can move tomorrow and not too much pain."

"She'll still probably be too drunk to feel pain tomorrow."

"Good night, *Dottore*." François grabbed Carl by both biceps and squeezed, rubbing his arms up and down.

"*Buonanotte*, François. Let's hope tomorrow goes a little better," Carl stuttered, hope missing from his voice.

Chapter Twelve

Where's The Bacon

Carl's clients started arriving in the dining room at six o'clock the next morning, startling and annoying the waitstaff who used those early hours to set tables for breakfast. Disregarding the sign that ordered they wait to be seated, one of Carl's particularly rotund couples, Lucas and Lacey Mae Long, took seats at a table already set near the yet empty buffet. The waitstaff, busy running back and forth, ignored the Longs.

"What is this? They're going to make us wait 'til eight o'clock? I'm starving," Lucas Long complained.

"Me, too. At least they could bring us some coffee." Lacey Mae chimed in, distraughtly wringing her fingers.

The waitstaff tried to work with their backs turned to the interlopers, but when Lucas grabbed one by the elbow, who happened to be the *maître d'*, he turned to address the offending couple. "*Signora e Signore*. You please wait until eight o'clock. You please wait in lobby. Staff has work. We may not be food ready if you come in dining room when we work here to get ready."

"Well, of all the…" Lacey Mae said as she stood up indignantly. "Let's go, Luke. I'm sure we can find coffee in the neighborhood."

"Yeah, Lace. Let's get outta here. These rude foreigners. Somebody should teach them some manners. The food's probably awful anyway."

World Tours clients had filled the dining room when Carl arrived at eight o'clock. They had obviously overwhelmed the staff before opening time. As he walked past the table where Sophia and Sally sat, Sally grabbed his shirt sleeve. "You're late this morning. If you're late, you make the whole group miss part of the tour."

Wrenching his arm free, Carl responded humorlessly. "Breakfast isn't supposed to start until eight o'clock. So, I'm exactly two minutes late." Carl checked his watch to be sure. "An hour is plenty of time to eat breakfast. The bus isn't going to start the tour until nine o'clock, whether you're waiting for it or not."

"Well, you should check on the passengers and make sure everyone is okay," Sally added haughtily, shaking her teaspoon at Carl.

"Suppose I just deputize you to do that, Sally," Carl said as he moved on, then stopped in his tracks as if he had second thoughts. He walked back to the table. "Just enjoy your breakfast, Sally. I'll look after everyone."

Carl sidled to the buffet. Even the rushing waitstaff could hardly keep up with demand.

Ida Sue saw the look of dismay in Carl's face. "I gotta admit, these are the eatin'est people I ever seen."

"You can say that again, Ida Sue."

"These are the eatin'est people I ever seen."

Carl shook his head and, looking away, rolled his eyes.

Jimmy Gage grabbed Carl's shirtsleeve, which started to show the marks of greasy fingerprints. Jimmy was dressed, as usual, in a shiny, worn-out-looking warm-up suit complete with food stains. "There's no bacon. I have to have my bacon in the morning. What kinda place is this, anyhoo? Y'all check that out before you book a place like this?"

Carl looked at Jimmy, who had the shape of a pregnant bull stuffed into a sausage casing. "Maybe Italians don't eat bacon. Did you notice there's lots of sausage?"

"I don't want their sausage. Who knows what's in that stuff."

"Calm down, Jimmy," his wife admonished, shaking her head. "A few days without bacon won't kill you."

"Yeah, but a few more days of bacon might kill him," Carl said, under his breath.

Carl sat down at a table where François seemed to be in a rush, drinking coffee and eating a single fresh-out-of-the-oven croissant.

"*Buongiorno*, François."

"*Buongiorno, Dottore.*" François laid his hand on Carl's and provided his toothiest smile. "You mind I have no breakfast for you. I discuss directions with driver. He came from Milan for tour, and he not knows the Rome tour as regular driver. Excuse me, please." He got up and left the dining room.

Carl sat blessedly alone. Most of his passengers had finished and now clogged the lobby where they'd wait the hour until the tour bus departed. Carl looked with longing at all the delicacies on the buffet. Eggs done any way one desired. A sandwich counter that offered every imaginable lunch meat and assortment of cheeses that no one would find back home. One counter displayed cold cereal and hot cereal. One section of fruit had items probably flown in from Egypt, where anything other than local produce came from.

The bread section tempted Carl the most. Nothing existed, anywhere in the USA, like the bread made in Italy, or France, or Germany, or England, or anywhere in Europe for that matter. But the Italian bread surpassed all the others. And such variety. Carl could forego anything except the bread. He broke down and selected a chunk of plain white baguette. With butter. His eyes rolled back in his head as if he'd had a vision of heaven. He moved on to the cold cereal counter, which offered grain cereals mixed with dried fruit and nuts. Dried fruit toppings ranged from prunes to apricots, pineapple, and all sorts of nuts.

"Is that all you're gonna eat?" Brianna zoomed in after all the other passengers had finished. "No wonder you don't gain weight."

"No, Brianna. I'm this way on purpose. It really isn't much of a hardship to stick to a cold cereal breakfast with such interesting variety."

"That's how we can tell you're not from here…I mean Mississippi, 'cause there'd be at least fifty pounds more of you. You don't eat the way we do."

"I get indigestion if I eat all that greasy stuff in the morning. Normally a bowl of oatmeal is it," Carl said, between meager bites.

"I don't know what would happen to me if I ate that bird food." Brianna grabbed a gooey, sugary-looking pastry, a paper cup of coffee, and headed to the lobby.

Carl stood at the curb while the passengers boarded the bus. François had boarded already, trying to get everyone settled. Carl saw Sophia lumbering toward the bus with her large suitcase. "Sophia, we're just doing a tour of Rome today. You didn't need to pack."

"It's empty. It's just for my shopping."

"Sophia, there's no room on the bus for a suitcase that large."

"Put it underneath and I'll get it each time we stop to shop."

"We can't load and unload it everywhere we go. We'll be in city traffic most of the time. Put it back in your room. You have time. Don't you have a couple of shopping bags?"

"Yeah, but I don't think they will be big enough."

"I'm sure some of the stores will give you a bag if you buy enough junk."

"It's not junk!" Sophia whined in her southern drawl. "It's gonna be gifts! I have a lot of people to buy gifts for."

"Fine, Sophia. Put the suitcase back in your room."

"*Dottore*, can you assist. Here." François had turned slightly red, hair not quite perfectly quaffed as at breakfast, and he seemed somewhat distraught.

"Is the façade beginning to crack?" Carl asked rhetorically, too quietly to be heard.

"Here I am." Carl pushed his way onto the bus with passengers trying to squeeze backpacks, hand luggage, coats, and hats into the overhead storage or under the seats. François led him to the back of the bus.

"This might be problem, *Dottore*." François pointed to Nora Sweets. "She not sit with roommate."

Nora wagged her finger for Carl to get closer so she could whisper. "She's too big. She takes up more than one seat. There's no way for me to sit next to her."

"There won't be enough seat. There only fifty seats on motorcoach and you and me must have whole seat," François explained to Carl.

"I'm not sitting with her," Nora whispered and crossed her arms, stubbornly.

François stood with a hand on either hip. "It will be problem when we rotate seat. There not enough seat."

"And I'm not rotating seats! I like a seat near the back of the bus and I'm going to stay here for the whole trip. In this seat. Get it, bub?"

"You can't do that, Nora. It's against company rules. It's not fair to other passengers if a few hog the front while others are stuck in the back. And you can't take up two seats. Ann is your roommate, and she has to sit with you."

"Then you can just rotate around me."

"No, Nora. This is an issue of fairness. And you meet more people if you move around on the bus."

"I don't want to meet any of these people. Anyway, I know most of them already, so that's not a very good argument. And you can't make me move."

Carl turned to François. "We might have to leave Nora behind."

"World Tours doesn't like that," François responded.

"Nora wouldn't like that either," Nora chided.

"If we don't have enough seats, someone has to go—"

Carl's attention was caught by Latrisha, transubstantiated into the hung-over sister, lumbering up the steps, eyes bloodshot and puffy, her whole face puffy. Her right arm rested in a makeshift sling, apparently made of a pillowcase borrowed from the hotel. A whole wad of small bandages were stuck to each knee and a large one covered her chin. Spandex shorts revealed her girth, if not more. The passengers became suddenly silent.

Carl kept his distance. "Are you okay? Maybe you should spend the morning resting in your room?"

Mahalia continued to push Latrisha up the steps, as the third sister, Eugenia, seemed to be guarding from behind so that they couldn't plummet backward off the bus.

"I'm not okay. Can't you see! I'm sick! I feel like the hind quarters are bad luck. But I paid good money for this trip and I'm not missing any of it."

Joseph, sitting in the second row, stood up. "Georgia Mae and me will move back a few seats so that Mahalia and her sister can sit up here where it'll be easier to get on and off."

"I'm going to set you and Georgia Mae up for sainthood. Where is Georgia Mae?" Carl looked around. "Luckily we're going to the Vatican later," Carl said but no one laughed. "Here you go," he said to sisters Latrisha and Mahalia, indicating the vacated seats, forgetting Georgia Mae in the confusion.

François made his way to the front of the bus and grabbed the microphone. "First we do a little driving tour and then we stop at Spanish Steps for lunch and shopping."

Sophia's hand shot up. "What is this with Spanish Steps. I thought we were going to Rome. That's supposed to be in Italy. Are we in Spain instead?"

"The Spanish Steps are Rome. Rome in Italy. I will explain later, when we arrive, why they name Spanish Steps," François continued. "We drive around Colosseum, and we show you where you meet motorcoach and then drive to Roman Forum where we get out and stretch and maybe use facility. You know what means facility?"

Nods of approval came from the passengers. Only a hand or two went up, which were quickly pulled down by seatmates and whispers confirmed the explanation to the unknowing.

"Then we drive more to see Baths of Caracalla, Castle San Angelo, famous Trevi Fountain you throw three coins in, and we arrive at Spanish Steps where you find easy lunch and shop and have two hours and I show where motorcoach pick up. Afternoon Vatican and Vatican Museum. Have to be on time. All day on time. Okay? We have everybody? I count."

"Georgia Mae still isn't here. She went to grab a breakfast," Joseph said, either flushed from last night's wine or embarrassment.

"We say we leave nine o'clock. We already ten minute late. You go get Georgia Mae now or we leave with no Georgia Mae. We have schedule. If we not at museums on time, we not go in. Ruin for everybody especial François. Time important on tour."

"Okay. I'll get her," Joseph said, begrudgingly.

Carl held up his hand, motioning for Joseph to stay seated. "That's okay, Joseph. I'll run in and get her. I can run faster."

"Suit yourself," Joseph replied, shrugging his shoulders, a look of relief that he didn't have to exert himself on behalf of his wife.

Carl skipped down the steps of the bus and moved quickly into the lobby. Georgia Mae sat by herself in the dining room, in full view of the loaded bus, drinking coffee and noncommittedly picking at a croissant.

"Georgia Mae! You're late. Everyone is waiting on the bus. It's ten minutes late!" Carl could hardly hide the irritation in his voice.

"I just have to go brush my teeth."

"If you do that, we leave you here. Now we're going to be fifteen minutes late. Think of all the people on the tour having to sit there and wait for you."

"All right. But I wish you wouldn't be such a stickler." Georgia Mae grabbed her jacket and oversized pocketbook and followed Carl out the front door and up the steps of the bus. As soon as Georgia Mae appeared at the front of the bus, passengers broke into applause.

Carl quickly snatched the microphone out of François's hand, almost taking a few fingers with it. "Please don't applaud. Please don't encourage people to be late. This is a bad precedent to start a tour. Please don't do that."

He handed the microphone to wide-eyed François who lifted his shoulders in incomprehension of Carl's outburst and watched Carl proceed to the seat next to his roommate, Owen. Owen seemed somewhat less than competent this morning, blankly staring out the window. All the seats, at this point, had been taken by passengers spreading out. Carl noticed that the three sisters, as oversized as Mahalia's luggage, had spread out. Seeing no empty double seats, Carl, by default, took the seat next to Owen.

The motorcoach headed into the ancient part of Rome along the Via di San Gregorio until the Colosseum stood straight ahead. François picked up the microphone. "As we approach Colosseum, you see cross in front of you. Cross to remember martyrs, the Christian martyrs we talk more about later at Catacombs but cross important today. Cross is where I meet you after time to walk around. You look. Take picture. Remember where cross is. Important you meet here after we walk around half hour."

The bus pulled to the curb in front of the cross. "You see Colosseum still biggest amphitheater in world even today. It start built seventy A.D. so not so old for Rome. Not B.C. like old things. Damage from earthquakes. Damage from Catholics. Renaissance stole marble for build St. Peter's Basilica." François paused, put up a single finger. "First recycle job." Despite the lack of laughter, François continued. "Colosseum once used for games. Fill with water on bottom for pretend ocean battles."

"Didn't they kill all the Christians here?" Sophia asked.

"Not all. You see you still here!" François tried to make a joke, but again it fell flat. "Kill some Christian. Public execution criminal, too. Some lions and Christian true, but not so much. Exaggerate. Mostly athletic games to entertain. Take mind off terrible politics. Like today? Like people pay attention to football instead of attention to politician so politician get away with murder while all in the people head is the football?"

"It's like football back home," Sophia concluded, seeming satisfied with the explanation, restating the obvious.

It took a full five minutes to empty the bus with passengers checking all around themselves for personal items stashed into seatback cubbies and the overhead compartments. François got on the microphone. "People. Hurry to get off. You don't need to bring things. We back on half hour. Motorcoach stay locked. You not to worry about things. It almost nine-thirty now. You be back on motorcoach at ten o'clock."

The passengers dispersed, some, but not many, to climb as far up in the Colosseum as possible, others to explore the labyrinth below, to find evidence of lions and torn limbs.

François beckoned Carl flirtatiously with a wave of his hand, and Carl followed like a puppy.

"You were so right about football. In the South, where we live, it is practically a religion. It's almost the only thing people talk about. They know nothing about history but can recite all these weird football facts and statistics to you. It's not even professional football. It's just some college games. Anyway, so what do you do when you get home to Paris for a break? Watch football?"

"No football for sure. Maybe sleep a lot. Tired after tour. Tour sometimes sixteen hours in a day, sometimes for ten days. Sometimes go to museum. Sometimes the music. Sometimes just coffee with friend."

"You have a lot of friends in Paris?"

"Not so much because never there. Some friends still from school. From lycée and university. I enjoy when client like you can talk to."

"Thank you, François. I'm really enjoying talking with you, too."

"Most passenger dull. Dull like knife not cut. Dull like round stone. I think like we talk about last night. We talk about with too much things. The people with too much thing get dull somehow. No?"

"I guess so. But I still say some collectors have great passions and that makes them interesting. They know the world in a different way. Because of the art and artifacts, they know so much more about history and culture. I think some of them are very interesting."

"You always talk collector, and I talk about the most people. Suppose goal for most people to get rid of things as get older. How you say downslide?"

"I think it's downsize."

"Get rid of collections and money. Change goal in life. Change for people so most successful the ones who die with nothing. The goal in life to make simple. Goal to die with nothing instead of the ones who die with billions. Spend most life giving away the things and make life simple. How different world be then."

"Yeah. Then instead of my clients buying all this junk, and lugging it home, they could bring junk they already have at home and give it away on tours. It would create good will wherever they went, instead of being considered ugly Americans."

"I think you make joke about way François think."

Carl sat silently for a moment then laughed. "You imagine World Tours groups going to China and bringing back all the junk? It would cause an international incident. Any idea taken to an extreme becomes absurd."

"*Dottore* good at absurd."

"I know, but when you think about it, giving stuff away instead of accumulating it would solve most of the world's problems. Certainly poverty and the environmental problems, probably even crime. I think you're on to something, François. But how do you change people?"

"The electronics change the people but it not the good way. Most people have the junk electronics and stuff from China. Always on the phone, always look up the nonsense information on the Google, listen to the headphones."

"I don't know, François. Maybe they get some emotional connection through these things. A connection to their friends." Carl hesitated for a moment before continuing. "Maybe not a connection to the world. Without their electronic things, most people would feel totally isolated in this world. I guess it works both ways, connecting people to their relatives or circle of friends but cutting them off from things happening right around them."

"Then it even more sorry when person like you say, with electronic connection, lose that connection. Better to be with real people and not want so many more things. Better to have other wish not materialis…"

"Materialistic. And distracted or preoccupied with electronic stuff. I was in Munich last year and wandered into the beer garden that's right in the middle of the city park called the English Garden. Everyone had great big steins of beer in front of them and a brass band played in the gazebo. Everyone seemed to be having a great time in conversation with the other people at their table and listening to music. They all listened to the same music instead of separately on earphones. And I noticed that not a single person talked on a cell phone. There wasn't a single cell phone or electronic device on any table that I could see. Hundreds of people. Can you imagine that scene in the USA?"

"There is difference…" François's response was cut short by returning passengers.

"We didn't want to be late, plus there's no shopping around here so there's nothing to do," Sophia said.

She tugged at Carl's sleeve and dragged him away from François's side. "I have trouble understanding him. Is he speaking English?" she whispered. A few of the other passengers joined Sophia and Carl.

"Yes, Sophia. He speaks English rather well."

"His accent is too strong. He should talk without the accent."

Carl continued to whisper. "I think it's because he leaves out some pronouns. Maybe a few articles and a few verbs that it makes it difficult to understand. I guess I'm just used to it, and you will be, too, in a day or two."

"Well, if I don't, I'll still enjoy the shopping…and the scenery."

François walked to where the huddle formed. "You still have fifteen minute. Walk and enjoy. Look at view of Forum over there. Beautiful view." The other passengers that had gathered turned around, looked and pointed, but didn't seem sure what they should be looking at.

"It looks sorta like parts of the Bronx I seen last year. You mean those falling down buildings out yonder?" Lucas asked François.

"Yes, two-thousand five-hundred-year-old falling down building."

"They ought to fix 'em up if people are going to come all this way and pay all this money to look at 'em," said Lucas, who because of his girth, would not wander too far from the bus. Certainly, climbing the steps of the Colosseum was out of the question.

"Yeah. Look at Disney World. You pay less to go to Disney World than you do to come here, and they got the real thing there. It's all standing up with spit and polish and nothing falling down at all. Everything's perfect in Disney World in the good ole USA," Lucas continued.

Carl put his hand on his forehead and François looked at him out of the corner of his eye but didn't laugh. François poked Carl in the ribs. "Good if all American go to Disney World instead Italy." He paused. "Except you." He poked him again.

By ten o'clock all the passengers had returned to the bus, Georgia Mae and Joseph, strolling arm in arm like newlyweds, not too far behind.

"Now we drive only few blocks, short distance to Forum. When we get to Forum, we get off motorcoach at entrance and you remember you return to entrance. Motorcoach not stay and wait because too busy. Too many tourist and too many traffics so motorcoach go away for half hour and come back. You be ready exactly eleven o'clock. You be at entrance exactly eleven you get on motorcoach quick, so we not hold up traffic. If you want, I give tour of Forum. If you not want, you walk on your own. You read sign and you know what going on. You ask guards. They speak English good as me so you can ask. Bathroom behind information office. You know facility? I know you all like bathroom. No more bathroom until lunch so you go bathroom. Yes?"

"How come you say motorcoach and Carl says bus?" Sophia asked.

François thought about it for a few seconds. "Motorcoach more dignity than bus. World Tours like us say motorcoach."

"Oh."

• • • •

Within minutes the bus pulled up at the entrance to the Forum. Most of the passengers gathered around François once they got off.

"You know almost five million people come here to see Forum during year. As many people as in big American city just to visit Forum. Forum the center of Rome for government and business. You have like that in American city?"

"I guess it's like Main Street," Sophia offered.

"Yes," François said. "Like USA Main Street but Forum many streets in blocks from here."

"Yeah, but our Main Streets aren't all falling apart like Rome," Lucas interjected.

Ida Sue joined in. "Yeah? Have you been to Tupelo lately? Or other towns that are just rotting to pieces because Walmart moved in and took over? And the flimsy way they build stuff there won't be anything at all left of American cities in two thousand years. Not even the walls."

François took the conversation back. "Rome built to last thousands years. All built brick inside cover with sometime marble sometimes concrete. You realize Rome have concrete two thousand years ago. Formula lost. Now only hundred years or so we have figure out concrete formula again. But here they have in Rome. This is old part of Rome. Some of this seven and eight hundred years before Christ. Seven and eight hundred year older than Colosseum. Not many realize. You realize Forum built on marsh. Yes, swamp. You know great American city built on swamp?"

"Jackson, Mississippi was built on a swamp. Everything in the south is built on a swamp." Cory said, now seated on her walker, having given up trying to maneuver it on the rough brick pavement.

"I think more like Washington DC built on swamp. No swamp no more. The swamp more just political saying. Drain swamp."

Only Carl laughed. The passengers had no reaction. François's humor almost never registered.

"Okay, we go for walk and François explain. You don't want walk, there benches, there facilities. We not be long time."

At eleven o'clock everyone, including Georgia Mae and Joseph, had ascended the steps of the bus and Carl smiled. Until he got to his seat.

"Where's Owen?" He looked around. "Where is Owen? Did anyone see Owen?"

Chapter Thirteen

Follow That Bus

"He was in the Forum. I saw him walking to the other end of the Forum," Sally volunteered.

"What seem to be problem?" François moved down the aisle toward Carl.

"Owen isn't on the bus," Carl said, rolling his eyes and shaking his head.

"You not to worry, *Dottore*. I go run through Forum and find Owen. He the old man, right? Soon I know all the name, but first day I not know all names. Owen old man?"

"Right. Owen old man. François, it will be faster if I go down one side and you go the other. We meet back here in ten minutes even if we don't find him. Hopefully, he has his tour book with him or remembers the hotel or at least that he's with World Tours."

"Yes. Police very good at finding tourists and returning them to owner. Police good for lost dog and for people."

Just as François and Carl disembarked, a taxi swerved in front of the bus, nearly knocking François down. A string of Italian invectives spewed from the otherwise calm François. François spoke Italian more comfortably than English. At least faster and louder. Italian lent itself to loud and fast, François's default language for cursing. Italian curses just rolled off the tongue, unlike the French ones that required the effort of more facial muscles.

No sooner had the cab come to a stop than Owen oozed out of the back seat. He went to the driver's window and tried to hand the driver a ten euro note. The driver pushed it away. Owen insisted. The driver grabbed Owen's wrist, took the ten euro note and squeezed a five euro note back into Owen's hand. Owen looked at it, in admiration, as if he'd received a gold watch.

"Owen, where have you been?" Carl could hardly disguise the annoyance in his tone.

"I went back to the cross by the Colosseum like you said. Nobody was there so I worried I was in the wrong place. Then I see our bus circle around the Colosseum, and I see the World Tours sign on the side of the bus, so I say to myself, that's our bus, so I see taxi cabs in line in front of the Colosseum and I get into the first taxi, and I say to the driver, follow that bus! And the driver turns to me and says, 'Who do you think you are, Humphrey Bogart?' I don't know what the guy is talking about. I just think it means something in I-talian, so I say again, Hurry up. Follow that bus. That's my bus. I'm supposed to be on that bus. I think he finally understood and even though he was far behind, he seemed to know where the bus was going and here we are. That's why I gave him ten euros. He saved my life, but he only wanted five euros to save my life, so I got this back." Owen displayed the five euro note as if were some sort of miniature banner of honor.

"Holy sheet!" exclaimed François.

"You can say that again. Holy shit!" Carl said as he indicated the bus door to Owen, and they set off for a short driving tour to the Spanish Steps.

• • • •

They disembarked at the top of the Spanish Steps and François gave as much information as he thought the passengers could process. "The bad news. There one hundred thirty-five steps. The good news is you only go down, not up. We pick you up in Piazza di Spagna, Spanish Square, down there." He pointed to the end of the square below. "Cost twenty thousand Scudi, like twenty thousand dollars to build Spanish Step. Imagine how cost today."

A hand went up. François pointed to the owner of the raised hand, as in a school room. "Why are they Spanish Steps?" Sophia asked.

"Question excellent," François answered. "Because down there, in Spanish Square, is old Spanish Embassy and so Spain pay to make nice area. Name stick. You okay I explain?"

"Okay. I believe you," Sophia said, sounding skeptical.

"Okay kids, you go down steps and work way to right, through Spanish Square, where you shop all you want and have lunch. François stay on motorcoach and do paperwork and learn names."

Carl felt dejected to not have François's company. "I'll try to keep an eye on everyone even though they'll spread out in Spanish Square. At least it's a self-contained area."

The two women with walkers, Cory and Helen stopped next to him. "We'll keep an eye out for Owen so that he doesn't wander off again. We're slower than everyone so it's no problem for us to watch him."

"Thank you, ladies. I appreciate your help," Carl said as he sat on the top step, enjoying the view of the square. Fifteen minutes later, as he headed down the steps and into the Square, he noted a cluster of uniformed police along the south side of the square. Upon closer scrutiny, he noticed that the police had surrounded a group of his clients like Indians around a wagon train.

Chapter Fourteen

Police Dance

Carl approached stealthily. Sophia, seeing Carl, broke away from the crowd. "The police here are so friendly. And look how handsome! Look at the arms on that one!" Indeed, Carl's eyes were drawn to the biceps bulging from the too-tight uniform shirt of the handsome policeman. "And can you believe it, they don't have any guns. No guns! Can you believe that? How do they keep crime down?"

"They probably have to worry more about keeping crazy women down then they do crime," Carl commented, trying to disguise his own fascination by tearing his eyes away from the display of manhood.

"Come here and see." Sophia pulled Carl into the crowd, which now attracted even more tourists and natives alike. Briana stood on the end, feeling the enormous bicep of that devilishly handsome cop who obviously wore his shirts tight to elicit just such an effect. Nora and Holly, between two other cops, apparently tried to teach them to line dance, while two other cops joined them, clapping their hands, trying to create a rhythm to the cacophonous singing of "The Electric Slide." The other clients, together with the Italians, line danced with the police and sung at the same time. The police displayed big smiles and looked so focused, as if dancing and singing were part of the job. Since no one complained, Carl moved on.

He wandered the square and stopped in a jewelry store. He asked to see an unbelievably thin gold watch with small diamonds in place of numbers. He recoiled slightly at a glimpse of the price tag. "I'll have to think about it," he told the clerk.

When he went outside, the police gathering had broken up and Piazza di Spagna returned to normalcy. Carl ducked into a chocolate shop where he had a better chance, maybe just barely, of justifying an extravagant purchase on a smaller scale.

Just as he paid dearly for a few grams of dark chocolate-covered seedless, dry pomegranates, the door burst open and Briana stuck her head in, dance-damaged big hair first. She seemed breathless from her dancing exertion.

"Do you have any free samples?"

The proprietress looked up dumbstruck. In Italy and anywhere in Europe, for that matter, one never enters a shop without a greeting and an inquiry as to the health of the proprietor or a comment on the weather. But Briana announced her Americanness in the next most obvious way, after the big hair. As if the proprietress would understand the question repeated, slower and louder, Briana asked again. "Do you have any free samples?" She raised her fingers up to her mouth repeatedly, imitating the motion of greedily consuming candy.

Carl tried to make himself as small and invisible as possible, turning back to the counter, hiding his face with his right hand.

Too late. "Carl, what did you get?"

Carl turned toward Briana, but the proprietress interrupted, answering Briana. She did not try to hide her disdain and spoke haughtily in deliberate but almost unaccented English. "No *Signora*. There are no free samples."

Not to be dissuaded, Briana spoke again. "Honey, at home the candy stores all have free samples. That's how they get you to buy things. You need to visit the USA to see how things are done right." The strength of Briana's southern accent ensured a lack of comprehension by the proprietress.

"I am sorry, *Signora*, but you bring in the flies." The proprietress shushed Briana away with a wave of her hand.

"Well, ah nevah!" Briana said, loudly, as she slammed the door to a clatter of bells and the shaking of the display cases, and through the glass, you could just barely hear Briana's utterance. "Foreign bitch!"

"Let me apologize on behalf of all America...." Carl said but couldn't quite control his giggling. The proprietress, humorless, waved him off just as she had Briana. Carl left the store but couldn't stop the uncontrollable giggles for quite some time. Carl started crossing the square, looking for a place to have lunch. He changed course when a man, a certain tall, dark, handsome tour director, waved to him from the front window of a restaurant.

Chapter Fifteen

Gone But Not Forgotten

At two o'clock most of his clients waited on the bus, two hours of free time being too much for many of them. Having everyone there on time was almost too good to be believed.

It was too good to believe. François came aboard and counted. "We are missing one."

Carl stood and quickly scanned the seats, looking only for an empty seat. "All of mine are here."

"Peggy isn't here. She not your group. She one of Canadian. What part of here and two o'clock she not understand?"

"I don't know, François, but I will help you look for her. I think she was the one with long brown hair. Really long hair. That might be obvious. Not too many women in Rome seem to wear their hair like that anymore."

"But don't go far, *Dottore*. We give her five minute. Motorcoach not allowed to park more than fifteen minute at Piazza di Spagna and we here already more than fifteen minute."

Carl and François scanned the square. Carl climbed the steps. Peggy was nowhere to be seen. On the way back, François looked briefly through the windows of stores and restaurants on the right and Carl did the same on the left. Still no Peggy.

"I do not like to do this, *Dottore*, but we have to go. If we late for Vatican, we not get in. Appointments are on time appointments, not come when you want appointments."

"What time is it now, François?"

"It more than two-twenty. We have to go."

"I guess if it was one of my clients, I'd have to argue with you. But I'm not responsible for all of World Tours' clients. You make the decision, François."

"We go."

François specified a route to the driver, taking them past the Trevi Fountain where so many tourists crowded the fountain and mostly hid it from view. "Motorcoach best way to see fountain because up higher can see above tourist," François commented. "Baths of Caracalla, you see on right. You see set up like theater? Opera and play now in baths instead of water. Ancient Rome the people come for the bath, the natural hot water spring under baths."

They eventually crossed the bridge in front of Castel St. Angelo. "Maybe Castel St. Angelo most famous for Tosca? Opera by Puccini… you all hear?" Most of the passengers scrunched up their faces at the mention of opera.

"I know Tosca," Ann said. "I've seen every opera."

Carl rolled his eyes.

Carl's youngest passenger, Holly, in the seat across the aisle, was focused with intense concentration on her iPad. "Holly, you're missing some of the most extraordinary scenery on earth!"

"I can see it better on my iPad. Without the heads in the way. Without turning around all the time."

"But you're missing the real thing."

"That's okay. These are really good pictures on the internet."

Carl just shook his head in dismay. François, who heard the exchange although facing straight ahead, rolled his eyes and held a raised hand to either side of his head as to not hear any more.

Following the Via della Rotonda, the Pantheon appeared on the right. François announced, "Here on right one most famous building from ancient Rome. Pantheon."

"Wait a minute Francene or whatever your name is, isn't the Pantheon in Greece? Yeah, it's in Athens. I saw it," Sophia burst out.

"That you saw Athens is Parthenon. This Pantheon."

Sophia didn't give up. "I bet they made it confusing on purpose so you wouldn't know where you were."

François chose to ignore the comment. "Here proof of ancient Roman brilliant engineer. Whole dome made concrete. Biggest dome in world until St. Peter's you see in a few minutes. Remember I say before formula for concrete lost until nineteenth century. No one know how does it. Still standing almost two thousand years. Still good shape. No? Was temple to Roman gods, now Catholic church inside."

• • • •

The group encountered no problems entering the Vatican Museum. April was still off season, and the gymnasium-size entrance allowed for the crowd to spread out. World Tours had agreements with most museums that groups did not have to stand in line but received tickets and entered separately from regular single tourists. François warned that the amount of walking required in the Vatican would be the most they had on this tour and that inspired Cora and Helen to bring their walkers into the museum.

"Almost everywhere we go you apologize about the amount of walking, then say it's the most amount of walking we'll have to do. Everywhere can't be the most amount of walking," Sophia said.

"It get better. You see. You get in better shape by end of tour."

Carl's group entered the large first gallery of the Vatican Museum. So far, so good. The first challenge, a set of what seemed like a staircase with at least one hundred steps, was conveniently located next to a door marked elevator. Carl headed up the steps with some of his clients, the others waited for the elevator.

At the end of that gallery another set of stairs, albeit shorter, descended. Carl heard the walkers squeal to a halt beside him.

"I don't see an elevator here," Cory complained, with Helen at her side.

"Let me go look in the hallway around the corner," Carl offered, sounding reluctant. A minute later he returned. "I don't see any elevator here. You can stay and see the rooms on this floor."

"I want to see the whole thing," Cory whined like a child.

"Okay, can you walk down the stairs if you hang onto the rail?"

"Sure."

"Okay. I'll take the walkers." Carl took the walkers from Cory and Helen. Cory's folded but Helen's weighed more, and the folding mechanism stuck.

"What the hell do you have in this thing?"

"My wallet is in there. Oh, and a doggy bag because I couldn't eat all my lunch back there on the Hispanic Steps."

"Spanish Steps, but you have an included dinner tonight so why would you carry food around?"

"I don't want to waste it."

Carl took the folded walker in one hand and the unfolded one he held out in front. He negotiated the steps with obvious difficulty, like trying to walk while locked in a cage, nearly tripping over the metal frame as he descended. Cory and Helen caught up to him within a few minutes. Carl set the walkers down and moved away from Cory and Helen, ignoring the exhibits in the immediate vicinity. He tried to get as far away from Cory and Helen as he could.

The plan didn't work for long.

Carl toured a few of the galleries of Renaissance art and came out to another staircase, where Cory and Helen waited like two grim reapers.

"Oh, it's a good thing you showed up, Carl. If we want to go to the Sistine Chapel, we have to go up this way. That's what the sign says." Cory pointed to the sign on a wall next to the stairs.

"Did you look for an elevator?"

"There is none here. Only back at the beginning or the other end. We asked the guard."

Carl was silent. He was trapped. He crossed his arms behind his back and straightened, demonstrating the pain in his back. "You sure you can handle the stairs?"

"As long as there's a railing," Helen insisted, pushing her walker toward Carl.

"If you can walk up all these stairs, how come you need the walkers?" He directed the question to both Helen and Cory.

"You never know when you'll find a place to sit down. It's more about a place to sit down," Cora answered. Helen nodded her head in agreement.

Reluctantly, Carl reassembled his cage of aluminum bars and vinyl seats about himself and began his precarious ascent. He kept accidentally banging the walker wheels on the edge of the stairs in front of him, nearly losing his balance each time. About one-third up the endless steps, he shifted his burden and heard a plastic/metallic clank, a clatter, and turned to see one of the wheels had fallen off a walker and rolled and danced and pattered down the stairs. "Stop, stop it I say," he called.

The wheel clattered within inches of Helen and Cory who made no effort to stop it.

"You'll have to go back down for the wheel. That happens all the time when you lift it. It's uneven if it doesn't have all four wheels. I guess I should have told you," Cory said.

Walkers reassembled, the Sistine Chapel was now within reach but after his double climb Carl headed toward a marble bench where he reclined, trying to straighten his back against the cold stone. Until a guard came.

"You no lay there. You go to hotel to lay down. Vatican museum not for bum." The guard waved for Carl to get off the bench.

Carl made his eyes into death rays to no avail. The guard just stood in front of him. Carl moved on and joined his group in the Sistine Chapel. Most of the tourists rolled their heads back painfully to look up at the ceiling.

"It hurts to look at it," Ava Jean noted.

"See the tables with the mirrors, and the mirrors roped off on the floor?" Carl pointed.

"Yeah," Ava Jean said. "Oh, I get it. You can look down instead of up."

"This looks different from pictures I saw," Holly said. "The colors are almost like a comic book, they're so bright."

"It was restored a few years ago," Carl explained. "There were hundreds of years of soot on the frescos and when they were cleaned, this is what they looked like. Unfortunately, there are a lot of books out there that have the old pictures in them and that's what people expect to see."

"I think the old way, all dark and dirty, looked more holy. They should have left it alone." Holly concluded.

Exiting the Sistine Chapel, the group assembled in front of St. Peter's Basilica. François pushed to the head of the group. "We very lucky. Very lucky. We all here together, all peoples here together."

"Except Peggy who you left in Hispanic town or whatever," Sally reminded him.

François took a deep breath before he continued. "I walk you through St. Peter's. We stop to see Michelangelo *Pietà* and many dead pope. Real dead pope you see under glass. *Pietà* under glass, too, because vandals years ago. When we come out, we go through gate there. You remember first gate, and through that gate is shopping. Very good shopping. Leather and jewelry. If you not want St. Peter, you go shopping all the time. But motorcoach be on that street outside gate at four o'clock exact. And you be ready for motorcoach. I think you stay with me for quick look at St. Peter then you still have hour to shop. Plenty time. You follow me but you remember motorcoach on that street at four o'clock, St. Peter or no St. Peter."

Carl's clients stayed mostly together for the tour of St. Peter's Basilica. Only a few headed to the shopping street right away. A few fell behind. Those who protested that looking at dead popes in their glass coffins would be too gross spent an inordinate amount of time staring at the desiccated and shriveled bodies in their glass sarcophagi. Some couldn't be torn away, the way one might be spellbound by a scene of horror.

• • • •

The clients dispersed through the colonnade of St. Peter's Square and onto Piazza del Sant' Uffizio where François recommended shopping. Carl found a stone bench in the sun and pressed his aching back against the cold marble. François sat down beside him and reached his right arm around Carl's shoulder, gently massaging his back. Carl was getting used to such shows of affection and he enjoyed it, judging by his leaning into François.

"That some nice group you have, *Dottore.*"

"Aren't they awful," Carl said, chuckling. He looked around, seemingly nervous that clients might see him with François's arm around his shoulder so intimately. The coast was clear. All the clients had entered various shops.

"Hard to judge awful." The arm tightened on Carl's shoulder, and he allowed himself to be pulled even closer to François.

"They seem the worse," François admitted. "But some might be great."

"Great? Great big assholes, you mean."

"No. You know what I mean. You not know person. One person on tour might be great artist. Might be great author. Difficult personality but might be great to do something."

"I doubt it, François. They're just ordinary people. Maybe not even."

"You just see Van Gogh painting in Vatican? You think Vincent Van Gogh on tour bus he be nice passenger? He be asshole I assure you. That mean we kick Van Gogh out of tour? Then Van Gogh never see the sunflowers. Never see the starry night. Never paint. Never the inspiration."

"Well, as far as I know, none of my passengers ever wrote a great novel or painted a picture."

"They might could someday."

"Now you're sounding like a Southerner. Might could."

"What you mean?"

"Might and could don't belong together in the same sentence…oh, forget it, might could is okay."

"No. I mean even silly person might go very deep. Might have idea for great painting, great art, great story but not have opportunity? Need inspired but need opportunity too."

"Who's stopping them, François? If they want to paint or write, nobody's stopping them."

"They work. They raise kids. She clean and he cut lawn or eat the weed you say. I think you call opportunity? They no opportunity for the create."

"Well, you might have something there. Maybe it's not only opportunity, maybe it's power. Everyone has opportunity, a few minutes here and there to scribble down a few words or to smear some paint on a canvas. But to do something with it, becoming well-known, that takes power."

"Yes. You need the power. Ordinary housewife not the power. Like the Oprah Winfrey, she have the power. She say you paint these benches we sit on blue, you bet even Italian government go round paint every fucking bench blue and then be proud to say Oprah Winfrey say to do. François say paint bench blue, François arrest and lock up for crazy. Maybe charge fine for suggestion of ruin public property. You right about power."

"Getting the power might be more difficult than the creativity. There are plenty of people who write book after book, and they go nowhere. Some get the power a little at a time. They keep on with it. One book sells a little. Then the next sells more. Then suddenly everybody wants what they have but by that time the writer's bitter at the world. That happened to Jack London."

"If Oprah say book good, sell like hot cookies."

"I think you mean hotcakes. But yes, like that."

"But so, you think your passenger like that? How you say potential to create?"

"Maybe. I still doubt it."

"Maybe create much smaller. Just make home the create. Maybe the having kids the creation. Little hobby the creation. Who to say what the great is. Not need Oprah to tell Sophia that postcard she send sister great writing or her arrange things she buy Italy great art."

"I think maybe you're going too far now, François. I could love them all to death and nurture their talents, but it doesn't mean that the tour directors will like them any better. I appreciate your accepting attitude, François, but I worry soon no one will want to take my groups." Carl stared down at the ground.

"You too much worry. I always take your groups. If you with them I take them," François said, squeezing Carl's shoulder.

"If they need correction or scolding…I feel like I'm talking about dog training school, but you can let me do that, so it doesn't ruin your tips. If you scold them, they might not give good tips."

"You not worried they come again if you scold them?"

"No, it doesn't seem to matter. They come anyway. Some I'd like to get rid of, but they keep coming back. I don't want them not to like you."

"You not worry. I think François tip because what François look like, not always what François do."

"You might be right about that, you probably could have gone to Hollywood." Carl slapped François on the thigh. They sat silent for a minute, faces turned up to the warm sun.

"Do you ever lead the really upscale tours. The ones with only really wealthy clients?"

"Believe or not, not like the rich group so much. Sure, better hotel, better restaurant. But some dull. They quiet and polite. Not so many question. Not so alive. It like the luxury make them dull. They like tell you all the places they go. Strange places. They no go Rome or London, or Paris. Say, 'I been already.' Go strange places like in Africa you never hear of. Can't wait to get to Vietnam. Iceland. Some small island where nothing is. Just to say did it. Just to tell it to bridge club or golf buddies. Then I notice we driving through Rome and magnificent monuments, Castle St. Angelo, Baths of Caracalla. Even if you see every day you still look up at magnificent. Not these luxury traveler. They read novel. They read tour book. They check messages on I-phone. Like your Holly person? She do that little while ago. I say, you see Castel St. Angelo in morning sun like this? Magnificent. Can you picture Tosca there? They say 'Who?' They say 'Oh, I was here last year. I been to Rome at least five time.' I like do Rome with you, *Dottore*, you appreciate. You here five time probably but always you want to see again. I know you always want to see again."

"I hear that all the time from my clients. I announce a trip to Italy, even this trip, and they say, 'Oh, I was in Italy twenty years ago. Been there, done that.' They like to use that phrase, 'Been there, done that.' I could slap them, but I say, Oh, are you going to the beach in Gulfport this year? And they'll say, 'Of course. We go every year.' And I think, you'll go to the messy, oil-stained beach in Gulfport, with its miles of ugly strip malls and crap, bad greasy restaurants, every year but you won't go to Italy twice in your lifetime? I don't get it. I'd like to just give up but then enough people show up to make the trip worthwhile, so I go. I think it's meeting people like you, François, that makes me want to come back. It's really what the memories are made of. If I just sat on the bus and talked to the other people from Mississippi, maybe I wouldn't want to come back. I'm really enjoying the time with you."

"And I like maybe spending an evening with you, *Dottore*. Maybe after group eat dinner and go away."

"If only they'd go away. I never did anything like that on a tour before, François. I thought you were not supposed to be too friendly with the tourists."

"You not really tourist. You colleague. You in travel business like me. We have good time tonight." They sat still for a time. "Time to go. Almost four o'clock and your awful but maybe special talent people need to get on motorcoach," François said, finally.

"Oh yes, we must attend to the awful talented people." Carl stood, hesitatingly disengaging from François's arm.

"I take you out tonight dance club."

"Okay," Carl said quietly, sounding uncertain.

The bus parked illegally along the median strip, so they had to board quickly. Once on board it became apparent that Georgia Mae and Joseph, the lovebirds, had not returned.

"Should we do the same thing we did at the Spanish Steps to look for them?" Carl asked François, standing toward the front of the bus.

"I know where they are," Sophia offered, as if she considered withholding a great secret.

"Where?" Carl demanded.

"See that there jewelry store." She pointed. "The second one from the corner. Georgia Mae was in there trying to bargain for a gold necklace or something. Joseph was watching her. I was in there, too, but I didn't buy anything. At least not in there. I did fill one shopping bag. See." Sophia held open the shopping bag that rested on her lap. "I'm sure she is still in there."

"I'll go get her," Carl offered to François.

"I think you should not," François cautioned, scrunching up his face and shoulders as if in grave wariness. "I go."

"Don't worry about me. I'm from New York. I can handle myself," Carl said as he descended from the bus.

Chapter Sixteen

Shoppus Interruptus

Carl approached the counter where Georgia Mae stood. The proprietor, a wispy little bald-headed man, had at least three gold chain necklaces of various thicknesses and design spread out before Georgia Mae. She picked up each one in turn and said something to the proprietor.

"Georgia Mae! The entire bus is loaded and we're already twenty minutes late! We're illegally parked. Come on…"

A hand clasped Carl's shoulder, but not the now-familiar squeeze of François. Carl winced. He turned and a rough-looking character, with a dark face and swampy skin like an acne-surviving ex-boxer, stood beside him, pulling him away from the counter.

"You leave alone. You leave alone 'til she finished buy. You get fuck out."

"Georgia Mae. Now! We're not going to wait."

The ex-boxer practically lifted Carl off his feet like a sack of potatoes and dragged him around the counter toward the door. Just then the bells on the door jangled, turning everyone's attention to François who quickly descended the two steps into the store. The boxer relaxed his grip on Carl, somewhat, but didn't let go.

François stayed some distance from the boxer but put up his hand and pointed to him, issuing forth a string of angry sounding Italian. Once again it sounded like the fastest-spoken language in the world, especially when uttered in anger, and apparently François was angry. He ended the brief diatribe by pointing to the proprietor, then raising both hands as if in surrender. The boxer let go of Carl while at the same time pushing him away as if he were foul-smelling garbage rather than merely a sack of potatoes. Carl, upon gaining his balance, moved toward François and the door.

"Georgia Mae! Joseph! *Attencione.* Shopping *finis.* You come with me," François ordered.

"I just want to buy this one necklace. I'm almost done," Georgia Mae said, pleading.

"You not buy necklace. Necklace junk. Nothing in store real. All fake jewelry," François said, looking the still and silent proprietor directly in the eye. The boxer started to move toward Carl and François and all François had to do was raise a finger toward him, utter a few extra Italian words, and the brute stopped in his tracks.

Georgia Mae looked from face to face, bewildered and nervous, as if suddenly recognizing the potential danger in the scene. She gathered up her shopping bags and purse, grabbed Joseph by the sleeve and circled the counter from the opposite direction and exited the shop, emitting a loud, declamatory grunt and shaking her raised head as she rushed past Carl and François. François grabbed Carl, likewise, by the sleeve and pulled him to the door.

"Narrow escape," Carl commented, in a shaky voice.

"I tell you. You not believe. Those characters should be Gypsy street corner, not fine Vatican store. They rip off my tourist. Tourist find out. Tourist blame me. Happens all the time. François should have warned but not think. Why François bring us to such a place. Just get on motorcoach. We get hell out of here. They no bother us anymore or they know I make report to police. I should make report to police but so much trouble and they be back anyway. Best to stay away."

"You don't have to worry about me. I'll stay away."

As they pulled up to the hotel entrance, François grabbed the microphone. "Tonight, dinner in hotel. You finish seven thirty and we back on motorcoach to go light show at Augustus Forum. Not be late or not good seat."

"Do we have to go? I saw it already," Ann complained.

"You couldn't see it. Last year first year. Light show new in Rome," François countered.

That shut Ann up.

"Do I have to go?" Helen asked. "My neighbors, the Haskells, they do a light show for Christmas on their house and the whole yard is full of snowmen and Santa and reindeer and elves, and it's a two-story house, so it's got to be better than anything here. Plus, I'm tired. These days are too long."

"I think you should see. Not like Christmas lights. You see. You tired not go. Tell me at dinner in hotel if not go. If not on motorcoach at seven thirty, stay in hotel. We not wait." The impatience in François's voice grew.

Sophia's hand shot up. "Will all the stores be closed?"

"There no stores in Augustus Forum. If want shop, stay home please." François sounded spent.

When they arrived back at the Cielo Borgia Hotel, Peggy, the Australian at-large, waited for them in the lobby, one hand on her hip, the other holding a glass of what looked like whiskey, face red with rage. François and Carl walked in laughing and reenacting Carl's near murder in the jewelry store, François acting the part of the boxer brute, shaking Carl, who acted like a silly rag doll.

"What's the meaning of this! You two are so busy fooling around with one another that you left me at the Spanish Steps!"

Carl looked at François, who stopped laughing and suddenly focused on Peggy, his face expressionless.

"Ms. Peggy." With his accent it sounded like Miss Piggy, and Carl didn't bother to stifle a laugh. He unraveled himself from François's arm and stood a distance apart. "I tell you again and again two o'clock. What part of two o'clock you not understand?"

"I was there at two o'clock. You were not there."

Carl reinforced François by saying, "We were there, Peggy. Two o'clock."

"Well, I was there by at least ten after two." She hesitated. "You waited much longer for that dumb old American guy. You even went and looked for him."

"We look for you, too. *Dottore* and me we look for you all across *Piazza*. You nowhere…right, *Dottore*?"

Peggy lashed out. "Stop calling him a doctor. He's an asshole."

"I really am a doctor but that's beside the point," Carl said. "Peggy, we did look for you. We were there until two twenty. I remember checking the time. We had gone through the whole square, and I even went up and down the steps just to be sure you weren't waiting at the top. The bus waited in the exact spot where we said we'd be."

"Well, you waited longer for him." She pointed to Owen who formed part of the audience that began to circle the verbal combatants like spectators at a boxing ring. "I'm going to call World Tours or whatever you are and report you. You're getting one bad review, François. You too doctor asshole."

"That's good, Peggy," Carl chimed in, needlessly. "I hardly ever get a review!"

"You're an asshole, Carl. I don't know why these nice people travel with you."

A few members of the crowd started clapping. Carl glared at them. "All y'all are going to end up on the no travel list if you keep it up."

"Hardy har har," Sophia volunteered.

"Anyway, François, you owe me fifteen euros for the cab ride back to the hotel."

"How you figure I owe you?"

"Either you are going to pay it, or World Tours will."

"We see." François turned to Carl. "We need some fun tonight."

Peggy wandered off in a huff.

Chapter Seventeen

A Night To Remember

Only twenty-one of the passengers showed up to the bus for the light show at the Augustus Forum.

"It's too bad they are missing this, but in a way I am relieved," Carl offered.

"Maybe I not sell it good enough?"

"No, François. The interest and attention span is limited."

"Anyway, good thing. Less to look after. Less to get lost." François reconciled himself.

On the way back, Carl and François sat together in the front seat, holding hands in the dark. "The show was spectacular," Carl commented. "And in a ghostly way, brought you back two thousand years to the day when the Forum was alive and the architecture was not only grand, but pristine."

"Amazing what do with light and laser. Soon light shows in Rome to show what ruins once like."

When the bus unloaded at the hotel, Carl and François stayed behind outside the front door. Ida Sue lagged behind also. "Don't you mind Helen, the light show was much better than the Haskells at Christmas."

"Thank you, Ida Sue," François said.

"You two boys have fun tonight," Ida Sue said, clicking her tongue, making her usual exaggerated wink, and entering the hotel.

"Some of them seem to know more than others. Too much."

"Never mind. We go to have fun. I show you where is fun. You ever been gay dance club?"

"Sure, when I lived in California. I'm not sure there's such a thing in Mississippi."

They took a cab to Via di Portonaccio, to the club Muccassassina that François selected. He seemed to know the bouncer who admitted them into the nondescript older building immediately, even though a few younger men waited in a line to get in as well as three or four women who seemed to be together.

Inside, François led Carl through the dark foyer that opened onto a dance floor with a garish light show overhead and on the walls. Color lights flashed from everywhere alternating with a strobe, and what looked like scenes from current events on large LED screens. Most looked like scenes from international gay pride festivals, but none flashed long enough for anyone to decipher the content. Even the floor blinked and splashed color on the figures who writhed and danced. Tables stood around the perimeter. A *maître d'* led them to a table near the end of the horseshoe arrangement of tables around the dance floor. François spoke an order directly into the ear of the *maître d'*, since normal conversation could not be heard above the din of what passed for music. Carl winced at the cacophonous sound. The drinks arrived quickly, and Carl savored the light whiskey, maybe rye, in his glass, with plenty of ice. He relaxed into his chair.

François stood up and took Carl's hand and led him to the dance floor. Bolstered by wine from dinner and the whiskey he'd just imbibed, Carl did his best to dance. He and François gyrated, grinding hips and butts, and undulated in the shadow of their raised arms. When the music turned slow, François grabbed Carl and held him tight, in a slow one-step, more comfortable to Carl, slowly moving as a couple across the dance floor.

Exhausted and sweaty, they eventually sat down to find another set of drinks already at their table. An expensively dressed middle-aged man joined them.

"How good of you to join us, François," the man said with a refined British accent, or as refined as it could sound above the din of the non-stop noise.

"Genève!" François stood up and hugged the man who bore a great wide toothy smile but held the sweaty François at arm's length.

"You certainly danced yourself into a fit, young man." Two other young men snuck past Genève and joined Carl and François at the tiny round table. "You children enjoy yourselves tonight," Genève said. "If Holston gives you a *conto* tonight, you just give it back and say give it to Genève."

François blew him a kiss.

The smaller, more handsome of the two who had joined their table, leaned over, and whispered into François's ear. Carl, no longer the center of François's attention, shifted uncomfortably in his seat. Their conversation didn't take long and then the two newcomers began kissing one another.

François leaned to Carl. "You interest in ludes?"

"What?"

"Ludes. I not say any loud. How you say in American…quaaludes?"

"That's how you say it. Jesus, François, I'd be a wreck if I took anything like that. I don't do anything like that on a tour. I don't do anything like that at home. When I was younger, I did plenty."

All François heard above the din was the negation. He shrugged his shoulders.

"Oh, I forget manners. This Giorgio," he said, pointing to the smaller guy who still hung on François's arm even though he was kissing the guy next to him. "This Bela," he said of the bigger, less attractive of the two.

Giorgio leaned and tried to encircle François's shoulder and aimed a big wet kiss at his closest cheek and whispered something in his ear. François turned to Carl. "You mind Giorgio and François to dance?"

Carl settled into his chair and looked relieved to not be pulled out on the dance floor once again. "No, I don't mind. You two go right ahead."

Carl watched Giorgio's paws resting on François's chest when the two men found a place on the dance floor. Giorgio, lithe and small, his head reached only to François's shoulder. Giorgio seemed all oily, oozing around François as if about to melt into a puddle on the floor, when he gracefully, and in time to the music, encircled François close, with the practiced steps of a professional modern dancer. It looked like a primitive mating ritual. Then taking François's hand they broke into a wild gyration, turning front to back toward one another, again and again. Then François swung Giorgio by the hand, out wildly, then toward him. Any sign of drunken impairment vanished. Both dancers seemed hugely in control. Practiced.

Bela leaned over the chair vacated by François to speak to Carl. "François and Giorgio great dancer. They make show whenever here. Crowd like. Genève like. That why he like François and Giorgio come here and never charge. It like free show and better than most dance show. Give Genève reputation with the lively people."

Indeed, a crowd had formed around the two dancers. François, lightly touching Giorgio's hand, spun him around on the floor on his backside. Giorgio sprang up and slid between François's opened legs and back again, pulled up by François. They launched into an extremely fast one-step with one or the other, or both, breaking off for a lightning-fast spin without interrupting the forward movement, hands like salutes, frenetically reaching out to alternate sides. The audience cheered wildly.

"Giorgio especially, it like he speak dance language. It like the dance live in him like angel. Maybe a devil. He not even Giorgio when he dance, he become the dance itself. Hard to describe but you see," Bela said.

Both looked like professional modern dancers, the moves so swift and calibrated, all the arms moving exactly in time, no mistakes, the moves so fast and energetic if you blinked you missed something. After a mad spin for both dancers, they stopped and a crowd closed in, patting them on the shoulders, giving sweaty hugs, and a few wanted demonstrations of the more complicated dance moves.

Meanwhile Bela moved to the seat next to Carl. "You just meet François?"

"Yes. Just yesterday. He is the tour director for a tour group I brought to Italy."

"François very nice man."

"Yes, he is."

"He need guy like you. He come here mostly himself. Sometimes a boy, never same one."

"A boy?" Carl scrunched his face in obvious disapproval.

"I not mean boy like teenager. I mean young man we call boy like you or me."

"Oh, yeah, we say the same thing."

"But young man not good for François. François need stable."

"You mean François likes horses?" Carl asked, laughing at his own joke.

"I mean stable like same man all the time."

Most of Carl's jokes didn't translate well. "Oh, stability. Yes. Most people need stability."

"I can tell François like you. Well, you come here to Rome live and give François stability."

"It's too soon to think about anything like that."

"But you think about it." Bela sat back as François and Giorgio returned to the table, sweaty and pulled-apart looking, shirts becoming untucked. François wagged his finger for Carl to come out for the next dance, but Carl put his hands up in protest. François seemed relieved to sit down. Giorgio breathed heavily, just taking time to suck on his next drink that appeared miraculously.

"You could do dance if you want," François said to Carl.

"Are you kidding? I would snap in two!"

"What's this snap?"

"Never mind."

"You think we should go, *Dottore*?"

"We have a long day tomorrow. And it's one o'clock now."

François interrupted Bela and Giorgio, who had returned to wet kissing and heavy petting, and said something to them, presumably in Italian. They both got up and accompanied Carl and François out of the club and into the fresh air.

"Bela and Giorgio drive us home," François announced.

Bela and Giorgio wavered on the sidewalk. "You think that's a good idea?" Carl asked François.

"No easy get cab so late. Cab think everybody drunk and spit up in cab. No want club people in cab late night."

"Jesus. They can't even walk," Carl said.

This got Giorgio's attention. "Bela no can walk, but drive good," Giorgio insisted. He stepped to a late model Porsche sedan and clicked open the lock. François opened the rear door and ushered Carl into the fine leather-fitted interior. As Bela tore away from the curb, leaving some of his tires behind, François leaned into Carl. "You have nice car like this at home?"

Carl answered, hesitantly. "Sure."

Before François could react, horns blared, punctuating their apparent near collision with an ambulance or police SUV. The vehicle skidded by so fast it took Carl's breath with it. The ride home, an event in itself, took place at a speed twice that allowed. Just like a movie of crazy Italian drivers, everyone drove too fast, with no traffic pattern. Bela drove around a traffic circle more times than necessary, faster each time, as if trying to throw his passengers against the car doors, like a giant centrifuge. Then Bela gave up and cut straight across the diameter of the traffic circle.

"Where are the police when you need them?" Carl said to no one in particular.

"You enjoy your tour of Rome?" Giorgio asked, turning around and slapping Carl's knee, a big grin on his face. He popped something, probably one of those quaaludes, into his mouth like a breath mint. François had one hand braced on the windowsill and the other on the seatback. Even he seemed a little nervous. After an unnecessarily circuitous route, the Porsche came to a screeching halt in the *porte cochere* of the hotel. Luckily, it was too late for anyone, even the porter or doorman, to be outside the hotel. The four awkwardly kissed goodnight over the seats of the Porsche. Carl and François poured out the back doors, and the Porsche skidded and screeched off into the night.

"You have good night out?" François said.

"It was something." Carl sounded as if he forced enthusiasm.

"We have more like that before you go home. You like to spend night with François?"

Carl, surprised by the invitation, was momentarily confused, and hesitated. "I really would, François, but if I don't get to my room and to bed, I'll fall asleep right here on the sidewalk."

"I take you upstairs," François said, taking Carl by the arm into the lobby of the hotel.

Chapter Eighteen

Loaded

The following morning, Carl walked past the table where Jimmy sat eating breakfast and Jimmy grabbed his shirt sleeve. "Look! They discovered bacon. I don't know where it came from, but it's the best bacon I ever had. I have to give it to these I-talians, when they cook somethin', they get it right."

Carl looked at Jimmy's plate and sure enough, a large lardon, the kind of thick slab of bacon that the French and Italians use for seasoning, lay across the plate.

"Lucky you," Carl said, but winced at the sight of so much fat. The amount of fat was disgusting, but cut up in tiny bits, it gave flavor to sauces and things. François, apparently, had asked the hotel to supply it to Jimmy for breakfast. That's how a tour director earns a big tip.

The group, congregating in the lobby, prepared to leave for Florence and the Tuscany town where they planned to spend the night. Carl went to the reception desk and purchased a few boxes of salty crackers, cookies, and even a box of individually packaged candies, American style. He planned to placate any irritation due to delays on the road with junk food. He carried the boxes to the bus where he intended to store them in an overhead compartment toward the back.

Carl saw François in the lobby, near the door, checking luggage against a list, so that nothing would be left behind, as the porter loaded them on a dolly to take to the bus. François looked as fresh and starched as he ever did, no sign of his late night of dancing and carousing. Carl, however, appeared with unusual dark shadows under his eyes. He looked out the lobby window and the hair stood up on his neck. He saw Lucas energetically loading the bus. Lucas, under the bus, squatting in the luggage compartment, received pieces of luggage from the porter while the driver stood idly by, hands folded on his chest, watching like a business executive rather than the driver.

Carl ran to the bus. "Lucas, don't do that!"

"What?"

"Don't load the bus. The driver is supposed to do that."

"But I don't have anything else to do."

Lucas, overweight and at least seventy-five years old, walked with a slight limp to begin with.

"Lucas. Can you imagine the liability for me, World Tours, and the bus company if you hurt yourself? Plus, we pay the driver and porter to do this. That's their job."

The driver, understanding enough of what Carl said, stepped and grabbed Carl firmly by the arm. "Let him alone. He volunteered," the driver said, somewhat threateningly, but with surprisingly unaccented English.

"I will not leave him alone. Lucas, come out of there."

"Let me just finish up this back row, then I'll let them handle it," Lucas said, ignoring Carl's command.

Meanwhile François, having finished checking the suitcases, came out to investigate the ruckus at the bus. He disengaged the driver from Carl's arm.

"What wrong now?" François said to Carl.

"We can't have passengers loading the bus. What if they get hurt? He could bang his head or hurt his back."

"You right always, *Dottore*," François said, and turned to the driver. He uttered a long string of fast words in Italian. The driver merely shrugged his shoulders, shook his head, and grudgingly, as if it weighed several tons, picked up the first suitcase that he saw.

Meanwhile, Lucas jumped out of the luggage compartment but stood up without clearing the cantilevered door overhead. He stood quickly, as if to prove his agility, and banged his forehead hard on the bottom edge of the suspended door.

"Ouch, goshdernit." Lucas raised his hand to his forehead. He lowered his hand and looked. Blood. He put his hand back on the wound.

"Let me see," Carl said, putting down the boxes of snacks and running to Lucas.

"No. It's nothing," Lucas insisted.

"It's not nothing, Lucas. Let me at least see it."

François brought a roll of paper towels from inside the first compartment and Carl wadded a few pieces and handed them to Lucas. The driver hurried up the stairs to the bus and came back with a first aid kit.

"Hold this and keep pressure on the wound. I think you could use a stitch or two in that," Carl said.

"Nothin' doing. Look, it's already almost stopped." Lucas pulled his hand and the wad of red soaked paper towels away and a small stream of blood oozed from the inch-long wound.

"For God's sake, Lucas, keep the pressure on it. Don't keep lifting the towels. You opened it up again." Lucas pressed his hand to his forehead. "Are you sure you won't see a doctor?"

"Yeah, I'm sure. Worse things than this happen to me all the time."

"Jesus. What do you think, François?" Carl turned to François who looked like he might be a little queasy from the sight of blood. Not a good reaction for a tour director.

"I think he keep the pressure then later we put plaster, or you call bandage. If problem we call doctor in Florence."

"You okay with that, Lucas?" Carl asked.

"Yeah. Just let me get on the bus. Stop making a big deal outta this."

"Okay, Lucas. Let's have you go to the back of the bus. You can lay down, but you've got to keep your head up. Don't lay flat or the blood won't clot as fast."

"Who made you such a know-it-all, Carl? Never mind. If you hadn'ta come out and bothered me loading the bus, this never woulda happened."

"It had nothing to do with…" Carl didn't even finish the thought as Lucas had already climbed onto the bus, his wife, Lacey Mae, nervously following behind him. She turned to Carl and François. "I don't know how he gets himself into these things."

"Oh, shut up, you old nag," emanated from Lucas, inside the bus. Lacey Mae just shook her head. Carl picked up the boxes of snacks and boarded the bus.

Once everyone settled, François grabbed the microphone. "Today very long day. Very long, long day. But nice day. You maybe catch nap when riding. First Catacombs of early Christian, right outside Rome. Then Etruscan tombs. Then enough tombs and dead we go to see the living in Florence. Sophia and Sally enjoy the shop in Florence. Then a little time in Siena for the more shop, maybe snack, but big event the dinner dance at Tuscan vineyard. All the wine can drink? You like that?"

Various forms of hurrah and applause rose from the passengers, while a few Baptists made disparaging remarks about the wine. Sally commented to no one specifically, "Well, if you have to drink alcohol to have fun…"

"Live band at dinner dance and other tour folk from other group they be there tonight so maybe you meet new husband or wife. Maybe one night stood."

"One night stand," Sophia shouted the correction.

"I see, you Sophia experience what François try to say. But we stop at hotel near Siena and near vineyard so can change to party dress for dance. Dance as long as want. Dad say you stay out tonight as long as want, as long as wine last, and no turn into pumpkin." François finally succeeded in provoking a few giggles.

The bus stopped first at the Catacombs of Priscilla on Via Salaria in the northern part of Rome. François turned on the microphone. "Catacombs once Roman quarry and then when done Christian use to bury dead second century A.D. to fourth century A.D. when persecution until end of persecution when Christians take over. There tombs and chapels so used by Christian not just dead Christian some dead Jewish. Thirteen kilometers of catacombs so not see all today but see art and design. Just you wander and read sign. Go to gift shop. You make Catacomb ladies happy if you buy in gift shop. Got that Sophia. Everybody happy you buy in gift shop."

"I don't know if I want all that Catholic stuff. I'm a Baptist," Sophia commented.

"You okay. All Christian here."

"That reminds me," Sophia cut in again. "We drive out here, we go through the city and everywhere you look a Catholic church or cathedral, bass-silly-car, or whatever you call those big old churches."

Carl corrected her. "It's basilica."

Sophia ignored Carl and continued. "And I don't see any new ones.

Like where people might feel comfortable. I didn't see a single Baptist church anywhere. Come to think of it, I didn't see a single protestant church anywhere. How come?"

"You remember Sophia, Italy mostly Catholic country. That say, Italy not very religious. Maybe old lady religious." As soon as he said that, he lowered the microphone and his head and winced. He came back apologetically, "I mean the young people not want the religion. Some older people still want Catholic mass and rules and things they are mostly the ladies, the men what you call sexular..."

There were laughs and giggles and people repeating the new word *sexular*.

"I think you mean secular. You better say secular otherwise it sounds somehow sexual," Sally warned.

"Italy secular society, thank you, Sally. That say, we not see, but four, maybe five, not sure, Baptist church in Rome. Most for American. Outside Rome, not so much. But Italian most not interested. Italian think of church and days repressed. Repression? They think the kings and dukes and jerks like politicians they use religion as weapon or rules to make miserable and not want better life. Be happy with what have you, get better when dead. Better in heaven so not to worry now you have nothing because duke or pope took all. Some now like churches to keep as museums. As art. As architecture. But not to take serious as message. As rules. I hope nobody offend by François but tell like is. Sorry, but that like it is. It history."

A blanket of silence fell across the passengers.

"You okay no churches?" François asked.

"I feel like we're with heathens. Maybe pagans," Helen said, the first words she'd uttered all day.

"You're so backward," Ann commented. "I've been everywhere in the world, and nobody goes to church as much as Americans. Maybe Muslims, but that's not church. Jesus isn't really involved there."

"Okay people, let not have argument. Let enjoy dead in catacomb. They enjoy quiet so we too. *Andiamo!* Be back ten thirty no later. You want to be left in catacomb eventually you be dead, too. Then not to worry."

• • • •

No one seemed to want to extend their stay at the catacombs, not even inadvertently, so the passengers loaded on time for once. The bus headed out of town to the autostrada north. The scenery included rolling hills but lots of factories and industrial sites, and not particularly attractive while still so close to Rome. François took up the microphone. "I like to take time to talk about Italy when scenery not so special you have to look, to concentration on beauty. So, I talk a little about Italy. Nobody mind?"

Some heads already nestled, asleep, in the seatbacks, some looked out the windows, a few had taken up books or electronic devices. Sophia and Mary, replied in stereo. "Yeah," and "Let's hear it."

"Okay. So, I tell you about Italian school. Very good school and free. Free I mean no cost to go."

"Even the private schools?" Sally asked.

"No. Private schools different. Charge fee. But few private school because public school so good…and free. Not much private school. Maybe a few Catholic but not much no more. Used to be school for American, but not so much no more. Anyway, school can start at zero age."

"How can a zero-age kid go to school? You mean they're not born yet?" Mary asked.

Ida Sue chimed in, "Yeah. I heard a these private schools in New York City where people enroll their kids before they're born so they have a place."

"Not like that," François took back the conversation. "What you call day care we call *Asilo Nido* for age zero, means infant, to three. Then for age three to six we have *Scuola Materna*, like kindergarten but can go for three years. All volunteer to go, but parent who work, even other, like send kid school. Free day care for all. Kids like school when baby. Get the social skill. Then age six to sixteen no is voluntary. School obligates. Primary age six to eleven, secondary eleven to thirteen we call *Media* what you call middle school, then secondary for age fourteen to nineteen but can leave age sixteen if want do something else. Sometimes call secondary *Liceo* or you call high school. High school specialize. Specialize classic, scientific, linguistic you call languages modern, technologic, artistic, or musical are some. For not academic high school professional technical can have economy, tourism, *technologica*, the farm studies, health care like medicine. If no interested then technical school learn plumber, electrical, hairdresser. Something for everybody. Everybody get skill they need. Then not so many how you call juvenile delinquent."

"Well, it sounds just about the same as at home. So, what makes you think it's so good?" Sally sounded defensive and confrontational.

"One thing is test. To get to science *liceo*, take test. Not pass test go do something else. So, student try hard. School mean something. Don't go to school because daddy say. Don't go school to fool around. Don't go to school to play with the ball. Go to school to do only what good at and try hard."

"Hey. What about football?" Lucas woke up as the discussion became louder. "At what age do they start football?"

"No such thing American football. Italian football what you call soccer. Soccer play for town, for civic team what you call little league. Saturday, maybe Sunday afternoon for football. School not for football. School for study."

"Even in college? What do they do in college if they don't have football?" Lucas persisted.

"I not yet explain college. Now I explain college. First after high school take test *Esame di Maturita*. If pass you get I translate Degree of Maturity. You get degree of maturity in the USA?"

"Hardly," Carl answered.

"So, university in three cycle. First cycle for three year. Continue study from high school. Second cycle two year unless special like physician more like six year. Second cycle all special but different years to take. Two or three year in second cycle it depends. Third cycle highest maybe master degree or doctor degree to teach the college."

"And you're saying it's all free? There's got to be some catch," Sally countered.

"Most free. Some university have register fee."

"I knew there was a catch to it!" Sally sounded triumphant.

"Most any registration fee fifteen hundred euro for year. Much less most university. Some twenty euro, like that. How much you pay for college in the USA?"

"I can answer that," Sally chimed in. "I just paid one of my grandkid's college tuition last month, and she goes to Ole Miss, which is a state school, and I still paid twelve thousand dollars this year and that didn't include her apartment, which is going to be another twelve thousand dollars 'cause you can't let them live in a dump. She wanted to go to Vanderbilt…that's private you know. It was more than sixty thousand each year and I told her, sorry, no way."

"So, you spend hundred thousand…more state school, you spend two hundred forty thousand private college, or you study Italy and spend five thousand."

"Yeah, but if you don't live in Italy you're not going to school in Italy," Lacey Mae, Lucas's wife, added.

"True you have to live Italy to go school Italy, but not have to be citizen. Just to live Italy. Some family come to Italy to live to get school."

"It can't be very good if it's free," Sally chided again.

"It very good because tests. You no get to college because daddy pay lots of tuition. Daddy have nothing to do with it. Get to college because work hard and not play the football and drink self silly at fraternity house."

"Waiiittt a minute, buster," Sophia interrupted. "Fraternities and sororities are important parts of college life. So's football."

"In Italy learn to do something more important. Bang head in football when done with school or not go to school. Drop out at sixteen and bang head in football if that's what you like."

"This school doesn't sound like much fun," Sophia added.

Lucas was sitting forward in his seat, visibly agitated by the talk of no football in college. "If there's no football in college, what's the point?"

François made a ridiculous face, tongue stuck out the corner of his mouth, cross-eyed, as if just too dumb to get the point.

Carl laughed, but not many others joined him. "If you live in the South, football is serious stuff," he said, quietly, mostly to François.

Lucas happened to overhear. "You're just a damn yankee. You don't understand anything about football."

"And the teachers can't be any good if school is free. How do they get paid? They must make almost nothing," Lacey Mae challenged.

"Average teacher seventy thousand to ninety thousand euro per year. That like ninety to one hundred twenty thousand USA dollars. University some higher not always. How that compare to USA?"

"I can tell you that," Eugenia answered. "I taught for forty years in Mississippi, and I can tell you I made half that only near when I retired. Half the lower amount. I hear tell of New York City teachers who make more than a hundred thousand a year, but it would cost that much to live in New York, so it's all relative."

"Most Italy teachers get housing benefit so not cost like that. Teaching different in Italy, in Europe almost always. Teacher profession like medicine or law. It respected and pay good. People go to be teacher like profession, not like just to find something to do. For summer off."

"Don't kid yourselves, folks. They pay for it. They pay for it with taxes. Their taxes are what, fifty or sixty percent of what you make?" Lucas nestled back in his seat with a look of satisfaction, as if he'd finally cornered François.

"Depend. You make thirty thousand euro each year you pay no tax. Still get education. Still get benefit like health and retire. Make more than thirty thousand euro and you start pay a little tax."

"Yeah, I bet before you know it, you're paying fifty percent. This stuff's got to come from somewhere." Lucas wouldn't admit defeat yet.

"Well, we make compare. Maybe teacher make ninety thousand euro in a year and say pay fifty percent back to tax. You in USA make ninety thousand dollar you pay maybe only twenty percent, maybe if lucky. Then you pay maybe another tax to state maybe five percent maybe higher, let's say five. Then you pay more than seven percent what you call socially secure? Boss pay another more than seven percent for you, you could have if boss didn't have to pay. So socially secure…

"Social security," Sally corrected.

"Sorry. Social security then cost you really fifteen percent. Where are you now? You have tax twenty and five and then you have social security fifteen so you already at forty percent. Then you save for retire? You save ten percent if smart? You save zero if dumb or no money then you be poor when old? Say you save ten percent. Then you at fifty percent same as Italian fellow. What about health? You pay for healthy? You pay no percent but pay what, a thousand each month? Even if you not pay, boss pay, and money could be for you money if boss not need to pay health. So, you more than fifty percent what you make. You pay more than Italian or French or German."

"And then you have to tithe. Don't forget your tithe!" Lacey Mae looked excited that she had something to contribute that no one else thought of.

"What you mean tithe? Other tax I not hear about?" François asked, cupping his hand to his ear to encourage Lacey Mae to explain.

"To your church, you're supposed to give ten percent of your income," Lacey Mae explained.

"That's ten percent after taxes," Lucas interjected.

"No, it isn't. I specifically remember pastor saying ten percent *before* taxes. Gross, he said. That means before taxes. I think," Lacey Mae argued.

"Well, pastor will never know. Church isn't like the feds who know everything you do," Lucas countered.

"But now everyone else on the bus knows you're stingy!" Lacey Mae said then folded her hands on her lap as if resolved to keep quiet from now on.

"So, some have another ten percent to pay to make it sixty percent!"

Carl added fuel to François's fire. "And don't forget that most of you pay tuition for those private schools. Kindergarten through twelfth grade. At the Capital Day School in Jackson, the tuition is twelve thousand dollars per year all the way through. That's one hundred forty-four thousand just to get your kid through grade school. Even if you go to a state school, you've already spent one hundred forty-four thousand on grade school. I don't know what part of a salary that is, but it is like another tax."

François, wide eyed, acted as if he couldn't believe it. "A hundred forty-four thousand for grade school? I could buy summer house Portofino for what you send one brat to grade school! And you think taxes too high in Italy?"

"Even if you have insurance, you still have to pay some medical and out-of-pocket stuff too," Sophia added.

"I think medical and retirement be question for another day. You like hear about Italian life?"

"Yeah, I guess so, but I still like America best," Sophia concluded.

Chapter Nineteen

Tuscany

François interrupted a bunch of naps as the bus approached Tuscany. "Okay, we now at Tarquinia and we see Etruscan tombs. Etruscans before Romans maybe eight hundred B.C. There people here for thousands years but what we call Etruscan from eight hundred B.C. Tuscany named for them. They carve tombs out of tufa stone. Nobody know how they live but can tell something from painting in tombs you see. We have guide to us, and he tell you everything. If François talk, he make mistake, so I give you to guide. Have lunch in snack shop because long time to dinner.

For those not interested in these early inhabitants of Italy, there was an extensive gift and snack shop where the group was to meet after the guide conducted a brief tour. Carl and François went for their own walk, away from the group with the guide.

"I like that you talk about these things in Italy, the taxes, the schools, retirement. One of the reasons I like to bring people to Europe is it widens their perspective. They see that the way we do things in the USA is not the only way. There are different, maybe better ways."

"Your clients what you call conservator."

"I think the word you want is conservative. Most of them are conservative, but there are a few that I would call right-minded or liberal. Liberals are afraid to speak out because they're a small minority."

François shrugged his shoulders. "That nice idea you open minds, but you hear Sophia. She like way USA do better. You might waste time."

"Your message might be subliminal. They'll all, at least the ones who were listening, think about it. They've been so brainwashed to think all these things are socialism and convinced to hate anything socialistic without even listening to the ideas. They can't tell the difference between communism and socialism, and they don't know what either means anyway. They were taught that both were bad words. But as I said, there's a few quiet ones who are well-informed."

"USA like to do everything own way. Churchill say something like American do right thing after try everything else."

"That's one of my favorite quotes. And it is true. The USA is still in the middle of trying everything else."

Carl and François completed a large circle around the tomb area and ended up back at the gift shop where the guided tour had finished. Carl went in with a group of his clients to have lunch and only a few remained outside with François.

Fred and Martha, the retired police officers, approached Carl at a glass counter displaying leather products, mostly wallets and small purses. "Carl, we'd like you to see something."

"What?"

"Just come here with us," Fred suggested with a wave of his index finger.

Carl followed. They stood beside a wooden bookcase filled with travel books and maps, in full view of Victor in profile, where Victor was unlikely to notice them watching.

"Watch," Martha said. Sure enough, Victor stood at a snack counter that displayed bags of salty snacks, American style. Victor held an open bag of potato chips. When he finished, he parted a few bags on the shelf and slipped the empty bag in between, concealing it. He picked up what looked like a Mars bar, made short work of it, and shoved the wrapper in a crevice between counters. Victor moved his head slowly to the left and right, obviously checking if anyone close by watched him.

"What should we do?" Carl asked, emphasizing the *we*.

"What *should* we do?" Fred asked in return. Carl shrugged his shoulders. Fred turned to Martha. Martha shrugged her shoulders.

"I can say something to him. Maybe if he knows someone saw him steal, he'll cut it out," Carl offered.

Carl crossed the floor and came up next to Victor, now breaking into a Milky Way. A strong smell, unwashed body odor, like a wall, met Carl as he approached. He reeked much more than underarm, not like a day without deodorant, but with an aggressive smell, like maybe the second twenty-four hours of a decomposing dead body. Carl gagged and took a step back. Two steps back, but not a total retreat.

"What are you doing, Victor?" Carl asked, from a reasonable distance.

"Just having a snack."

"Did you pay for those?"

"I'm going to pay for them. See. I'm keeping the wrapper."

"You didn't keep wrappers. I saw you stuff at least three wrappers where no one will find them."

"Okay. I won't do it anymore. It doesn't hurt anybody. But I won't do it anymore."

"You better not do it anymore. If you get arrested here, there's nobody going to bail you out of jail, you get me?"

"Yeah. I understand. I won't do it anymore."

"And what if one of our other passengers is standing next to you and the cops think you are in it together? Did you ever think of that? You could both be arrested, and there isn't anything me or François could do about it. You'll involve an innocent person."

"I guess you're right. I'm really sorry. I won't do it again."

"People are watching you, Victor. You won't get away with it. Rather than have anyone else in the group blamed, if I see you do it again, I will have you arrested."

"I mean it. I won't do it again."

"Go to the cashier and pay for that candy bar." Carl watched as Victor walked to the cashier and handed her the empty wrapper that she took disdainfully, as if he'd handed her a dead rodent. Carl left Victor at the cashier. Victor certainly earned his place on Carl's blacklist, where he joined, surprisingly, only five or six other former clients.

• • • •

The group looked forward to the three hours in Florence because it offered endless shopping after brief visits to the Academy to see Michelangelo's *David* and a driving tour past the Pitti Palace, the Duomo, and other important landmarks. As the passengers disembarked from the driving tour, François made an announcement. "I walk to Ponte Vecchio. If you want, you come with me. You be happy. See one oldest bridge in world, built thirteen forty five. It replace Roman bridge so even older. Even great flood, November nineteen sixty six it still stand up. Stand up forever Italian build so good."

"Why would we want to see some old bridge?" Sophia interrupted.

"I say you be happy. Especially Sophia be happy because bridge covered with stores."

"A bridge can't be covered with stores. You're making that up."

"No. You come see. All come see. Bridge full of stores. The expense jewelry store for Sally. The souvenir for everybody. Everybody follow then we all come back to motorcoach take off for Siena." François started walking.

"You mind if I join you?" Carl asked, sidling up to François. François still appeared no worse for wear considering the partying he had done last night.

"*Dottore* always welcome," François smiled and put his arm around Carl's shoulder and pulled him closer, really a hug.

Sophia watched with a scowl and admonished him. "You I-talian guys get away with that here in Italy, but if you did that there gay thing back home, you'd get beat up."

François loosened his hold, only somewhat. "You see guys, they hold hands, they touch. You American are weird one. So many have the issue with the men."

"I don't know about that," Sophia said, shaking her head, and then fell back in the crowd.

Carl and François slowed down as they approached the bridge and let all the passengers get ahead of them. The passengers apparently forgot their reluctance to see an old bridge when they saw the mass and variety of small shops. Even Victor, usually oblivious to the shopping opportunities, lightened his step and ducked into Fratelli Piccini, one of the more exclusive jewelry stores. François led Carl to an empty bench. Several minutes later Victor exited Fratelli Piccine quickly, looked both ways, and hurried to cross the street through thick pedestrian traffic on the busy bridge. Seconds later a man in a dark blue suit came out the door and looked in all directions. Looking for someone.

Chapter Twenty

Florentine Felon

Carl looked at François, "Do you think what I think?"

"I not want think. Never had passenger arrested. But first time everything."

François and Carl stood, and Carl started walking in the direction where they saw Victor dissolve into the crowd. Carl turned to François who lagged behind. "I just want to see what he's up to next." Carl spied Fred and Martha, the retired cops, in the next block and caught up, François still trailing slightly behind.

"Have you seen Victor?" Carl asked Fred.

"As a matter of fact, he just went in there." Martha nodded and Fred pointed to the jewelry store named Dante Cardini.

"He's suddenly taken an interest in jewelry, I see," Carl said.

"Expensive jewelry," François added.

"Do you think we should go in and break it up? Warn the proprietor?"

"I don't know, Carl," Fred answered, "If they're on to him and we come in showing we know something's going on, we're likely to all be arrested. Or, just as bad, we'd be detained by cops asking a lot of questions. We don't want to stay here hours or even days answering police questions. I think we should let it play out."

"He be caught. Shop not stupid. They watch," François added.

"Okay, so be it." Carl conceded. "It's time to head back to the bus. Let's see if we can scrounge up some of our passengers on the way."

Carl, François, and the Singers turned back the way they came.

As the passengers settled back on the bus, Sally placed a package in the overhead rack above her seat. Following her, Eugenia, one of the sisters, who had been sitting behind Sally, also placed a package in the overhead rack.

"Don't touch my things!" Sally shouted, attracting the attention of the nearby passengers.

"I didn't touch your things. You don't own the overhead," Eugenia, who was usually silent, countered.

"And every time you pass my seat, you don't have to grab the seatback and shake it," Sally added.

"Oh, stuff and nonsense!" Eugenia said and reached for Sally's seatback to help settle into her seat, thought better of it, and just plunked herself into her seat.

The late afternoon drive to Siena proved spectacular, the rolling hills and vineyards of Tuscany in bright sunshine with dramatic dark clouds forming far to the west. World Tours planned Sienna as a three-hour stop, long enough to wander the town, have a snack, and then drive some distance to the hotel to get ready for the dinner dance at a vineyard later in the evening. The temperature fell and dark clouds filled the sky, like playground bullies, before the bus reached Siena. The bus pulled up a block from the great town square that would have been magnificent in nice weather but was just dreary and forbidding on a cloudy, late afternoon. The group disembarked and François gave his orientation.

"Siena festival two time each year. Great horse race. Ten horses for the ten, how you say neighborhood? They wear the silk colors and compete. They names like Aquila, means Eagle, and believe it Chiocciota means snail. For fast horse? And there even Tartucca, the tortoise even worse, and Lupa, the she-wolf expect fast. They put dirt in square to make nice soft for horse also because rider all the time fall off and lots time horse finish race with no rider! You imagine? Rider not important. Horse important to finish. Then the young men with the flags put on show. Luciano Pavarotti give concert in square. Acoustics good in square but Luciano use microphone anyway and then too loud. One time no sing but voice come out of speakers anyway. Not so good for good old Luciano. No dirt on floor when Luciano sing. No dirt and no horses. All cleaned up for Luciano."

Most of the passengers lost François back when the riders fell off the horses, and a heavy cold rain broke loose and spat down rudely just as he finished his comments. Most passengers huddled under the few umbrellas that had not been packed in suitcases under the bus. They looked miserable. Carl conferred with François and then raised his voice. "I really don't want anyone catching cold by getting wet and freezing out here. If everyone agrees, we can just go to the hotel and get warmed up. Maybe tonight, if the rain stops, we can come back and walk around for a little while before the dinner at the winery."

"Difficult to believe Siena when sunshine and festival in square. But the local they come out more at night, so you see." François put his hand on Carl's shoulders and added, "We can only do if everybody agree. It must be everybody. If anybody go back and say to World Tours, we no see Siena, then I have trouble. So, everyone agree? You tell me if everyone agree."

"Let's see a show of hands. How many would like to go to the hotel?" Carl said.

Seemingly all the hands went up.

"Okay, then," Carl concluded.

"Let be sure. Is anyone want to stay in the miserable rain?" François added.

Two hands shot up from behind drenched umbrellas. The crowed moaned. The two hands belonged to Georgia Mae and Joseph.

"Jesus Christ," Carl said, not loud enough for anyone other than François to hear.

"That it then," François said, deflated, throwing up his hands in surrender. "I wait motorcoach three hours. When get to hotel, warm up fast, ready for dinner dance tonight at vineyard. We leave here, Siena, seven o'clock on money, how you say? Three hours what we say and three hour what you get."

The bus came back to the Siena town square at about six thirty and already a line of drenched, shivering passengers waited to board. At six forty-five François took a count, hoping to leave at least fifteen minutes early. "Of yours I have forty-three, *Dottore*. Forty-three. You tell me two who missed. No. I guess. I not seeing…" François's right hand went to his mouth then raised hands to both ears as if trying to squeeze the consciousness out of his head, like crushing a ripe melon.

"You don't have to tell me," Carl said.

Then the crowd started chanting rhythmically, "Joseph…Georgia Mae…Joseph…"

"I can't believe this," Carl added, so red in the face an egg could have been fried on his forehead.

"I know where they arrrrrrre," Sophia sang in her childish, sing-song voice. For someone so daffy, she sure observed everything.

Carl turned around and started to raise his hands as if to strangle her, jokingly, but stopped short and braced his hands on his hips in a not very masculine fashion. "Where?"

Sophia continued. "When we were getting on the bus, excuse me, motorcoach, Joseph and Georgia Mae were just sitting down at a table in that there restaurant on the corner. Me and Sally just left the restaurant when they came in. Just a few minutes ago."

"Umghhhh," Carl growled and turned toward François, who listened to the exchange. He pushed Carl down into his seat roughly.

"I handle this one. I wish to."

"Be my guest," Carl said, rubbing his shoulder that François so carelessly and briskly handled, contrary to his usual caress. Carl looked through the window at the driving rain.

Chapter Twenty-One

Saving For A Rainy Day

François ran down the block holding his spiral-bound plastic-covered guidebook over his head through the pouring rain, trying, in vain, to preserve his beautifully styled hair. The wind blew too strongly for an umbrella. When he reached the restaurant, he burst through the door. There sat Georgia Mae and Joseph, among very few clients. The gray-haired waiter stood next to them taking the order, tapping his pencil on the order book impatiently.

François did not pause for pleasantries. "Why you wait six forty-five to have snack when you know we leave at seven o'clock?"

"We thought fifteen minutes was plenty of time to get a quick bite," Georgia Mae whined, looking up startled at the disheveled and dripping François. "You look awful, François," Georgia Mae added.

"Sit down and have a little drink," Joseph slurred.

"You thought fifteen minutes? You not think! You know better! You come in restaurant during dinner, and you expect eating in fifteen minutes? You think this McDonald? You think it like American fast-food crap?"

"Well, we didn't know and there's no reason to be rude and profane. Did you hear the profane, Joseph?" Georgia Mae demurred.

Joseph turned beet red, took another deep slug of his red wine, and replied, tentatively. "Yes, dear."

"Waiter!" François waved to the waiter who had retreated behind the carved, polished mahogany bar, not wanting to get near the fracas. The waiter came forward as if summoned by royalty. François had a commanding presence among proprietors, probably because with his recommendations they stood to make the most money.

"Alphonse." he knew the waiter by name. "Alphonse, you get these people the take-out. The fast take-out."

Alphonse looked puzzled. François switched to Italian, telling the waiter to prepare something, he did not care what, food to go for these two and make sure they pay. François stood by with his arms folded across his chest. Joseph refilled his wine glass and polished off the rest of the bottle. "No sense in letting it go to waste."

Within a few minutes, the waiter came out with four shiny waxed paper bags neatly folded and sealed and presented a cash register tape to Joseph. Joseph looked up at François who moved his arms from his chest to his hips. Joseph took out his wallet. "How much tip?"

"You never mind tip. Pay and we get out."

Joseph left a generous amount, more out of blunder about the value of the euro than out of generosity. The three left the restaurant and walked quickly toward the bus, Joseph and Georgia Mae hunched under Georgia Mae's umbrella and François making no attempt to shelter from the driving rain. He still looked handsome even with his black hair plastered flat to his head. Georgia Mae and Joseph entered the bus first with François close behind. Sophia, in the seat behind the driver, started to clap. François reached out and grasped her hands. "You clap, and I break fingers."

The bus remained silent for the drive to the hotel.

The guests, to a number, were too tired to complain about rooms or arrangement, and anxious to get changed for the dinner dance that promised free wine.

Carl, once again, waited with François in the lobby to fend off complaints. They waited for ten minutes after the last client received their key and heard no complaints. "This proves that complaining is a sport for some of my clients. Something to do with time to kill upon arrival at a new hotel."

François agreed, "Complain not something to do when wet, or tired, or in hurry."

The hotel, probably once grand, like many older hotels throughout Europe lost business to modern, American-style, anonymous and characterless hotels. This hotel, outside Siena, had a lot of character, big floor to ceiling windows, marble floors, dusty old crystal chandeliers, and red carpet worn through in spots, especially on the black marble stairs. But the hotel seemed clean, and the staff uniforms reflected the elegance of a by-gone era. Everyone left on time for the vineyard. The idea of all-you-can-drink free wine motivated everyone, even the Baptists.

The Vineria Ascarello, in the outskirts of Siena, was only a ten-minute drive from the hotel. The restaurant, an enormous event tent set up at the end of a parking lot, nestled between rises of grape vines on either side and an ancient-looking villa served as the offices of the winery. Modern buildings housed the kitchen and wine-making equipment.

The rain had not entirely abated and the more than one hundred guests drenched the floor of the tent as they entered. The dance floor, a large, raised parquet platform toward the back of the tent, held a three-piece band that played American popular music from all eras while the guests arrived. Everyone sat down at first but as soon as a waiter uncorked the wine and people had a few sips, they started making their way onto the dance floor. Mostly women at first, doing fast dances together, but then when the band struck up a line dance, the floor became crowded.

Wet mud got tracked onto the dance floor, making it very slick. To give the vineyard personnel their due, they closed the dance floor periodically for mopping, but couldn't cure the wetness. Unfortunately, mopping up the gritty mud may have preserved the floor from scratching, but made it even slipperier.

Carl sat with François near the end of one of the long tables set up for guests. The volume of the music did not encourage conversation, so Carl sat silently, listening to the music, much of it nostalgic and enjoyable. The dinner consisted of regulation chicken with pasta, but prepared in Tuscany, it had more taste than usual banquet fare. "It's amazing that they can get pasta to taste so good when it is prepared for more than a hundred people," Carl tried to say to Francois, but Briana interrupted him, her big hair badly repaired after the drenching. She asked François to dance.

François didn't hesitate for a moment and got up on the dance floor with Briana. Although Briana wasn't much of a dancer, François knew how to make her look good by doing most of the work and shuffling her about the dance floor gracefully. From the smile on Briana's face, everyone knew she felt genuinely happy with the attention from handsome François.

The dam broke and François became inundated with requests. Every single woman, and some not so single, even those not from François's group, wanted to dance with François. He could not sit down. He let some of the women cut in so that he could satisfy everyone. When the waiter came to collect his hardly touched dinner, Carl waved him away and protected François's place so that he'd be able to eat eventually.

Some of the overflow, the women who realized that François wouldn't have time for everyone, came to Carl and asked him to dance. He began to make a motion to dismiss but relented and danced at least three songs in a row with different women, two of whom he didn't even know. He moved closer to François who, despite the chill of the night, was covered with a fine layer of perspiration. François reached out for Carl and Carl recoiled, as if François planned to make an exhibition of dancing with him like at the dance club in Rome. François, merely wanting to sit down, grabbed Carl and led him back to the seats, ignoring the trail of women who still wanted to ask them to dance.

"You save my life," François shouted. They both turned their chairs to watch the action on the dance floor. Warmed up, the women started asking, maybe forcing, the few husbands on the tour to dance. The husbands got passed around in lieu of François's and Carl's presence on the dance floor. Stewards opened second and third bottles of wine on the tables and some of the passengers were obviously getting drunk. The dancing became wilder and bawdier, and François continued to decline when women with slurred speech asked him to dance. He and Carl watched. Then François got up and walked outside the tent, apparently for fresh air.

Carl continued to watch until a fast line dance started, and the stage became a little too crowded. Holly was really putting effort into her line dance, totally engrossed in exaggerating the movements, when she slipped and fell on her butt. Those around her stopped dancing and helped pick her up. Being the youngest, she didn't seem to be hurt, but Carl strained to see what happened. Next, Ava Jean, the cosmetic queen, fell into her neighbor, who broke her fall to the floor, so she didn't seem hurt either.

Carl walked toward the tent's opening to find François, who stood to the side, talking to the manager of Ascarello's events. "I think it's time to go," Carl announced.

"Oh no! They like. Highlight of tour. Most times guest want to stay two o'clock, maybe four o'clock. They enjoy the dance. Lots of drive tomorrow to catch up on sleep."

"I think most have had enough," Carl rejoined.

"No, *Dottore*. You let have fun. We keep band extra hours if you like."

"Look, guys." Carl addressed both François and the event manager. "When someone falls on their ass because they're too drunk, it's time for them to leave. When two people fall on their asses, then it's time for everybody to leave."

"If you say so, *Dottore*. You boss," François relented.

"I say so. Just think of the liability for World Tours…and us…if someone gets hurt and we should have known better because the floor was wet and they were drunk. Any other night it would be fine to keep going, but the rain makes this different."

"Okay, *Dottore*, you win. You safety queen."

"I think you should call me the safety czar, not queen."

François looked at Carl, rolled his eyes and affectionately poked him in the stomach.

The manager asked the band to announce one last slow number, then he and François herded everyone to the bus. So satiated with wine and exhausted, no one seemed to mind the party ending at one o'clock.

"I don't think anyone will have trouble getting to sleep tonight," Carl said as they arrived at the hotel. Carl went to the room he shared with Owen after he'd made sure everyone settled down for the night. Owen, already in bed, in his pajamas, watched some Italian sitcom without subtitles, an unlit, but still smelly cigar stub dangling from his mouth.

"I didn't know you spoke Italian," Carl said.

"I don't. I'm trying to guess what they're saying," Owen replied without taking his eyes off the television. Carl shook his head and headed toward the bathroom.

"Woah!" he whinnied, but not louder than the raucous cacophony of the television sound. Across the shower curtain rack hung the largest pair of stretched-out old-man underpants that Carl had ever seen. They had obviously been rinsed out, but not enough to divest them of several faint and not so faint skid marks, and they dripped water onto the tile floor.

"Jesus Christ." Carl did his business, brushed his teeth, washed his face, and went to bed, avoiding dealing with the shower until the next morning, when things might seem brighter and drier. Owen drifted into the sleep of the dead and Carl switched off the TV. Carl tossed and turned. Then the snoring began. Not normal snoring. It sounded as if some great factory loudly exhausted explosive bursts of burnt gas, or like ten baritone chain saws angrily cutting through huge tree trunks at the same time. This alternated with talking. Not simple talking but arguing. Then, worst of all, the punctuation of farts. A symphonic duet of bowel and colon expelling, at full volume, a gas one could almost see. Carl always traveled with ear plugs, which maybe cut the sound in half, and eventually he drifted into an uneasy sleep.

Around three o'clock Carl awoke to a knock on the door. It couldn't have been the first knock, but a very loud knock. Loud enough to penetrate the ear plugs needed by sharing a room with Owen. It woke him up from a deep, dreamless sleep. The knock came again, sounding more urgent this time. Carl removed an earplug. Without turning on a light he went to the door. "Who is it?"

Chapter Twenty-Two

A System For Health

"It is me, François, open please." Carl could hardly hear for the decibel of sounds coming from Owen. Such sounds could not possibly emanate from a sole human being— gurgling, coughing, talking, farting, moaning, a one-man band of the grotesque.

Carl opened the door but forgot to release the chain guard. François stood there in a white dress shirt, unbuttoned half-way down, exposing his darkly haired muscular chest. Glancing below, Carl noticed the boxer shorts that left exposed above mid-thigh François's remarkable muscularly defined legs, etched thickly with the same even dark hair as his chest. Carl fumbled at the door to release the chain. He held onto the door and looked wobbly. Carl blushed as he anxiously motioned for François to enter, temptingly half-clothed.

François, about to speak, cupped hand to ear and wrinkled his handsome, usually placid forehead. "You have trash compactor in room?"

"What?"

"That sound. How you stand that sound? That sound like trash compactor. Smell worse. Smell bad in here."

"That's just Owen. It's okay," Carl said as he removed the second ear plug. François just shook his head and extended his lower lip in an endearing look of childish sympathy. Then, rectifying his face, returned to seriousness.

"We have problem here."

"We do?" Carl frowned.

"We have sick passenger. One of yours. Olivia, roommate of Helen you know?"

"Yes, I know those two. What's wrong?"

"Olivia think she have flu. How you say influensis?"

"Flu will do. This is terrible. I'm not surprised after getting soaked and freezing. Damn Joseph and Georgia Mae. Flu could spread to everyone."

"That's why National Health have strict rule. Strict rule is quarantine for flu. World Tours make same rule. No travel, no participate with other traveler for person with flu."

"Are we going to tell her? Tonight?" Carl's face showed a sickly white color. That meant leaving Olivia behind. He'd never done that. Olivia would be furious.

"We get dressed and go to room. She say on phone can't sleep anyway."

"Okay. I'll meet you at her room in a few minutes."

Carl arrived before François and knocked. Helen immediately opened the door. With all the lights on, Olivia sat up in bed. The hotel manager, along with a man carrying a medical bag, the hotel's on-call doctor, appeared beside Carl.

"You please stay outside," the doctor said to Carl and François, who had also appeared, fully clothed, beside Carl. The doctor slipped on a facial mask, went in, opened his medical bag on a bedside table, and extracted a modern digital thermometer. He placed it in Olivia's ear for a second. "Mild fever. Not so bad. You have stomachache?"

"Oh, do I," Olivia moaned, placing her hand on her abdomen for emphasis.

"You maybe have influenza. When you to travel?"

"What's he asking me?" Olivia asked Helen.

"I think he wants to know when we're supposed to leave here," Helen answered.

"We're supposed to leave first thing tomorrow," Helen added from the doorway.

"You no go anywhere for two days after symptoms," the doctor retorted.

"What do you mean? We can't all stay here for two more days. The group will miss half the tour!" Olivia, now animated, struggled to get up from the tangled sheets.

"Tour go. You, *Signora*, you not go. You stay at least two days."

"I will not. When all y'all go, I go."

"The law is you stay. You not get on and infect other peoples on bus."

"You can't stop me. I'm not being left in this godforsaken place."

François came to the doctor's aid, leaning on the doorframe. "Sorry, *Signora* Olivia, doctor correct. I not let you on motorcoach if influenza in you."

"This is an outrage. I paid good money for this tour!"

"We at World Tours very sorry about rule. But hotel bring you food for two day and then if you feel better you take train catch up. Maybe catch up Venezia."

"Where the hell is Ven-neet-zia? I didn't see any Ven-neet-zia in the tour book."

"I mean Venice. You say Venice, we say Venezia. You catch up with us in Venice if you feel good. If doctor say so. Hotel help you get train."

Helen pulled Carl down the hall a few feet."I don't think she really has the flu. She's really a drama queen. She ate a whole quart of strawberry ice cream or gelato or whatever it is this afternoon when we were in Siena. She's lactose intolerant and she said she thinks she's allergic to strawberries, but she ate the whole thing anyway. I saw her do it. Right in front of me. Telling me how sick it could make her. I told her to stop. I couldn't believe how stupid."

"Let's tell the doctor," Carl said, hurrying back to the room.

"Olivia," Carl said, poking his head into the room. "Are you sure you don't want to tell the doctor what else this might be?"

"What are you talking about, Carl. I'm sick to my stomach. I don't feel like all this nonsense."

"Did you eat something that might make you sick?"

"No. I didn't. What do you mean?"

Helen, standing behind Carl, offered an answer. "What about the strawberry ice cream? Is that why you could be sick? Not the flu?"

"That's it!" Olivia practically shouted but had to turn to retch into the ice bucket that Helen had placed next to her on the bed earlier in the evening for exactly that purpose. Everyone screwed up their faces and turned away. The retching sounds made Carl look particularly queasy, and he backed out of the doorway. "I'm allergic," pleaded Olivia.

The doctor considered for a moment."You cannot change story so easy. You report the flu, the quarantine start. If symptom all gone in twenty-four hour, then we say maybe allergy. But fever and vomit are flu because that what you say first. Tomorrow night we see and maybe you go then."

"Dammit. That goddamn ice cream. I thought I'd get away with it just once. It was so good."

The doctor packed up, shaking his head, silent and visibly annoyed to have been called out late on a rainy night because this fat American woman couldn't control her eating habits. The hotel manager stayed behind to say, "You not to worry, *Signora.* We bring breakfast and lunch tomorrow, and dinner and then doctor say if you go. We bring you to train next morning. Group still in Venice?"

"Yes. We in Venice three nights. You not miss Venice, *Signora* Olivia," François consoled.

Ignoring everyone, Olivia said, "Helen dear, will you go to the lobby and fetch me a couple of Co-Colas?"

"Sure, honey—"

Helen was cut off by the hotel manager who interjected, "Helen not stay in room with flu. We give her other room. She isolate."

"What? I need Helen. I need my Co-Colas."

"You better not drink Co-Cola when you're sick. You are dehydrating and you need water. Co-Cola doesn't count as a liquid when you're sick. Helen, don't give her anything other than bottled water," Carl insisted.

"I don't drink water. I hate water. I want Co-Cola."

"I bring you one Co-Cola, but I bring you much water," the hotel manager seemed happy to agree with Carl. "American they drink the Co-Cola, morning, noon, and night, making them blow up like balloon, like so much sausages."

"But I bet it's profitable," Carl added.

"Nothing is going right! I hate this! I hate it here! I hate Italy!" Olivia smacked a pillow and pouted like a child. "At least I'll have Helen to help me get to Venice after tomorrow."

"No. Helen stay with group. She go Pisa with us tomorrow and then night to Venice. Helen not allowed to stay with *Signora*," François said in a voice so authoritarian no one could argue.

"What? I can't go alone."

François continued, "Sorry, *Signora* Olivia, but those are rules. Passenger not stay behind. Only sick one stay behind. And Helen have mobile issues. Use walker not much help to *Signora*."

"That's so damn stupid. I might just go home."

François, his patience thinning, folded his arms across his chest. "You not go nowhere until health better."

Helen grabbed her yet unpacked suitcase and followed the manager to an empty room down the hall. Carl and François moved down the hall in the opposite direction, said a brief goodnight, went to their separate rooms, both looking too tired and annoyed to initiate any further conversation.

Chapter Twenty-Three

Pisa With Pizza

The sun rose brightly the next morning. The rain moved on, leaving the air crisp and clear. The hilly drive to Pisa was pleasant and uneventful. Recent spring rains made the hills green, the grape vines in luscious new leaves. The sparse palm trees and tall cypress gave the landscape an exotic, almost tropical feel. No hurry today, François called for a rest stop at a gift and snack shop along the way. Having had a big breakfast, Carl wandered around with François.

"Can you always tell the hand-crafted gift items from the ones imported from China?"

"You want to know, you ask François, I tell difference."

"I don't want to buy anything. I was just curious. If I bought things on all my trips, there'd be no room left in my house. I need to get rid of things, not buy more. I'm curious if all the Chinese and imported stuff is ruining the Italian economy."

"It not good. That for sure. Italy try some laws against import stuff and you buy only Italy made stuff, but you can see not working. The cheap stuff more people to buy and more job for the sales, but less job for the good craft people. France do much better keep out the import and you buy stuff made France. Work better in France. Too much junk Italy."

"That's too bad. I hate to see the fine leather, wood, and jewelry craftsmen disappear."

"Still the very good stuff here. The shoes. The jewelry. The clothes.

You go Milan and you still see best in world."

As they approached Pisa, still in the countryside, a grand villa appeared on the right side of the bus.

"What's that?" Sophia asked, in a voice that could cut glass.

Ann, because of the seat rotation, now sitting across the aisle from Sophia, answered her. "I've seen that before. It's nothing. Just an old house."

François answered in the microphone. "The villa on right Palazzo Borgo di Corliano."

"I thought Corliano was them there mafia people in New York in the Godfather movie," Sophia interrupted.

"Not same Corliano. This Corliano merchant from Florence. Built summer house here fifteen-hundreds."

Sophia was fixated on the old villa. "It looks like it's all covered with graffiti. What's that about? Who woulda done a thing like that? It doesn't look like new graffiti."

François turned to the driver and said a few words in Italian. The driver motioned for François to hand him the microphone. "The decoration on the Villa is typical decoration of the time. We call it Mannerist art. It is Florentine from the sixteenth century, the time of construction of the villa. It depicts harpy eagles, fruit arranged in crowns, flowers, birds, all the symbols of fortitude or strength, abundance, and good fortune." The driver handed the microphone back to François. The group was stunned that not only did the driver know something that François apparently didn't, but he spoke in an English of which Queen Elizabeth would approve.

François got on the microphone to explain. "I forget to tell you when I introduce Guido, our best driver, that he degree in art history. He from Cairo so no legal to be tour guide in EU but he be great tour guide if he can get license. He great driver, too."

"Not much of a luggage handler, though," Carl added.

As they approached Pisa, the road became more congested with the traffic of many cars, scooters, and motorbikes, but soon the motorcoach pulled into a parking lot designated for tour buses. Slightly pre-season, only a half-dozen tour buses parked in a lot that could hold a hundred.

François held the microphone as the bus pulled into its designated parking space, in full view of the famous Leaning Tower.

"Here you are. You see where you are? Maybe most famous thing in Italy. You go look. On sides is shops. Shops and the restaurants all around. They all fine. All good. All different price. You look at board on sidewalk before you go in to see price and what you get. Very good deal. You get five course for ten euro. Very good food. You get simple thing, sandwich for three euro."

"Can you get pizza? Is this where pizza is from? Is that why they call this place Pizza?" Sophia asked enthusiastically.

"No. Spell different. This is P-I-S-A, and you talk about food the P-I-Z-Z-A," François spelled both words. "Which all it means is pie in English and started in Naples but now everywhere but everywhere different. Not start in Pisa. You find some pizza here if you want. Good pizza all over. Now you listen to me close. Motorcoach stay here. You see next to Leaning Tower. You see motorcoach from Leaning Tower. Eleven o'clock now, we stay here until two o'clock. That three hours. You look at Leaning Tower first then you eat. Or you eat then look at Leaning Tower. If you Sophia, you shop. You do what you want but you be on motorcoach at two o'clock. No ifs or ands. Your butts be on motorcoach at two o'clock. You not order five course dinner at one-thirty. You get me? You understand what I mean, Joe and Georgia Mae? You get on motorcoach to leave exactly two o'clock. We have wonderful, beautiful drive over Italian Alps, Apennine they called, this afternoon. Maybe if lucky we still see snow. Maybe if we not lucky it snow on us. No. We be lucky. We be in Venice early tonight for very good dinner in hotel. Very good hotel. Big modern hotel. Now you come back before two. I walk you around Leaning Tower and tell you story if you like. Or you just get lost. Just kidding. No place get lost in Pisa. Small town. But you stay where you can see tower so you can find motorcoach."

Carl followed along, slightly behind, as François gave his brief and sketchy history of the Leaning Tower and the small city of Pisa. "Pisa have ninety thousand people. Pisa formed by Etruscans. Where you hear about Etruscans before?" François looked into his small crowd, getting eye contact but dumb stares, rather than recognition. "You just came from Etruscans!" he added.

"Thaaaats riiiiight," Sophia offered, "That Eat rust-can graveyard we just was at yesterday. Why did they bury them all the way down there if they lived all the way up here? Couldn't they find a closer cemetery?"

"Etruscans living all over, up here, down there," François responded, not entirely able to explain the disconnect involved in Sophia's question.

"So, Leaning Tower you see part of Duomo, the cathedral. Campanile or bell tower for cathedral is leaning. Built all the way back in eleven hundred, you believe so old? Not why it leaning because old, lean because foundation not right. Lean even while construction but after built nobody know how to fix and now nobody want to fix because then maybe tourist no come. So, it about two feet tall on one side than other. Enough? Still tilt. Start out four degree but nineteen ninety it five and a half degrees afraid fall. Engineer put stabilize under nineteen ninety three and even two thousand one and now lean only little less than four degree but enough so tourist still come to see. Yes?" Some stared up at the tower and others looked past the square at what sort of restaurants might be safe for their palates, scouting out possible fast food places.

"So, you see tower and I point you see motorcoach at end of square. You come back to motorcoach you come to tower you look north you see all motorcoach. You come on time two o'clock, you remember what time?" François raised his hand to his ear and maybe half the participants responded with the time.

Allen, one of the Australians who had joined the group, tapped Carl on the shoulder. "Might I have a word, mate?"

"Of course. How are you enjoying the tour so far?" Carl looked for François, who remained aside, pretending not to be listening.

"Sure, mate. You know your Victor. Victor is traveling alone without paying a single supplement, and I am traveling alone, same, without the single supplement, so they put us in the hotel rooms together."

"Well, that's a chance you take when you don't pay the single supplement. Sometimes it works out that you get a room by yourself, and sometimes you share. It's happened to me so now I always pay the single supplement unless I have to share, like with Owen, who really can't travel alone."

"Hold on mate. This is about me, not you. It's about Victor. I never knew a human being, if that's what he is, to stink like that."

"Stink?" Carl acted startled, raised his eyebrows, blinked several times in phony disbelief.

"Stink. This is the third day of the tour, and he has not been near a bathtub. He doesn't seem to have any change of clothes. I can't stand it. I'm not even sure he was clean when we started. This is more than three days-worth of stink if you ask me."

Carl gingerly put his hand on his stomach as if to be reminded that the stink made him queasy. "I don't know what to say. I really can't control my clients. I'll ask François what we can do. Maybe we can get you your own room. I don't think we can do that for two people. Let's see how much influence François has for the rest of the trip. Maybe Victor and Owen can share a room. I don't know that Owen would notice. Then I guess you and I would have to share a room. I don't have any bad habits…I guess you don't either. How does that sound?"

"It sounds better than the way it is, mate."

When the crowd dispersed and Allen joined his friends, François spoke to Carl. "I show you excellent restaurant. Lunch on me today."

"You don't have to do that. I have tons of money."

"No. I show grateful. You bring to me forty-five whatever rich American tourists, so I make a bunch on tips later. I spend on friend now."

"That's genuinely nice of you. I've never had a tour director do that. Maybe a drink or two. Never lunch."

"I'm better than normal tour director. You see."

"I do see," Carl said quietly and looked admiringly at François. "*Andiamo!*"

François led Carl through several winding blocks of white limestone buildings, commercial and shopping streets, to a quiet area. Through literally a hole in the wall they entered an ancient, but glass-fronted one-story building in a courtyard. Tables stood inside, set with heavy white linen tablecloths, shining crystal stemware, and real silver eating utensils. A *maître d'* seemed to know François, bowed deeply and graciously, and directed them to a table by the window.

"I don't think the dreadful people find us here," François said, waving a hand toward the enclosed courtyard.

"Even if they did, they wouldn't stay when they see the prices," Carl added.

François partly raised his hand in the aisle and a wine steward came to the table. When the steward returned with a bottle, he poured a small amount for François to taste. He nodded in approval.

"I almost never drink during the day while on duty," Carl said, as he tasted the wine.

"You American have the hang-ups about wine and the alcohol. When do you enjoy?"

Carl took another sip. "Now."

"You like the scallops, Carl?"

"Love 'em."

"Okay. For appetizer we order the fresh scallops in radicchio salad with slices of melon in season," François read and translated from menu. Carl followed along in his own copy of the menu. They didn't ask for English versions of the menu, which might not have been available in this authentic, non-tourist restaurant. For the second course, François selected a tasty consommé with the tiniest pearl onions and flakes of what looked like parsley floating precariously on top. Next, a very small pasta course appeared, compliments of the house, an angel hair pasta lightly swathed in olive oil and garlic with a thick sprinkling of the fluffiest parmesan cheese Carl had ever seen. The pasta wound around in a sort of braided circle that Carl couldn't imagine doing at home. Barely a taste, really, as not to spoil the appetite. They each ordered a main course, François opting for veal with mushrooms and Carl a sea bass, poached in wine and herbs.

"This food is out of this world. I'm not used to this," Carl offered, taking a break from eating.

"You not have good food like this at home? I guess I know answer to that. America terrible reputation for food. Almost bad as England."

"America is worse, believe me, François."

"What wrong with America food?"

"In some big cities it's good, but a little city like where I live, all the restaurants, almost every single one, is part of a chain. Mostly fast food but also chains of steak houses, chains of seafood, what they call barbeque. Nothing regional or inventive about it."

"That so too bad. So, you cook yourself."

"I don't cook myself, but I cook for myself." The distinction went over François's head, and he furrowed his brow a bit.

"I like to cook, and I really have to, where I live."

"I'd like to try you cook some time for me."

"That would be fun. But I'm sure, being French, you'd be the better cook. I guess there's no time for that on a tour."

After enthusiastically enjoying the main course, Carl and François slowed down but the waiter brought, unsolicited, small fresh fruit salads with citrus, kiwi, and halved grapes combined. Merely a taste. Also followed, unsolicited, a dish of sorbet, "to clear the palate for last course," the waiter explained. When the waiter returned, Carl held his hand to his stomach. "No more. Terrific, magnifico, but I ate too much." The waiter bowed to Carl and then to François, who winked at the elderly waiter. The wink turned out to be some sort of secret signal, for a few seconds later, two plump chocolate truffles appeared on plates in front of Carl and François, along with those tiny cups of extraordinarily strong hot coffee. "I'll have to force myself," Carl protested as he bit into the dark chocolate truffle, stuffed with even darker creamy chocolate filling. Carl closed his eyes as he savored the chocolate. Ecstasy lit his face. François bit into his and, as a joke, wrinkled his mouth as if he'd bit a lemon. They both laughed because there really was no hiding the superiority of the chocolate.

They remained quiet for a while.

"I bet a lot of your passengers would love to cook for you. Or give you presents, chocolate like this and things?" Carl said.

"Yes. *Si,* ladies and even sometimes men get crushes."

"Crushes? Really? Does crush mean the same thing in Italy?"

"Sure. Why you not think François handsome to have the crush on him?"

"No. You are terrifically handsome. Among the best I've ever seen. You must know that."

"You think so great. You nice looking man. Maybe you know what I mean."

"I know I'm ordinary looking. I'd never say, boy, is that one terrific looking guy." After a pause Carl continued. "I'd say, he's a nice looking fellow, or something like that if forced to describe myself. As we say in America, 'nothing to write home about.' But you're a different story." Carl laughed.

"What I mean is I know people look at me and unfortunate I think I know what they think. They think François some prize. Some token like to win at carnival. Like trophy. They see nothing more. Since little boy I always try to figure out if people like me because François cute or because he nice or because he smart, but always same François think because he cute only reason like. Then get older not cute anymore but can tell François get handsome then older even more handsome than other man. Don't say to be haught."

"I think you mean haughty. No, you really are handsome, and it wouldn't be haughty or overly proud for you to admit it. No one would see it differently."

"You see what I mean. François get older it get worse. Girls like François in high school and college. Never ever François believe it because François smart or nice or generous. All want to look. Worse. All want to feel, to touch." François shivered and crossed his arms on his chest as if warding off unwanted physical attention. "But not touch real François. All touch the body, the only thing they see. They not see real François. François sometime very depressed over."

"I feel terrible about this. I think I'm guilty of the same thing."

"No. Not guilty. You talk to François. We share thought. We friends already three day. If love that be okay, that be good. François want somebody understand. Nice looking, how you say, nice looking fellow understand and real love not looking love." François reached and grabbed Carl's hand with the fork in it. Carl put the fork down and squeezed François's extended hand.

When Carl looked at their hands together, he noticed his watch. "It's a quarter to two already. We need to go. Are you sure I can't pay for this?"

In response, François handed a credit card to the waiter who disappeared for only an instant and then returned the card, asking for his signature. They rushed from the restaurant and François led on a shortcut back to the bus. Everyone appeared to be on board, even Georgia Mae and Joseph, with only a few stragglers waiting to climb the steps.

"You musta had a really good lunch. I ain't seen you smile like that since before we left the USA!" Ida Sue said to Carl but she sounded a little facetious. Ida Sue appeared to have a knack for uncovering, maybe even creating, the prurient.

Carl looked at Sophia who listened intently, trying not to mind her own business. She held an enormous shopping bag on her lap.

"You must be right, Ida Sue." Carl dismissed the comment. "Would you like me to put your stuff overhead, Sophia?"

"Would you do that for me please? Do you know if in Venice I'll be able to get me another suitcase? A really big suitcase. Like the one Mahalia has with her?"

"Why would you want to do that, Sophia?"

"I just bought so much stuff. I have a shopping bag at least that big from what I bought in Rome, and we still have a couple of cities to go."

"I suppose so. Remember, you're going to have to pay the airline for the extra suitcase and for the weight."

"I don't care. I have to buy stuff for people."

"She's like the world's record holder for shopping," Sally said. "I thought I was bad."

"You are bad, just not as bad as Sophia," Sophia's seatmate Joan commented.

As Carl turned to his seat, he stopped abruptly. "Where's Owen?" he asked the passengers who sat close by. "Is Owen in the back? In the bathroom? Did anyone see Owen?"

Chapter Twenty-Four

Among The Missing

François came to the back of the bus to see what had agitated Carl.

"Sophia and I were keeping an eye on Owen, Joan offered. "Gosh dern, does he ever tend to wander off! A couple of times we had to grab him when we went into stores. Then we found an outdoor restaurant where we wanted to eat lunch and we asked him to join us, but he said he wasn't hungry. I know why he wasn't hungry, but I'll tell you later. That's the last I saw of Owen. He stood waiting just outside the railing for the outdoor restaurant, you know like the way people leave their dogs tied up while they eat? But next time I looked he was gone. That was more than an hour ago. So, I don't know."

"Anyone seen Owen more recently?" Carl raised his voice to be heard by everyone on the bus. Silence. A few heads shaking.

"Jesus Christ, François. Here we go again. I guess you go down the right side past the Leaning Tower and I'll go down the left side and then circle around the next side street and then come back."

"We really don't have much time, *Dottore*. Venice long drive."

"We can't just leave him. I wish I hadn't eaten so much," Carl said, suddenly gripping his stomach in anticipation of a post-lunch run.

"I just go. You stay here. Relax. I run and look. I find Owen."

"No, it will be faster if we both go. Each take half the town. Let's say twenty minutes?"

"Okay. We be back here Owen or no, at two thirty. No later. No more time."

"No more," Carl conceded as he moved to the front of the bus, François's hand on his right shoulder, as if guiding him toward the steps.

Carl started down the square at a jog while François did the same on the opposite side. Soon, with the crowds around the Leaning Tower, they could no longer see one another but kept on. Down past the Leaning Tower, Carl kept running but slowed his pace in front of restaurants and stores, not that Owen would be buying anything.

He circled around to the next commercial block beside the square where it was more likely for Owen to get lost. If Owen kept in sight of the Leaning Tower, he would have been able to see the bus. The street narrowed and the pedestrians impeded his way, but he kept up a jogging pace. Nothing. Old men lumbered along, looking like Owen, but as he approached, like a mirage, they morphed into anonymous old men. When the street let out into the far end of the bus parking lot, Carl took one last look up the main street, through the square, and returned to the bus about the same time as François. François had unbecoming sweat stains, leaching far out from his armpits, wet running down his chest with his hair uncharacteristically disheveled. Carl looked very much as disordered as François. When they approached the open door to the bus, both heard strains of singing. "68 bottles of beer on the wall, 68 bottles of beer…"

"Goddammit," Carl said.

François reached out a sweaty hand and rubbed Carl's back. "We did the best we could. We go now. Owen will found us in Venezia."

"I've had enough Owen. Let's get going. I've never had to abandon one of my clients, but I guess there's a first time for everything."

Carl preceded François up the stairs and into the aisle of the bus. An old, bald-headed, portly man stood in the aisle with his back to Carl, both arms raised, conducting the chorus. "Sixty-three bottles of beer on the wall."

"Owen!" Carl shouted above the din. Owen kept conducting.

"*Owen*!" Carl howled. The singing passengers fell silent and pointed at Carl to get Owen's attention. Owen turned around.

"Hey, boss. You look terrible," Owen said, looking from Carl to François. "Why are y'all sweaty? It isn't so warm out."

"Owen, where the hell have you been? François and I ran through this whole town looking for you."

"Oh, that. Well, I got lost. Once you get away from that leaning thing it gets confusing. All those winding streets and squares and more streets. And I said to myself, I said, Owen, now you done it. You're going to spend the rest of your life in Pisa. Probably eating pizza. Ha Ha. Well, I thought to myself, I thought who can help me? And I thought of only the police who seemed so nice in Rome and everything, dancing, not that I want to dance with a cop. Maybe line dance but for sure not a slow dance, but the line dance, I never learned that."

Carl stood in the aisle, wearing a fresh red blush of anger. François poked Carl in the back, trying to get him to relax, to break the tension. Carl just stood there with his hands on his hips but before he could say anything to stop Owen's diatribe, Owen continued. "So, I go to the nearest policeman and I say, I'm lost. He said something like 'No sprekenzy durtch,' or something and I said, yeah, I think you're getting it. I don't know where my bus is, and his partner, another policeman, an older guy like me, well, maybe not that old, you know I'm eighty-four. Or is it eighty-five? I even forgot it was my birthday until my son..."

"Owen, for Christ's sake!" Carl said.

"Well, this maybe older middle-aged cop comes along and says in this sort of I-talian English, he says, 'Whatsa matter for you, bub?' so I recognized the English in it, and I say I'm lost. I need my bus, and the older cop says, 'All the busses stay one place. One place only for the bus,' so I say."

Owen puts his right hand on his hip, almost coquettishly, and continues. "And where might that be? and the young cop says, 'I show you. You walk with me. I bring you there in five minute.' Well, I have a helluva time keeping up with this young colt of a cop but in five minutes we wind through these narrow streets and alleys all that I don't remember coming through in the first place, and before you know it, there's the bus right in front of us. All the buses but I recognize the World Tours sign just like in the cab in Rome and I say thank God for World Tours signs or I'd be up a creek."

Carl and François, dumbfounded, stood gaping with disbelief at Owen. Twitters, laughter, and applause fluttered through the bus and Owen realized he was entertaining an audience.

"*Enough*! Sit down. We're already forty-five minutes late! Let's get going," Carl scolded.

"*Andiamo*," Sophia shouted.

Carl, his last nerve apparently unraveling like an old electrical cord, admonished Owen. "You need to stay with a couple of other people all the time."

"They're too slow. Those women go from one store to the next. I can't stand it," Owen protested.

"I know what you mean," Carl admitted.

As the bus reached the smooth surface of the highway, Sally wiggled herself out of her seat and snuck up on Carl, who stared out the window, watching the country scenery. The shadow Sally cast could not be ignored.

"You should have had lunch where we ate," Sally almost sounded as if she were scolding.

"Now, why would I want to do that?" Carl said in a flat voice, not even looking up as Sally's voice was so brittle, irritating, and infinitely recognizable.

"It was for sure the best restaurant in Peetsa. We had these huge peetsas. I even brought some back with me. An individual peetsa was fourteen inches. I'm not kiddin', and you could have everything on it you want. All for ten dollars or ten euros or whatever they use here for money, and that included a salad and a glass of wine, but I had to pay two dollars more for my Co-Cola if you can believe that, and they acted as though Co-Cola was something strange to ask for, and they didn't even know if they had any, but they did, the good kind in the little bottle, which wasn't much for two dollars, but I'm sure it was the best restaurant in town."

"I'm sure it was." Carl said without turning his head from the window.

"Where did you eat? I bet it wasn't a fourteen-inch peetsa!"

"No. We ate way back in town somewhere. François chose the restaurant. There were something like five courses. Very fine food."

"Well, I know what them five skimpy courses is like. I hope you had enough to eat. Next time you just follow us, and we'll show you the best place."

"I'll do that. I'm sure François would like to know where he can get the biggest pizza and for the best bargain."

"You know it. I should be running this tour. Anyway, I'm feeling a little sick. I better sit down. Maybe I ate too much. It was so good and there was so much of it. I brought back on the bus what I couldn't finish in the restaurant. You want some?"

"No. No thanks. I'm really full."

"Well, when those fancy little five courses are all gone and you're starving in the middle of the afternoon, you just come back, and I'll give you a slice. It'll be cold, but you'll still be able to tell how good it was. That's if I don't eat it all by then. Anyway, you know where I am."

"I sure do." Carl pressed his eyelids closed tightly.

Without much traffic, they made up most of the forty-five-minute delay caused by looking for Owen, giving them extra time at a rest stop while crossing the Apennines late in the afternoon. Late season snow still clung to the ground and sat in plowed mounds like adipose snowmen around the parking lot. Mississippians rarely saw snow and never so much of it piled up. Some started making snowballs and threw them at one another, like children, amid the blasts of horns as they ignored cars entering and leaving the parking lot. Carl just shook his head and headed toward the service center building. François stayed behind to make sure no one slipped on the ice and snow. Just as Carl was about to enter the building, he saw Victor pick up a stone and pack it into a snowball.

Chapter Twenty-Five

Snow Job

"Don't you even think about doing that," Carl said loudly, getting as close as he dared to the stinking Victor.

"I wasn't going to do anything with it," Victor protested like an errant schoolboy.

"Drop it!" Carl spoke, pointing, as if to a misbehaving dog. Victor dropped the lethal snowball and headed toward the building, head hanging down at the shoulders as if really humiliated.

The rest stop was typical of those service centers on the major highways in Italy. To save space, the Italian architects located the commercial areas in a bridge over the highway. In this case a cafeteria, restrooms, gift shop, and as usual, an upscale restaurant occupied the space above the highway. Italians typically stopped for leisurely meals of several courses and hours in the upscale restaurants before continuing their journey. For all their fast, seemingly reckless driving, they felt no hurry as a culture. The driving was a sport and the eating a passion. Even the cafeteria boasted excellent food, from various pastas to steaks and roasts and mouth-watering desserts like found only in the best bakeries in the USA. Being typical of Americans in a hurry, Carl's passengers used the self-serve cafeteria and the rest rooms and were instructed to return to the bus in a half hour.

Carl held the door as his clients entered the building. Joan stood by and waited until the rest of the crowd passed. She wasn't usually a complainer.

Carl looked at her. "I bet you're saving some sort of gem for me."

"It's just about Owen. Nothing bad, really. I know you have your hands full." Joan hesitated, then continued. "You know why he never buys lunch when we stop to eat?"

"No. I never really thought about it. I haven't been watching him too carefully, and you can see the results."

"Well, here's the reason. Once the bus gets moving and everyone is settled down, he goes to the back, you know, where you keep the snacks in the overhead. He opens them and he takes stuff out."

"I thought he got up to go to the bathroom."

"No, Carl. He stuffs the crackers and candy into his pockets and then when we stop, he goes off and starts eating them. Other than the free meals, I mean the ones included with the tour, he eats all that crap. I don't mean it's crap, I know you bought them for us as treats. But they're meant to be snacks, not meals. I bet if you go back there and look, there's almost nothing left. I know you didn't pass them around yet, but they've got to be mostly gone by now, thanks to Owen."

"I'll go check. I planned to give them out this afternoon." Carl held the door for Joan and then walked back out to the bus. The boxes of snacks, every one of them, showed signs of violation as if by a huge rat. Owen had poked a hand-sized hole into the side of each box, then turned the boxes around, hiding the hole. Carl shook each one in turn and, sure enough, the candy box was completely empty, and the cookies and crackers were mostly gone. "I'll be dipped in shit." He shrugged his shoulders.

François grabbed a strong coffee and a pastry and walked around outside to the far end of the parking lot. Carl went inside to keep an eye on his clients but had nothing to eat. Standing near the gift shop, covertly watching Sophia fill another shopping bag with frou-frou and kitschy junk, Sally accosted him. "Do you know what's going on?"

"Probably not, Sally. Why don't you fill me in."

"You know Victor?"

"Oh no. Shit."

"So, you do know Victor. Why did you let him on this trip?"

"Why wouldn't I? I didn't know anything about him before this tour. What is he up to?"

"Why didn't you ask? I could have told you. He hangs around our church. He won't join but he's always there. He went on one of our overnight trips and the same thing happened and the pastor told him he could never go on another trip. That's probably why he came to you even though this is a lot worse than overnight. Nobody trusts him in the church either, and he smells so bad all the time, but pastor didn't kick him out yet, of the church I mean. There's just something about kicking somebody out of a church, you know what I mean?"

Despite running out of breath she continued. "But a trip is different. A trip is not as Christian a thing as church is, or something like that. You know what I mean. But you should do something like pastor did."

Carl waited until the diatribe ended but as soon as he opened his mouth, Sally, having caught her breath, started in again. "I knew the stories about him stealing, so I decided to keep an eye on him. In Pisa I saw him take some postcards and not pay for them. I was in a jewelry store in Florence and he came in and one of the bracelets I was looking at suddenly disappeared from the counter. Here he went through the cafeteria line and got a whole big meal. I mean like one of everything. Then he walks right past the cashiers. These I-talians are so trusting they're not even watching. He walks right past the cashiers, sits down with me and Nora and Briana and starts to chow down. Nora, who was watching, says, 'Aren't you gonna pay for that?' Victor says, 'I did.' Briana says, 'I saw you walk right past the cashiers.' Victor says, 'I'll pay for it when I'm done if it's any good.' Briana was so upset, she was almost done with her minestrone anyway, that she just got up and left. Nora and I finished but we didn't say anything else. Victor picked at everything. He really had a huge heap of food on his plate, and he ate not even half of it, except both the desserts he ate the whole thing, then said, 'this food sucks.' Can you believe he talks like that in front of women? And he got up and walked out of the cafeteria, and now he's there in that magazine or bookstore or whatever it is, probably robbing them blind."

"That's terrible."

"What are you going to do about it?"

"I'll take care of it."

Carl walked away from Sally out to the parking lot. Sally followed at a distance, intending not to miss potentially juicy action. Carl caught François's attention and waved his hand for François to join him. François raised his right hand to his forehead and even at this distance,

Carl could see that he rolled his eyes and stuck out his tongue in his little-boy, endearing way. Together they hurried toward the shop, which sold magazines, books, and tobacco products, with the curious and trouble-making Sally in tow.

"I'm tired of Victor and his stealing. I want you to translate for me if you have to."

"Are you sure we should do this, *Dottore*?"

"No, but I can't stand doing the rest of this tour knowing at any minute there might be a catastrophe with the police."

"I never have call for police on World Tours client. Oh, maybe once," François scratched his head as if recollecting.

They reached the cashier counter.

"*Buongiorno, Signore*," Carl said.

"*Buongiorno*. I may be help to you?"

Carl continued in English."You see that man in the back row? The bald man in the dirty jacket." He pointed, hiding his finger with the palm of his other hand, to Victor in the back aisle of the shop. François translated but didn't point.

"*Sì, Signore*."

François turned to Carl. "Yes, sir."

Carl waved him off with a smirk and a chuckle.

"Keep an eye on that man. He might be shoplifting." François translated but hesitated at the word shoplifting, as if not able to find a direct translation. The proprietor shrugged his shoulders and opened his raised palms as if to say, 'what do you want me to do?'

"Okay, then, François. We did all we could."

"That's right, *Dottore*. All we could do. Now it up to God."

"I wouldn't go that far."

• • • •

With passengers loaded, only a few minutes late, the bus entered the autostrada with about two hours to go before arriving in Venice.

Carl began to walk up and down the aisle and visit with his clients to hear their impressions of the tour. When he got back to Nora and Ann's seat, he stopped short. Nora had refused to rotate seats. Carl pointed to all the trash stuffed into the seatback in front of them. Even the vents along the window were packed with used tissues as was the crevasse between the seats. Carl spoke to Nora in a harsh whisper. "This is one of the reasons why we make people rotate seats on tours, Nora."

"Whadda ya mean?"

"The trash, Nora. If you had to move your seat every day, you'd be more likely to pick up your trash so no one else would see the mess you made. You really don't expect the driver or François to pick up used snot rags and stuff, do you?"

"That's why I don't want to rotate. Then I'm not bothering anybody."

"Nora Sue, tomorrow, when we get on the bus, you will go with the rotation and leave your seat clean. You do that or you find some other way to get home."

"You can't do that!"

"Try me. This is disgusting and it's a health hazard."

A cloud of stink struck Carl as he started to make his way to the front of the bus when he passed beside the seat where Victor slept, leaning against the window. Allen, his Australian roommate, perched on the edge of his seat, leaning into the aisle, to get as far away from Victor as possible while still sharing a seat. When he saw Carl trying to get past, he waved his hand in front of his nose, then pinched his nose and rolled his eyes toward the top of his head.

"Okay. I'll do something. I'll talk to François right now. Maybe he can call the hotel before we arrive."

"Do appreciate anything you can do, mate, but if you can't, ask the hotel for another room. Even if I have to pay for it. I'll demand World Tours pays for it. They can't expect me to put up with this."

"You'd sure have a good case. I'll do my best."

Carl made his way to the front of the bus where François sat on the fold-down seat across from the driver. Carl sat on the steps between them.

"To what do I owe the honor of the visit, *Dottore*? But of course, always good to see you," he said as he put his hand on Carl's knee, squeezed, and left his hand there. Of course, Carl did nothing to discourage the hand.

"I have to talk to you about Victor."

"Didn't we take care of Victor? Maybe next stop we just have to get in head of Victor and keep an eye."

"I guess you mean ahead of Victor. No one would want to get in Victor's head. This more involves the nose."

"Nose…I get it. Victor stink. What do you do about Victor stink, *Dottore*?"

"What do I do? This is your tour."

"When thing go bad it my tour, when thing go good it your tour!"

They both laughed.

"Just tease you, *Dottore*. Everything good and bad my tour." He moved his hand somewhat up above Carl's knee. "If that what you wish," he said enigmatically.

Carl watched the hand move up his thigh.

"Easy for François. François handle it. Happen sometime. Especially the old," he paused a moment. "And sometime the young, the teenage, stink, but I give soap and say to them use it. Sorry it embarrass, but very bad for all passenger. Only have mention it one time and one soap and then problem go away, at least for days."

"Is there any way, François, that you can get Allen, his roommate, a separate room? I think he's actually going to get sick if he has to stay with Victor. And with the stealing, it's really a special circumstance."

"You not to worry, *Dottore*. I already take care. You need different room too or you not sleep and get sick from that old geyser trash compact."

"I think you mean geezer."

"Maybe you get hurt by trash compactor or other dreadful."

"Dreadful? Where'd you get that word dreadful?"

"I read American novels. They dreadful but they use good words to learn English well."

"I guess so. Anyway, I'll trust that you solved the problem." Carl began to stand and realized that François's hand had moved mid-way up his thigh. Carl looked to the driver to see if he noticed. The driver watched out of the corner of his eye, his lips pressed together in a knowing smirk. Carl patted the hand in encouragement and then stood up and moved to his own seat next to the slumbering, sprawling, unconscious Owen.

François picked up the microphone. "You all…I get that right?"

Multiple y'all corrections came shouted from the passengers. Then Sophia piped up. "Technically if yaw gawna talk to all of us you have to say "all y'all. That's plural. Y'all is singular."

"That so?" François sounded utterly amazed. "How you want to hear about Italian retirement? Much time before Venice so I tell you retirement." No one looked or sounded excited. "François bet all you want retire. What age you retire in USA?"

Sally responded this time. "Starting at sixty-two but you get more money if you wait until sixty-seven or seventy."

"That better. Most retire Italy sixty-six but some if money, if tired, if want to, retire early. Retire paid by government no must save. But help to save because Italy retirement not so too much. Italy retirement, what you call social security, it thirteen thousand euro or maybe twenty thousand American dollar."

"Wow. That isn't much," Sally said.

"Maybe not so much in America but okay in Italy and by time sixty-six years old have own house or apartment. Or rent apartment for old only maybe six hundred euro the month most. Not so much the year. Plenty left after they travel, eat restaurant, go to opera, bet the horses."

"Bet on horses? Where is that?" Fred, the ex-cop, was suddenly excited.

"No. François only joke. Not the horses. But cost of living Italy much low USA especially house and transport. Live okay on twenty thousand and most have saving because never pay medical or school. If have little no money maybe live in special old-folk place. Some nice. Most nice. Pay for by Italy small amount to live there."

"But do you have some more taxes taken out like we do for social security?" Sally asked.

"No. The tax is the tax. I say yesterday, tax from nothing to maybe sixty percent for millionaire. Like USA millionaire not like pay tax but get caught sometimes. No extra tax. No even sales tax. Owner of store pay tax. Pay tax on profit but you tourist, you customer, not see tax added in store."

"That's right. I think that's why things seem so cheap here. What you see on the price tag is what you pay. At home you have to think an extra ten percent," Sophia contributed.

"Even restaurant no tax. You relax. You know what bill to get," François added. "So, you not need so much to retire. And no poor people when retire because all get same retire. Everybody equal when retire except rich who save."

"There's lots of poor old people back home," Ida Sue said. "I have an aunt who worked as a cashier in a small store her whole life and her social security is six hundred a month. That's what's not fair. She worked her whole life, and they took the same percent from her, which I can tell you was a bigger chunk of what she needed to live on, bless her heart."

"Didn't her employer give her a pension?" Sally asked.

"Sure. They took a little out of every paycheck and when she retired, she was told she'd get one hundred fifty each month. That was nothing compared to what she paid in all those years. Then the store went bankrupt or something and she got a letter saying that her pension was no longer coming. It was awful for her. These companies are ripping us off," Ida Sue concluded. "Somebody got my aunt's money."

"Oh, I no want interrupt but see big building on side of mountain, left side of motorcoach?"

"The white square looking thing?" Lucas asked.

"That Beretta factory. You know Beretta?"

"Sure," Fred said. "Everyone knows Beretta. That's what some of us used in the department."

"But I thought there were no guns in Italy," Sophia chimed in as if to poke a hole in the utopia François described.

"You know best customer Beretta?" François asked in way of answering.

"USA!" Fred claimed.

"You right. Beretta corporate headquarter in Texas. Sell most gun in Texas. Not sell gun here. Maybe some police but not most police here."

"Why do they make 'em here? Why don't they move the factory to Texas?" Fred asked.

"Old tradition go back to fifteenth century. Italy not want gun but want job. Give incentive to keep factory here. Craftsman here, too. Generation make the gun. Never use the gun but the skill here north Italy. Lots of Italians want factory gone, say move whole damn thing to USA, but how you say, money talk?"

"But what good is it if you can't own a gun in Italy?" Helen asked.

Lucas agreed. "Yeah. We have much more freedom in the USA. You can tell us all you want about social security and free education and God knows what else free, but you can't even own a gun. So, that's not freedom."

"Why you want the gun? You have so much killing by gun in USA," François pointed out. "You worse in America than war in Afghanistan.

In two year, the gun kill more than Viet Nam war."

"But I wouldn't feel safe without my gun," Helen protested.

Carl rarely participated in his clients' discussions with the tour director but commented on this topic. "You think you're safe with a gun, but if a burglar knows you have a gun, if you try to reach for it or have it in your hand, they're going to be faster and you're going to be dead."

"I just feel safer with a gun in my house, next to my bed," Helen insisted.

"How many in your city murdered with gun?" François asked.

There was silence, then Sally piped up. "It's about average one every day. It's at night and the next morning you hear about it on the news. I don't think a day goes by that there isn't somebody shot. And if a day goes by then the next day there are two or three to make up for it."

François nodded in agreement. "So, you live in where?"

"Jackson, Mississippi, and we're proud of it!" Sophia contributed.

"And how many the people live in Jackson?" François continued to try to make his point.

"What is it, about a hundred and sixty or a hundred seventy thousand people? Somewhere around there," Sally said.

"So, Italy almost sixty and a half millions of people and no murder every day. Maybe a few murder each year. Less murder than Jackson with hundred seventy thousand. Go figure. You think the gun not matter? Why you think so much the Americans shot if not because they have the gun?"

Silence fell on the bus before François continued. "And the murder in Italy mostly the foreign, not the Italian. Like the tourist wife mad at the tourist husband and kill. Is right for all person say they feel safe with gun make country not safe for everyone?"

Carl butted in again. "You sure don't see the kind of mass murders we have in the USA in countries like Italy. Does anybody know why that's true?" He waited a moment and concluded. "I think it's poverty."

His comment met with total silence.

Briana broke the silence. "Do they give free samples at the Beretta factory?"

François scrunched his face at Briana as if that were the dumbest thing he'd ever heard. "No. But you volunteer for practice see how bullet work. You volunteer for target and get to keep samples."

"Hardy har-har," Sophia said.

Chapter Twenty-Six

Venice

The driver located the Venice hotel in Marghera, the mainland part of Venice, not on the more desirable and tourist-infested islands. But the location of the hotel, within walking distance of the pier and the ferries that ran continuously to Santa Croce, was considered most convenient for a tourist hotel. The building stretched more than an entire block and rose six stories, one of the largest buildings in the area and one of the only ones that could accommodate large tour groups.

Built in the nineteen fifties, the lobby soared two stories, a glass and marble space, starkly and simply furnished in high fashion when constructed, a sharp contrast to the old-time grand hotel the group had just left the night before. An empty restaurant occupied the space at the far right, and a broad white marble staircase rose next to the restaurant, in the center of the lobby. François received all the hotel keys from the registration desk and distributed them without Carl's help.

Carl stood to the side, quietly, for a few minutes before Ruth Ann accosted him.

"Did you check if my credit cards arrived?" Ruth Ann asked.

"No, I didn't ask yet. They wouldn't give them to me anyway. You'll need your passport or some identification before they'll hand you the envelope."

"Come with me then. I don't speak I-talian and even though yours' stinks, it's better than nothing."

"If you feel that way about it, Ruth Ann, you can wait for François. He'll be free in a minute."

"No. Come on. I want my credit cards."

The desk received no envelope in the mail. The clerk, however, knew to look out for an envelope for *Signora* Swenson and promised to leave a message for her as soon as it arrived. If not this afternoon, then tomorrow afternoon.

"Sorry, Ruth Ann, but this seemed like the best place to catch up with them since we are here for three nights."

"Sorry…my…ass. That's the last time I'll take any advice from you."

"How much money do you have left?"

"That's none of your damn business."

"Ruth Ann, I just want to know if you are okay for the next couple of days or if you need anything."

"I'm just fine. I found my ATM card in my wallet. I guess I didn't take that out with the credit cards, or I put it back or something. Maybe I didn't call the bank, so it won't work."

"They usually work. There's an eight hundred number on the back if you need to call them from out of the country."

"You're always so helpful," Ruth Ann said with a smirk and headed toward the elevator bank.

François held the key for Owen and Carl, and the ones for Victor and Allen, the Australian, until last. He turned to Owen and Victor first. "We have problem in this hotel. They have one few room than we need, so I rearrange. Carl share room with me, it okay with him?" He looked at Carl. Carl nodded, a little too rigorously. "That leave Victor to Owen instead of Carl to Owen and Allen to his room alone…"

Victor followed the conversation vigilantly and interrupted. "Why does Allen get a room alone? I'm supposed to have my own room, too."

"No, you pay no single supplement. Allen did pay." François crossed his fingers where only Carl could notice. Victor raised his hand to protest but François shook his head and held up a finger, indicating Victor should wait a minute. "Here key for Allen. You go rest for dinner." François waited until only Owen and Victor remained. "I have something for you, Victor." François reached into his pocket and pulled out a small rectangular box wrapped in purple paper, concealing a bar of lavender soap. "I think you probably forgot soap when you pack. Maybe you not like hotel soap. Hotel soap very little. Maybe you need big soap that smell nice for change."

"Thanks, but I don't need that," Victor protested, putting his hand up to refuse the soap.

"You need. You not get on bus again if not use."

"You're not the boss of me. Carl's the boss."

"On tour Carl no boss. Carl just *Dottore* with nothing to say. Carl boss in USA but when he in Italy, I boss. He *Dottore* but I *Commandatore. Capisce?*"

François shoved the bar of soap into Victor's shirt pocket. "I mean what I say, Victor. You make other passenger no comfort. Comfort of passengers my business. You clean up. Come to dinner and stink then no dinner for Victor."

"Asshole," Victor said under his breath and then walked to the elevator.

"At least you know your name," François said softly. "Come, Carl. I show you room with me. You be surprise when you see. You be comfortable."

"I'm sure it will be fine," Carl said a little too eagerly.

Carl and François entered the elevator and François selected the button for the sixth, the top floor. François led Carl out of the elevator. This floor was a little different from the others, certainly from the natural light coming through the almost continuous skylights in the ceiling of the hallway, almost like being outside in that distinctive, bright, Venetian light.

"This floor all suites, *Dottore*. I here many time with big group and manager do favor for me. You like suite." François unlocked a door with no number, just the name Lido. He pushed Carl through.

More noticeable than anything else, a wall of windows framed a view of the islands of Venice, looking almost directly up the Grand Canal, however distant. The ferry landing was visible on the right and the island of Murano could be seen in the distance, far to the left.

"Wow," Carl said as he walked to the window. A wide terrace with a table, chairs, and lounge chairs opened on the other side of the windows, taking advantage of the view. The room was furnished in the same style as the lobby, with chrome, glass, and leather, black and white furniture. The only color came from an enormous arrangement of fresh flowers on a coffee table in the center of the room. The fragrance of the flowers almost overpowered the senses.

"Only one bad, Carl. Suite they give me only have one bedroom. I tell manager I think okay. If you make me sleep on sofa okay. But you make François happy if in bed. I no mind. I like. Suite so nice anyway."

"I think we can manage." Carl moved quickly and melodramatically flung open the sliding glass door, like a certain nineteen sixties sit-com movie star in her Park Avenue penthouse. François then opened one of the double doors and revealed a bedroom, probably twice the size of a regular room in this hotel, also opening onto the same terrace. The bedroom contained a low king-size bed, and like the living room, all black and white furniture and art. Another slightly smaller arrangement of colorful fresh flowers rested on a short table in front of the bed.

"What you think, *Dottore*?"

"I think I like it better when you call me Carl. The suite is terrific. It will be the best part of the trip."

"I hope not, Carl. I hope the time with François best part of trip," François said, looking down at his feet coyly, not looking Carl directly in the eyes.

Carl took a step closer and took François's right hand in both of his. "I think you're right."

Just then a knock sounded on the door, and Carl's smile disappeared. "Oh shit. It's starting already."

Chapter Twenty-Seven

The Romance Of Venice

François disentangled himself from Carl's hands. "Not to worry," he said as he walked to the door. In the doorway stood a uniformed waiter pushing a cart bearing a wine bucket containing what looked like champagne and a plate of assorted exotic-looking cheeses and breads.

"Oh, I forget," François turned to Carl as he waived the waiter in and indicated the terrace, "I order this before and forget to tell. Dinner not until seven so we snack?"

"We snack," Carl said, joining François and the waiter on the terrace. The waiter stood by, ignored by François, but it was obvious to Carl that he waited for a tip. Carl pulled a two euro coin out of his pocket and pressed it into the waiter's hand, and he disappeared with a bow. François opened the champagne and poured it into two glasses. "You sit and enjoy?"

"Yes, for a little while. I'd like a shower before dinner."

"Me, too," François raised his glass in a toast.

After admiring the view, taking showers, and getting dressed in coincidentally similar sports coats, Carl and François went down to join the group in the dining room. The management had roped off a section for World Tours. Several other tourist buses were parked in the hotel's parking lot and the tables bore the names of the various groups. Most of Carl's group had already taken seats. François grabbed Carl by the wrist and led him between the tables until they reached the table where Victor sat between Allen and Owen. François leaned over Victor's shoulder and sniffed loudly.

"You do us proud, Victor," François announced, after his nose was filled with the scent of lavender. "You sniff, Carl?"

"That's okay, I'll take your word for it," Carl responded.

"Why don't you two girls beat it, huh?" Victor said, continuing to look straight forward, not acknowledging Carl or François.

"You very funny, Victor. You a comedian in USA?" François asked.

Victor blatantly gave François the finger, without even turning toward him. Owen and Allen pretended to be concentrating on the menu. Allen held a hand to his mouth, suppressing a grin. Carl pulled François away and they sat at an empty table for four at the very edge of their group. They both picked at salads and the fruit course.

After dinner, Carl and François sat close to one another on the sofa in their living room, but neither moved nor spoke. The phone rang. Both made motions to answer.

"I get it," François insisted.

"*Buonasera,*" the receptionist at the front desk announced and then spoke in broken English, not knowing whether he had Carl or François on the line. "We have trouble in lobby. Too much noise. First and second floors they can't sleep. Come fix noise."

"What you mean noise?" François replied irritably, turning to face Carl, holding the phone toward him so that he might hear as well.

"You guests. They all on the stairs and they scream, they yell, they laugh. They all drunk, I think. You make them go to room. I try to tell, and they just laugh. They keep all hotel awake."

"We be right down." François put down the phone and motioned to Carl.

"Let us go down." He reached for his sports coat folded over a chair and Carl did likewise. They took the stairs in the event any of the troublemakers had gotten beyond the lobby. As they approached the doors leading to the second story staircase the din became audible. Opening the door, they were accosted by what sounded like a zoo. The women's voices carried much more irritatingly than the mens.

As they approached the broad marble steps that descended to the lobby, they had difficulty finding a path through the sprawled and writhing bodies, most with glasses in hand, and shouting to others at some distance.

"Party over," François began saying as he made his way through the bodies, poking shoulders to get attention.

Carl started doing the same thing on the opposite side of the broad staircase.

"Everyone need to go to rooms. It late. Early day tomorrow," François kept repeating and slowly the reclined bodies stood waveringly and headed down to the elevator bank in the lobby. Carl and François took seats opposite the elevator bank to watch their passengers compete for the elevators. Only two of the four elevators seemed to be operating.

An overfull elevator tried to close its doors when Victor stuck his hand in. At the last minute, rather than lose a few fingers, he withdrew but began pounding with his fists on the brass outer door. "Goddammit. Wait. This fuckin' thing…goddammit." The remaining passengers stood back from the crazed Victor.

The porter on duty and the desk clerk came running over. "Stop. You stop that." The porter and desk clerk each grabbed an arm. Victor put up a struggle, attempting to shove their hands aside. When he saw he lost the battle, he brushed himself off. "I was just kidding. I didn't mean anything. I didn't break it."

"We go with you to room. Please stay in room rest of night," the desk clerk said. François got up and joined the group. "I'm sorry," he said in Italian to the two hotel officials, and continued in English so Victor would understand, "I'll see Victor to his room and talk with him."

The two hotel officials released Victor into François's custody, leaving Carl with the few remaining clients waiting for an elevator. A third elevator, which had not seemed to be running this evening, opened its doors but started closing again before anyone could get in. Doug reached in to try to stop the doors, but they continued to close on his arm. He winced in pain. Luckily the porter and desk clerk nearby, shoved their fingers in on both door panels, and pulled them apart. From the sound of their banging together, the elevator doors had done some real damage to Doug's arm.

Carl raced to assess the damage and Jean Ellen tried to examine Doug's arm. "It could have been fractured," Jean Ellen said. "The doors hit him pretty hard."

"Doug, considering your condition, I don't think we should take any chances. We should have a doctor look at you," Carl suggested.

"Maybe an x-ray, just to be sure," Jean Ellen added.

Carl looked toward the desk where the clerk and porter had retreated. "Let's ask the desk clerk to call a cab. They'll know where the nearest hospital is." The desk clerk heard the request and began to make the call. "I need to find François and tell him where we're going."

Just then François appeared on the staircase. Carl took François aside and explained what happened: "Doug is in his eighties, traveling with his girlfriend, Jean Ellen, and it will probably be Doug's last tour. He was diagnosed with inoperable lung cancer that has been resistant to chemo and radiation. Doug told me about it months ago when he signed up for the tour. Visiting Italy being a lifelong dream, I encouraged him to go."

"Don't you start to blame self," François sympathized. "It nice thing you do for Doug."

"Jean Ellen was a nurse before her retirement and promised to take care of Doug to make this tour possible. I suggested to Doug that he take a day off, when necessary, stay in the hotel when possible and rest up when he felt he needed it. I encouraged him. Maybe I was overly optimistic. Most of my clients are elderly and fulfilling 'bucket lists.'"

"It not a bad thing. The accident happen."

"It's a sort of mission for my business to fulfill travel dreams. I think older people need something to look forward to, like travel."

"So far, he keep up good but now hospital need to go for arm." Jean Ellen wandered closer to François and Carl. "Jean Ellen you look?"

Jean Ellen responded, "At the very least he's going to have quite a bruise. I'd like to get him checked out, like an x-ray."

A cab pulled up at the front door.

"I go with Doug and Jean Ellen. You stay here. Get some sleep. You need Italian spoke at hospital maybe. I go," François insisted.

"Okay." Carl saw the three to the taxi.

Carl went alone to the room. He took out his cell phone and dialed his home number. After about three rings, Chuck answered.

"Why are you calling me at work?" Chuck scolded. "You have all day to call and then you get me at the busiest part of the day."

"Jesus. I forgot. Sorry. It must be four in the afternoon. I just had to send somebody to the hospital and I'm a little upset."

"How serious is it?"

"Maybe a broken arm. Stuck in the elevator doors. Kind of a freak accident."

"Don't you need to be at the hospital?"

"The tour manager went. Somebody had to stay in the hotel with the clients and I don't speak enough Italian to be any help in the hospital."

"Is everything else going well?"

"Yeah. I guess so. How's Ponce?"

"Ponce is fine."

"Is he eating enough?"

"Ponce is fine."

"Is he getting out enough?"

"Ponce is fine. I'm fine too in case you're curious. Anything else you want to know?"

"Give Ponce a kiss on the dry part of his nose for me."

"Sure. Bye."

Half a bottle of flat champagne remained from earlier in the evening. Carl poured a glass.

Carl sat on the terrace and watched the boat and ferry traffic to Venice. The lights grew dimmer in Venice and its silhouette against the sky became more and more ghost-like, ethereal, and otherworldly. By the time he had finished the bottle, Carl stood unsteadily and flopped down on the bed. He got up momentarily and took a shower. The clock next to the bed displayed two o'clock.

• • • •

François returned about five o'clock in the morning and crawled into the other side of the bed without waking Carl. François's arm had migrated to Carl's side of the bed and his hand grasped the bed covers pulled onto Carl's shoulders. Carl looked at the hand and arm but made no attempt to move it from his person. Carl stayed in bed until six o'clock, when he got up to take another shower.

François rolled and slept for a few more minutes. By seven o'clock, both dressed and ready for breakfast, they headed for the restaurant in the lobby. "Last night not go like planned," François said.

"Who could have planned a night like that? Jesus."

"Tonight be nicer. You see." Dark circles beneath his eyes marred François's normally perfectly handsome face, making him look older.

"How is Doug?" Carl almost hesitated to ask.

"Doug have sprain only. Sprain from pulling arm out. Elevator not break arms, but you sprain you pull out too hard. Doug be okay. He take day off. Tomorrow he see Venice when we take gondola. He stay home today, and Jean Ellen stay with him. They okay."

"Thank you for taking care of them. I know the Italian hospitals are particularly good and they never charge anything, even to tourists, so I knew they'd be in good hands."

As they entered the dining room, Jimmy called to them with a wide grin on his face. "Hey, they have bacon here, too! Or something that looks sort of like bacon. Tastes like bacon. These I-talians are catching on fast."

"How did you have time to order lard for the lard ass?" Carl asked, after moving out of earshot.

"François has ways."

Sally and the busybody, Ida Sue, at the nearby table, accosted Carl and François. "I bet you two had a good time last night. Heard you got a suite. I should be the one got upgraded." Sally teased, and Ida Sue gave Carl a huge, exaggerated wink.

"It was the only room left."

Ida Sue started to giggle, held a hand to her mouth. Carl moved on, following François to one of the only unoccupied tables in the hotel restaurant. François had his usual strong coffee and a single croissant, while Carl made a great heap of cold cereal mixed with yogurt and all sorts of fruit and hot tea instead of the strong coffee.

Everyone waited on the bus in happy anticipation of a day in Venice…except one.

"Where's Georgia Mae?" Carl asked Joseph.

"She's getting a little bit of a late start this morning. She should be down to breakfast by now," Joseph replied.

"Down to breakfast? Everyone is here waiting to go. You know this isn't okay."

"I'm sure she'll just grab something and come right out."

"No. Go get her. No, I take that back. I'll go get her."

Carl walked to the front of the bus and explained the situation to François.

"I go in. I look."

"No, François. This might start to get ugly because it's happening all the time. I'd better handle it."

Carl walked through the revolving front door, scanned the almost vacant lobby, and turned right toward the dining room. He waved off the *maître d'* who asked for his room number. "I'm looking for someone."

He walked quickly among the tables until he ascertained that Georgia Mae was not there. He left the restaurant and went to the registration desk. "*Buongiorno.* Can you call the room of O'Connor, please. That's Georgia Mae and Joseph O'Connor." The clerk picked up a telephone from behind the counter, dialed the room number, and handed the phone to Carl. It rang three times and finally a breathless Georgia Mae answered.

"You realize we're waiting for you," Carl said, in clipped tones.

"I'm on my way down. I got a late start. We didn't get a wake-up call."

"Did you ask for one?"

"I think Joseph did. Maybe not."

"Listen. Forget it. Come down right now."

Carl waited in the lobby between the stairs and the restaurant. Sure enough, Georgia Mae came out of the elevator and tried to circumvent Carl and head for the restaurant. Carl moved swiftly to block her way. "No, you don't."

"I've got to have something to eat. I'll get motion sick. Just a roll or something. A glass of juice."

"Nothing doing. You've now kept a whole bus waiting twenty minutes. Think about it. That's collectively hours of time. The bus ride takes five minutes to the ferry, there's coffee on the ferry. Fifteen minutes to Venice, then you can go to a coffee shop and eat all you want."

"You're just mean," Georgia Mae complained and stuck out her lower lip, as she made an about face and headed toward the bus waiting outside. Stony silence greeted her when she entered the bus. She beamed at everyone, smiling as though expecting another round of applause. The corners of her mouth fell when she saw the looks of impatience and even downright hostility on the faces of the other passengers, most of whom offered no eye contact whatsoever and preferred to look at guidebooks or magazines instead.

"I have talk with them tonight. This is it. This too much," François said to Carl as he walked by, behind Georgia Mae.

"So be it."

"Okay, people," François said into the microphone. "You have brilliant day for Venice. That the right word? British say everything brilliant. You say maybe we stop for tea, and they say brilliant. You say there's a detour, it take us fifteen more minutes to get to hotel, they say brilliant. I guess it mean nothing. But to me it still mean something. We meet brilliant tour guide Antonio when we get off ferry in Venice and he walk us to St. Mark's. Antonio best tour guide in Venice. He take us through basilica and explain. Then he take you to Murano Glass in Square. You look but you not buy, maybe. Maybe glass chandelier cost you thirty thousand American dollar. François whole house not cost more than Murano chandelier. Then we leave Murano, and we go into St. Mark's Square, and you have leisure lunch. If you want afternoon free on own, you have it. If you want you follow Antonio, you see Doge's Palace, you see Lido, you see neighborhood and other palace. You meet four o'clock at ferry. You remember where ferry is? Ferry at end of canal. You follow Grand Canal you no get lost. You get lost you ask anybody. Ask anybody except tourist. Tourist know nothing. They get lost. Venetian never lost. Venetians greatest navigators. Never lost. And you remember Roma."

Those still paying attention wrinkled their foreheads. One of the braver passengers asked, "What's Roma? Isn't that where we started the tour?"

"Roma not so nice to call jeepsie."

"Pickpockets," was murmured through the group. Hands dove into pockets and patted purses and fanny packs and clutched them tightly.

"Okay, we go. You hold on your stuff."

At least half the group headed off, ignoring Antonio, the magnificent St. Mark's Basilica, headed into the Square, which promised hours of shopping.

"You want to follow Antonio into basilica?" François asked Carl.

"No. I've been there many times. I might walk through later. It is glorious, but I don't want to see it with a noisome crowd."

"Good word, noisome. Mean full of noise? No blame there. We go have coffee or whiskey."

"Coffee, thanks."

As it was still early morning, hardly anyone sat in the outdoor cafes and restaurants that lined St. Mark's Square three quarters of the way around, in front of the grand and elegantly colonnaded buildings. Carl and François headed to Harry's Bar, the Hemingway hangout. François guided Carl by the arm. "Normal hours I not go to Harry's tourist trap. But early morning Venetian not even awake so nice even at Harry's and coffee good anywhere, not like shit American coffee."

They took a table toward the middle of the seating area, less likely to be noticed and interrupted by their own tour group.

"You ever been to the USA?" Carl asked.

"I go to New York years ago with wife." An immediate and total silence descended.

"No," François said, reaching out for Carl's hand. Carl recoiled slightly then allowed François to rest his hand on top of his. "That years ago. Not now."

"When were you married?"

"I marry right after high school. We both in the university together. We young. Thing to do but heart not in. It not last long, believe me."

"So, do you have a relationship now?"

"No, not to worry, Carl." François patted Carl and then withdrew his hand. "What about you, Carl? You married? You have relationship? The children under feet?"

"Under foot. Like you, I married young. Right after college. It didn't last long. The relationship was a lie and I realized I wouldn't change. A few years ago, I met a guy, Chuck, and I thought that was it. The real thing. The love of my life. But I've been realizing lately it's not."

"How you mean, it's not?"

"We have nothing in common at all. I love working and the things that money can buy, and he'd just as soon live on the sofa."

"Live on sofa?" François furrowed his brow.

"You know lazy? Couch potato?"

"Oh, yeah, I know lazy means. So, this Chuck lazy?"

"Just no ambition. So, I earn most of the money. I travel. He works a little from home, stays home with the dog, Ponce." Carl blushed and grew quiet.

After a few minutes of silence, François laughed. "So, we sleep together last night."

"Literally, we did. It's funny how sleep together usually means anything but sleep."

"Sleep together in most language, most time mean fuck. Why not say fuck?"

"Such a paradox. You know what I mean by paradox."

"You say one thing really means another?"

"Yes. Like that. We say sleep, which is the opposite of sleep when we really mean fuck, which by nature is not done while sleeping."

"Other way to say, make love. Make love like potter make vase. Silly to express."

"I never thought about it, but it isn't like you're making a real thing, like a piece of pottery, or a painting. You're making a feeling."

"At best you make feeling. Sometimes you make big mess."

"Big mess physically or emotionally or both." Carl laughed a little and then it turned into one of those uncontrollable laughing bouts and he almost rolled off his chair. François joined him in the laughing and grabbed Carl's arm so he wouldn't roll onto the cobblestones.

When the giggling had subsided, François continued. "François like sleep with Carl."

"Last night was really sleeping and was it even two hours' worth?"

"No, I get tenses wrong. I mean like to sleep with Carl future tense."

"That would be nice."

The conversation was interrupted by screaming and shouting in the middle of St. Mark's Square.

Chapter Twenty-Eight

Jeeped

"What's going on out there?" Carl asked as he looked past the surrounding tables.

"Seem to be some fight," François said, half getting up out of his seat to get a better view. "That Helen? The tall skinny one? Your client?"

"I think you're right, François. I think I should go to see what's happening."

A crowd of clients and pedestrians had formed a circle around Helen and Nora. Helen frantically rifled through her large purse, receipts and other papers, lipsticks and candy wrappers falling to the granite paving stones of the square.

"What's wrong, Helen?" Carl asked.

"I've been robbed!" Helen half sobbed, half shouted.

"Are you sure? Maybe you left your money in the hotel room," Carl offered in an attempt to be helpful.

"No. That's not the way it was," Helen protested.

Nora spoke up. "She opened her purse and started counting the money out of her wallet. This lady wearing this long hippy dress comes up and crashes into the both of us, so Helen dropped the money on the ground. All these people came from nowhere and dove for it."

"I thought they were being helpful. I thought they were picking it up for me. I started to say, thank you, thank you and they ran away as quick as they came. They got all of it. All I have are my credit cards still in my wallet."

"We warn you that," François said, not particularly consolingly.

"Where are the police when you need them?" Helen cried.

"Probably line dancing," Carl said, but immediately covered his mouth with his hand.

"Don't worry," Nora scowled at Carl and put her arm around Helen's bird-like thin shoulders. "I have plenty of cash if you need it. You can pay me back when we get home."

"You two okay?" François asked Helen and Nora. The other passengers who gathered for curiosity or moral support started to break off and headed back to the shops and restaurants.

"Yes, no thanks to you two. Hiding out, drinking coffee. You should be watching more carefully."

"François did warn you, Helen," Carl admonished.

"Well. It's still hard to believe that such things can happen in a civilized place."

"Yeah, civilized like at home. At home you probably would have been bashed in the head or shot in addition to being robbed."

"That's nonsense, Carl, and you know it."

"Hey, Helen. The crime rates speak for themselves," Carl insisted.

François joined the discussion. "No body shot here. No body mugged. Just the jeepsie. Nobody shot in ten years in Venice…except maybe tourist shoot one another or drug dealer. Very safe."

"Sure, François. You're full of crap." Helen said.

Nora pulled her toward the crowd of clients who had just left St. Mark's Basilica and headed toward the Murano glass gallery on the corner, with Antonio in the lead.

"Let's go in Murano's. We can buy a chandelier as consolation," Nora suggested.

"What the hell am I going to buy it with? My money was stolen!" Helen retorted as they disappeared.

"How much fuckin' money she carry?" François said, laughing. "So like American to blame somebody. All America blame somebody. Weather too cold they blame Canada. Economy bad USA blame China. Somebody listen in on phone they blame Russia. Europe only has self to blame."

"I think there's some truth to that, François."

"Come, Carl, I show you something special. You like opera?"

"I'm crazy about opera."

"I have friends in opera house. We go there and see what is going today."

"François, you must be exhausted. You don't have to show me around all day. You were up almost all night. You look exhausted." The dark circles had not quite disappeared from François's eyes. He looked a little older today but still strikingly handsome. "With Antonio in charge, why don't you go back to the hotel for a nap?"

"François never need nap. When home in Paris and not work, have nap every afternoon. Never nap on job."

"Okay. Let's go to the opera house. Speaking of not sleeping, I saw a performance of *La Sonnambula* there years ago."

"How old you anyway, Carl, that you go to *La Fenice* years ago?"

"I'm thirty-four now. I was twenty when I went to *La Fenice* the first time."

"You old man. Just kidding. François turn thirty in June. François getting to be old man."

"I think you have probably plenty of life in you. We'll see."

As they approached *La Fenice*, a soprano could be heard singing "Casta Diva" from *Norma*. It floated above the buildings, down to the watery surface of the canal, and bounced off the crumbling stone of houses and apartments. It sounded ethereal and lovely. The unaccompanied voice, with such acoustics, resonated exquisitely.

"That voice sounds familiar. Maybe it's somebody famous," Carl speculated.

"There school at opera house. Singer come for lessons. You hear."

"Yes, I hear. If it were USA they'd be inside, windows closed, air conditioning blasting, you wouldn't hear a note outside. This is wonderful. The way it should be heard."

"You like then."

François led them to either a stage door or an entrance for sets and stagehands. They found the door unlocked. Inside the door stood a tiny desk with a uniformed security guard, maybe early middle-aged, model handsome, who rose when he saw François, and they kissed on both cheeks. They exchanged a few words in quick Italian, too fast for Carl to decipher, and then the guard indicated with his hand that François and Carl should feel free to wander about. The security guard bowed to Carl and softly uttered a greeting. "*Dottore*, welcome."

François headed to the back of the auditorium. It had been green, green silk walls and velvet railings, when Carl attended the last time. Since the fire, it was now red, but just as sumptuous, and if it weren't for the change in color, one would not know that a tragic fire had demolished one of the greatest, beloved, although by no means the largest, temples to opera in the world.

They found a rehearsal in progress. The stage, set for *Norma*, displayed a half-constructed Stonehenge look-alike set. A concert grand piano sat in the orchestra pit, instead of an orchestra, and a long haired, skinny conductor stood in the bend of the piano. The conductor held an old-fashioned, low-tech cardboard megaphone in his right hand, the score spread out on the closed lid of the piano. Mainly he waved the megaphone around to get attention but spoke directly to the female chorus on stage. Shouting didn't work and finally he used the megaphone, surprisingly effective for a simple roll of cardboard. He spoke in American English.

"You are the slowest Druids I ever saw. You're going to worship, not to a funeral. Come on, the music is slow but at this speed half the opera will be your entrance!"

The women of the chorus looked at one another, some obviously not understanding, and some laughed, causing the conductor to put his hands on his hips in impatience. The conductor noticed that the women seemed to be lined up by size, the smallest coming on first and then getting larger and larger. By the time Norma stepped on stage she'd have to be sitting on an elephant or no one would notice her.

"And break it up girls. Don't line up by size." He brought a hand up to his mouth, seemed to realize that what he said might be either insulting or cause some sort of dissent among the Druids as to who was fatter than whom. Already they broke into clumps and seemed to be arguing with one another and pointing at one another's hips and asses, laughing. The conductor looked toward a man who came to his right side, probably the stage director, shouting something in Italian, too fast for Carl to understand, but causing guffaws from François. The chorus moved off stage, some shouting invectives with lots of suggestive hand signals at the stage director.

The piano started again and in somewhat faster stroll, the Druids entered the stage and managed alternating fat, skinny, fat, skinny, tall, short, tall, short. The conductor nodded approval to the stage director who just shrugged his shoulders. Last came the diva, Violeta Herrena .

Chapter Twenty-Nine

Déjà Vu The First Time

Carl turned to François. "I know her!"

François looked at Carl with raised eyebrows.

Just as she was about to begin "Casta Diva," the aria they had heard echoing outside, the conductor stopped the music. "I think you all need a break but that looks much better." The conductor turned around.

"That's David Gockley, who I've heard conduct dozens of times."

Just then, a tall young man came from backstage and spoke to Violeta Herrena and a few of the women of the chorus. "I know him, too," Carl said.

François looked at Carl as if he'd gone mad.

Carl moved closer to the stage to get a better look at the man.

"Hank. Is that you?" Carl shouted from the audience. The acoustics were such in the opera house that everyone heard him. All the Druids and everyone in the orchestra pit turned to see who'd shouted. Carl looked startled that his voice carried so loudly.

Hank walked to the front of the stage, raised his hand to his forehead to block the glare of the stage lights. "Who goes there?"

"Carl Minton. Just stopped in to see some of the rehearsal."

"Jesus Christ. I wish I had known. Violeta, here's someone I want you to meet." He grabbed Violeta by the hand and led her to the stairs at the side of the stage. Carl went to meet them halfway and François followed, hands in his pockets, looking awkward.

"Violeta, if it weren't for Carl, I wouldn't know all that Schubert lieder…or a lot of other music. He accompanied me all through college." Violeta gave Carl her hand, continental style, and Carl bowed slightly to her.

"You look some familiar," Violeta said.

"You couldn't remember me playing keyboard in the Mobile Philharmonic."

"Oh, love perform Mobile Philharmonic. Not for years. But I remember faces. You have face." She pointed and shook her finger at Carl's face.

"You performed there, it must have been a dozen years ago, but I remember the concert. We did scenes from *La Boheme*. I spoke with you backstage during the intermission. You couldn't remember that."

"I tell you I remember face."

"How long are you in town for, Carl?" Hank interrupted.

"Just through tomorrow. We leave the day after. I have a group with me. I'm in the travel business. I'm no longer performing."

Violeta held her hands to her cheeks and shook her head in sorrow, even though she had never heard Carl perform except as part of an orchestra.

"I'd like to leave two tickets for you for *Norma* tomorrow night," Hank continued, indicating François. "I can't really socialize before a performance, though maybe we can all go out on the town afterward."

"I'd love to, Hank, Ms. Herrena, but I'm responsible for this group of unwieldy Americans. I don't think I can get away."

François came forward and grabbed Carl's elbow. "You go to opera. I stay home with kids."

"Where you find such a devil of handsome man?" Violeta asked with a pronounced Spanish accent, pushing her way toward François, extending her hand as she had to Carl. François bowed and kissed the top of the proffered hand.

"He's my guide in Italy," Carl answered dismissively, sounding a little jealous of the attention François got everywhere they went.

"Oh, you keep this one. This one handsome as devil. I know devil and I know handsome. Unfortunately, all my husbands were devil and not so handsome as this!"

"I'll leave a ticket at the box office tomorrow. You come if you can and look for me after," Hank said.

"You leave two tickets so handsome devil maybe come too?" Violeta added.

"Somebody has to stay home," Carl cautioned, but François wrinkled his nose as if smelling something bad. He'd obviously warmed up to this group now that he became center of attention.

"We have to start back at rehearsal in less than an hour, otherwise I'd ask you to join us for lunch, but this is going to have to be quick and not too appetizing," Hank interrupted the gushing and cooing of Violeta about François.

"We'll continue our walk through the house," Carl added. "If I can't make it tomorrow night for the performance, can I get in touch with you through your agent, Hank?"

"Sure. I'd like to get caught up. My career, traveling all the time, hasn't left me with many friends. It's not much of a life. I'd like to chat, maybe get together when we're in the same city. You can email the agent at Rowe House, and they'll find me."

"Great. I know them. I'll be in touch if I don't see you tomorrow."

Violeta and Hank headed back up the stage stairs and François led Carl back out the center doors of the house. They turned left and went down some stairs where they could hear conflicting music coming out of several rooms.

"That's strange. A Beethoven sonata in an opera house."

"Not so strange. The practice rooms rented for lessons. Expensive lessons. And some of singers just come practice because not practice in hotel too loud for guests. More studio upstairs. You want to see? Hear?"

"It's getting late François. I'm starving to death."

"You go to die?" François took Carl's arm in exaggerated concern.

"No. Just an expression. I'm really hungry and it's getting late. By the time we eat it will be time to meet the group back at the ferry."

"I show you marvelous place we eat."

"Just as long as you let me pay for it, François. Not like yesterday. Today you let me pay."

"Then I show you really marvelous place to eat."

François led Carl several blocks to what seemed like a private palace along a canal. But for the small black and gold sign beside the door, no one would know it housed a restaurant. Through an open-air hallway they entered a courtyard of crumbly yellow stone, half covered in moss and smelling of boxwood and damp decay. On one side of the courtyard appeared floor to ceiling French doors, all open with a few tables set under a wide colonnade. Yellow watered silk wallpaper covered the restaurant walls and three matching Murano chandeliers with blue and green fruit and flowers of delicate hand-blown translucent glass hung from the high ceiling.

A waiter came and introduced himself in Italian and François took the lead in ordering. After a debate in fast Italian, François said to Carl, "He wants to know if we want heavy lunch or light lunch. Something makes think it not be much difference between."

"We have dinner at the hotel tonight and that's only a few hours away. Let's try the light lunch."

François instructed the waiter. In a few minutes, a dish came with portions of cantaloupe on a single leaf of lettuce, with a few slices of prosciutto.

"This is very light," Carl commented. The waiter brought a half bottle of some white wine and asked François to taste it, but François said that he thought the waiter could just pour it.

"I think more coming."

Then something shaped like an egg, rolled, however, in breadcrumbs and slightly browned, came on a tiny bed, more like a small nest of the most delicate angel hair pasta. "A new delicacy. It a fry soft boil egg. Everybody wants now."

Carl broke into the perfectly prepared egg. The yoke made a sauce for the pasta, which had tiny pieces of crisped bacon, garlic, herbs, and truffles tucked into it. Then came a light consommé with tiny rings of green onion floating on top. Hardly enough to fill one up.

"I interested. You not tell François you famous musician and you know all famous musicians."

"I was hardly famous. I accompanied Hank when we were both in college. He got famous and I didn't. I played in a second-rank orchestra."

"But still, you young. You could have got famous."

"I don't think so. I didn't nearly have the talent of those two we just met."

"But still. If heart in it. Would not the concert stage be better than the tour group?"

"I just don't think I had what it takes. The will. I didn't have the will." Carl turned back to his meal.

"All job have frustrations," François offered, consolingly.

The waiter brought a small piece of white fish, on a plate by itself, in a lemony cream sauce. Baskets of the most fragrant and perfect white bread, a whole small baguette each, appeared with the fish course. Chilled butter, rolled into rose designs, arrived with the bread.

"At least with this job I get to travel and see the world. Plus, I had terrible stage fright, so I never felt comfortable about performing."

"Then maybe all for best. Plus, you had experience as musician for memory. How rare that?"

"Yes. There are some great memories. Not many people get to have those memories of performing."

A slightly sour strawberry sorbet followed, just enough to clear the palate, to make it ready for a miniature bowl of *crème brûlée*, with a honey crust beyond description.

"You think food okay in Italy?"

"I can't even think of words for it."

"Even François, who always full with words, can't describe. The people must experience. In America eat because hungry. Italy, France, eat to enjoy. Nothing to do hungry. Food like art. Most American, even English not understand. They eat when necessary. Not like to think food is art."

Carl mused, "It's almost like there's something shameful about enjoying food too much or spending so much time making it. I guess it is part of the Puritan ethic that both countries have."

"Puritan or no. Makes for bad food," François concluded.

At three-thirty, when Carl finally wrenched the bill away from the waiter, he suppressed a gasp at the price of three hundred and eighty-five euros. As if he spent money like this every day, Carl took out his credit card and paid the bill. François looked quite the worse for wear, having probably two hours of sleep the night before and acting as guide all day. His hair appeared rumpled and his shirt askew. He led Carl by shortcuts to the ferry where their group waited impatiently.

"I suppose you two went for another of those five-course lunches," Sally accosted them as they approached the group.

"I think more like six or seven, wasn't it François?" Carl teased, even though he probably spoke the truth.

"While we, the peasants, eat in McDonalds. That's fair, isn't it?" Sally retorted.

"You not eat McDonalds. There no McDonalds allowed on Venice islands."

"Well, I'd rather have McDonalds than what we ate. Some kind of sausage. Who knows what."

"That favorite dish of Venice. Good for you find native dish!"

"Ugh…I can't wait to get home."

François shook his head and shrugged his shoulders. "Soon enough, *Signora* Sally, soon enough. You say you always found the best places. I glad we not follow you today."

"That's for sure," Sally said and turned to embark on the ferry.

• • • •

The bus arrived at the hotel at five o'clock and began disgorging passengers. Shopping bags and packages today seemed to outnumber passengers. Carl watched and just as he turned to enter the hotel, a cab pulled up. The big butt in stretch pants that backed out of the cab, preceding the rest of the body, caught Carl's attention. "Olivia! You got a train today. We weren't expecting you until tomorrow morning."

Olivia turned and scowled. "I'm not talking to you."

"Oh, Olivia. You're here, you're feeling better. Let's let bygones be bygones. It's not like it was my fault. I didn't have anything to do with your being kept behind."

"You should have insisted I could go with the group."

"I can't. Nobody'd listen to me anyway. You know nobody ever listens to me."

"Oh, go away. No. Carry my luggage. It's in the trunk."

"I'll call the porter and he'll take it directly to the room."

"I don't want to pay him. You take it."

"The tips are included in the tour, so don't worry. I'll get your key and the porter."

Carl disappeared inside. He gave the porter the key he got from the reception desk, saw an elevator door standing open, and ducked in, avoiding any more contact with the irascible Olivia.

Carl and François went to their room, as did half the clients. The other half headed toward the bar in the lobby.

"I have paperwork for little time. Do before dinner and email to office. You okay? You take shower and relax?"

"Sure, François. You're the one who probably needs to relax. I don't know how you survived all day with two hours' sleep."

"It okay. I have plenty energy. You see."

After Carl showered and dressed, he found François, head down on the desk in the living room, sound asleep. His head rested on a pile of papers that Carl recognized as the additional excursion forms filled out by his clients for the gondola ride tomorrow. François wasn't a pretty sight with his nose scrunched down into the papers and a small glob of drool escaping his mouth.

"Do you want to go down to dinner, François?" Carl put his hand gently on François's shoulder.

He jerked to wakefulness. "I think you handle it please. I stay here maybe order room service, maybe not. Big lunch today. Maybe just sleep."

"That's okay. I can handle the crowd."

Carl left and energetically took the stairs down to the lobby. Entering the dining room, he saw the few remaining empty seats at a table where Georgia Mae and Joseph sat by themselves. Late all the time, the couple had finally managed to estrange themselves from the rest of the passengers. Carl hesitantly joined them.

"Did you two have a nice day?" Carl asked innocently. Joseph appeared red-faced and inebriated already. Georgia Mae, sitting forward in her seat, turned to Carl, and looked as if about to pounce.

"I'm sick of being picked on. All these people are so anal about what time we leave for this or for that or how long lunch is. They're not fair."

"You have to consider the feelings of others, Georgia Mae," Carl said mildly.

"The feelings of others! Who cares how I feel?" Georgia Mae burst into loud sobs. "I'm tired of being picked on. I'm trying. I just lose track of time," she cried. "You're not being fair."

She stood and stormed from the dining room.

Joseph watched, then looked at Carl and rolled his bloodshot eyes. "She's very emotion…emotionive, emotion-al, emotional," he stuttered drunkenly.

"Maybe you better go check on her."

"Nah," he waved his hand in dismissal. "She'll be back. You…you… wait…you wait and see." He raised his glass of wine as if proposing a toast and guzzled it down. "Have a drink, Carl. There's plenty of wine. Plenty."

Carl and Joseph ate in silence.

Just about dessert time Georgia Mae returned, looking scrubbed and somehow refreshed in a change of clothes. "Sorry I'm late," she apologized, graciously, as if nothing had happened earlier. "Carl, can you get the waiter? Maybe there's some dinner left over. I'm hungry."

Carl summoned the waiter who had observed the whole evening's events at this table. He prepared to bring back her earlier courses, in elegant, covered silver dishes, getting the attention of the diners still in the restaurant. Georgia Mae found a surefire way of getting attention.

Carl excused himself and headed toward his suite.

A table, next to the door to the suite, displayed the remains of a plate of caviar, a few broken crumbs of crackers stuck in what looked like cream cheese, and an empty bottle of wine.

"Some dinner," Carl said quietly.

The lights were on in the living room but not in the bedroom. Carl entered the bedroom and saw the form of François, in his pants, but no shirt on, lying across the bed. He didn't turn the light on, not wanting to wake François, but undressed and slipped into the narrow portion of the bed not taken up by François's sprawl.

"Umm," François said as he turned on his side and placed a hand on Carl's hand and another over his nose. Gently, Carl removed the hand from his nose and placed it on his chest and lay awake for some time, expectantly. Eventually François turned on his other side, his back to Carl, and let out a gentle, sleepy sigh. Carl turned in the other direction and fell asleep almost immediately. Neither woke up during the night, for any reason.

• • • •

Like a miracle, everyone boarded the bus before nine o'clock the next morning, ready to go, even Georgia Mae and Joseph. Even Doug and Jean Ellen, Doug with his arm in a bandage, held in place by a sling. François, looking well-rested and perfectly groomed, took the microphone. "Lots of water today! We take ferry to Venice. Then we walk again to St.

Mark's where you go yesterday. Next, we get on gondola. Those who pay extra excursion for gondola. Rest have free time, two hours to walk around. I stay with you if you want. I give different walk tour. But most you enjoy gondola. I get best gondola. Best singer. Singer from opera does special for you. Then noon we meet back at ferry, but we no come home to hotel. We go to Burano Island. Burano Island unique. Still fishing village. Fishing and tourists all that there. Shops, restaurants. Much small than Venice. I think you say quaint? It quaint at Burano. You get lunch. You walk around. You shop. At four o'clock we get on ferry back to Venice. Five o'clock ferry from Venice to hotel. Dinner at villa in country. Long day. Got it? I be there with you. I tell you along the way."

Seeing Doug and Jean Ellen, François picked up the microphone again. "We have the five-to-ten-minute ride to ferry station, so we have time to talk, no? We have Doug and Jean Ellen back. Welcome back Doug and Jean Ellen! Doug have little accident. Good time for François to talk about medical system in Italia. How your visit to hospital, Doug?"

Doug sat up straight and seemed eager to talk about it. "It was fine. Everyone was friendly, polite. Most even spoke some English, but you helped."

"And how much cost you?" François asked.

"Well, that's the strange thing. It ended up costing nothing. After they took an x-ray and put this bandage on for the sprain, they gave me a receipt that showed forty-eight dollars for…"

Jean Ellen interrupted. "It was forty-eight euros, dear."

"Well, it didn't matter. I looked around for a cash register, a check-out line, whatever. I ask, 'Where do I go to pay this?' and nurse explain that there are no cash registers in the hospital. They don't use money in the hospital. They treat guests the same as Italians if they can."

"I don't believe it," Lucas said.

"No. Doug right," François took on the conversation. "Part of the big fifty percent tax you talk about, which really more or less, pays the medical. One reason can do is medical not so expensive as USA. You see x-ray for forty-eight euro. What you pay x-ray in USA? Anybody know?"

Fred put his hand up. "I just had my shoulder x-rayed last week. Something like nine hundred sixty-eight dollars charged to my insurance."

"You see medical not cost so much Italy. So, tax pay enough. And doctor no make million…millions for year work like in USA. Doctor pay maybe like high pay teacher like ninety thousand euro the year or maybe some more if specialist."

"I bet the standard of care isn't very good at those prices," Helen chided.

"Not so," said François, "World Health Organization rate France number one and Italy number two in world for health care."

Sally couldn't resist putting her two cents in. "I thought we were number one."

"USA number one expensive but something like twenty-three for the care. USA spend nine percent of total budget. Italy only three percent of total budget but more people cared, and nobody go without. How many go without USA, forty million?"

"It can't be that many," Helen said defensively. "I was a nurse and we had plenty of doctors who came from France and Italy and especially India and Pakistan because they could make more money in the USA."

"So, François ask, you want doctor who leaves, wants to make a lot money? Or you want doctor who likes being doctor so money not so important. Different kind of people. I think different kind of doctor in Europe. Not big money-making thing. You go in business if you want to make the money. You go to medicine you want to help the people."

"Ah, everyone wants to make a buck. Don't kid yourself," Lucas said.

"The Italian healthy, too," François continued. "Not so much the problem the obese, the diabetes, the heart problem."

Sophie wasn't buying that. "I see them eating plenty of junk. All that pasta and bread…and the wine everywhere," she said as she dipped a hand into a bag of potato chips.

The bus pulled up to the ferry station. "Maybe someday you see enough Europe to see different. Not same as USA."

• • • •

After the ferry landed on Venice Island, the crowd made their leisurely way toward St. Mark's and the gondola launch. Two of Carl's clients,

Cory and Helen, brought their walkers. The two struggled against the unevenness of the cobblestones and the frequent pedestrian bridges.

"Are you sure you can manage those things? You left them at the hotel yesterday." Carl asked as he fell behind the crowd and sidled up to the two women with their walkers, the seat compartments now filled with paraphernalia.

"It wouldn't be so bad and we wouldn't need them if there was somewhere to sit around here. Yesterday was real uncomfortable, all that walking and no place to sit. I can even sit in a store with this thing," Cory insisted.

"They must be hard to push on these rough cobblestones," Carl said.

"They have special big wheels for rough surfaces so it's okay," Cory replied. "We can pull them if we have to. The bridges are the only problem."

Speaking of which, they came to the first of many camelback pedestrian bridges that crossed the canals on their way to the gondola launch. Carl stood to the side. Both women bent their walkers and tried to close them, lifting the bags of junk first and putting them on the ground, then giving up because various items overfilled the seat compartments.

"What do you have in there? Couldn't you have left most of that at the hotel?"

"You're a man. You just don't understand," Helen said. It was about the hundred and eightieth time someone made that remark and Carl smirked.

"I might not understand why you need all that junk, but I understand it's going to be tough getting around like that today."

Cory, appeared flustered and annoyed. "Well, instead of complaining about it and flapping your trap, why don't you help?"

Carl stood there expressionless, eyes wandering as he contemplated flight.

"Well?" Helen, already halfway up the bridge, turned to Carl. "You're gonna make us late for the boat ride."

Carl tried to pick up a walker in each arm. Even full of stuff they were not particularly heavy, and Carl made a show of flexing his biceps. Stuff kept falling out of them. Finally, he put both walkers down, picked up one and carried it across the bridge, came back for the other and carried it across. Helen and Cory huffed along on their merry way. Carl sat briefly on the bottom step, catching his breath. He sat on the steps until Cory and Helen gained some distance.

"What are you waiting for?" Cory turned and shouted back to Carl. "There's another bridge up ahead."

Sure enough, in not more than a hundred yards, another bridge loomed larger than life. The portage was not nearly as easy on this next bridge as the steps appeared steeper, and the bridge seemed somehow taller. And the bridge after that. By the time they got to the gondola launch near St. Mark's, Carl was sweating like a hard-ridden horse, shirt half tucked, and breathing heavily.

"You really need to keep in better shape if you're going to do this travel business," Cory said, instead of a thank you.

It took three gondolas to hold Carl's clients. François remained behind and Carl got in the last gondola to load up and leave. The three gondolas headed toward the Grand Canal and then slipped into a side canal where the first gondolier broke into song, "O Sole Mio," naturally, the number one hit with tourists.

Carl sat directly in front of his gondolier and took out a five euro note and subtly offered it to him. "Caro Mio Ben?" he asked. It was an old Italian art song, often the first song to be tackled by an aspiring serious singer.

The gondolier produced an enormous smile, slapped his right hand on his chest, bowing slightly in gratitude while swiping up the five euro note. He broke into a glorious, full voiced version of "Caro Mio Ben." As though he once sang in the chorus at *La Fenice* but didn't make the big time.

The gondolier pointed out that on some of the ancient buildings, the lowest-floor windows appeared below the water line. He said they were lucky that the tour didn't occur during a high-water time in Venice, when tourists would have had to wear rubber boots to slosh through St. Mark's Square, or walk on the narrow, elevated boardwalk that kept them slightly above the high water. Venice appeared, at least for these few days, much the same as it had for many hundreds of years. The brilliant light gave everything a radiance, exactly like in those paintings by Canaletto.

The group disembarked back at the gondola launch, some shakily, but without incident.

"That was easy," Carl remarked to François, as if he had expected something else.

François guided them back to the main ferry station. The ferry ride to Burano was sunny, calm, and pleasant. Carl disembarked first, followed by many other tourists and ferry passengers. They flooded onto the main street of the town, a space that appeared more like a half-mile-long narrow square designated only for pedestrians. Not many cars existed on any of the Venetian Islands. Carl walked a brief distance into the square and then turned to his gathering passengers. François caught up with them, bringing up the rear.

"Well, this is Burano," François said to the few who listened.

"Duh…" Sally said, poking her index finger into her cheek.

"It still authentic fishing village but now make most of money from tourists. Restaurants and shops. No historic sites so you go around for three hours. Have lunch. Shop. Make sure you on ferry at four o'clock because the ferry leave four o'clock. Don't starting back to here at four o'clock and expect the ferry wait for you. The ferry exact on time. All the time. No exception for Georgia Mae and Joseph and Owen and who else?" François scanned the crowd, tentatively pointing at those who didn't seem to be listening.

"Suppose we want to go back early?"

Carl turned toward the voice. Other tourists, not from his group, gathered around as if François were some public entity, a free tour guide.

"Don't pay attention to François if you are not in my group. If you're not in my group, you can go back to Venice any time you want. Go now!" He shooed them away, impolitely, with a wave of his hand. Half the non-World Tours tourists grumbled and wandered off. A few still lingered, starting conversations with Carl's clients.

François began moving down the square with a large gaggle of clients and unknown tourists and Carl decided not to follow. Carl started walking at a fast pace in a different direction, glancing over his shoulder as if to make sure no one followed. He didn't get more than half-way down the course of the square when he heard all too familiar shouts and screams.

Chapter Thirty

Déjà Vu The Second Time

Helen screamed. "Stop that man. That man has my purse. Stop that man!" It sounded like a recording of the events from the day before with the very same Helen. Everyone turned to look while Carl ran back to Helen's side.

"What happened?" Carl asked.

"A man. A man in a hat. A man. He looked foreign. He walks toward me, not looking at me, then he grabs my pocketbook. I hold on to the straps and try to pull but he yanks really hard and gets it away from me or I would have fallen down. I even tried to chase him a little, but in these heels and my walker." She points down to her shoes. Sure enough, Helen had been trying to negotiate the cobblestones and her walker in shoes with high heels.

Carl scratched his head. "Jesus, Helen. After yesterday I thought you'd be more careful. Didn't François warn you about purses and pockets and carrying money with you?"

"Well, I was careful. I only had spending money for today in there and I left all my credit cards and passport in the safe at the hotel."

"I guess you averted disaster, Helen," Carl sounded consoling.

"Well, it was a new pocketbook. I bought it just for this trip. It wasn't cheap!"

"Helen, do you mean it was expensive? Or do you mean it just wasn't cheap?" Cory asked idiotically.

"What difference does it make?" Helen turned on Cory, looking as if she'd like to scratch her eyes out.

"I'm sorry to hear about the purse," Carl offered. "But nobody listened to François. You had plenty of warning."

Helen wrinkled her face and stuck her tongue out at Carl. He turned to walk away.

"Well, aren't you gonna do something about it?" Her voice rose to a screech.

Carl turned back. "I'm going to go find the police." Carl held up a finger, indicating he'd be right back.

Carl wandered for a half-hour, ignoring anyone in uniform, and finally found a pastry shop. Inside, tucked in a corner, if a really attractive man could ever tuck into a corner without still commanding attention, sat François, reading a newspaper with a cup of very black-looking coffee in front of him.

"Great mind think like," he said when Carl joined him at his small table.

"Yes, great minds think alike," Carl repeated, not meaning to correct.

"You English is so, how you say, precious?"

Carl laughed. "I think you mean precise…although I don't know. I guess you could say that. I've been speaking it my whole life. But I can imagine that expressions I use don't make any sense."

"Sense enough. So, you think, Carl, this worthwhile?"

"What do you mean?"

"I mean client sometimes, no, a lot times, pain in ass. Things to worry. But it worth trouble?"

"Oh, I think so. It beats staying at home."

"Better than where, Jackson, Mississippi?"

"That's it. But the tours and the constant complaining, things going wrong, they just wear me out."

"*Dottore, Dottore.* Just you look at this sight. The water, the sky like Venetian painting." François reached and placed his hand on top of Carl's, the one that wasn't holding a cup of tea. He rubbed the back of Carl's hand."I like hair. Hair very manly," he said in a low voice.

"I like it, too," Carl forced a smile.

"Tonight we have a good time. We have suite. We get back from dinner early…but you go to opera." François's tone suddenly seemed dejected. "See friends. See friends more important."

"I'm thinking about it but it's a tough decision. I really want to spend the night with you."

"You have other night. You not see these friends in so long. Nice for you to have memory with them."

"But I'm enjoying your company, too." He remained silent for a minute. "Do you often have clients that you like in this way?"

"Not so very. Or you say not so often?"

"You say not so often."

"Sometimes have dinner special, but rare. Rule not to be special to any client. Treat all same even if feel different about some."

"Do you feel different about some?"

"Sometimes, *Dottore*. Cannot help feel different about attractive client. Can't help want to have some fun with you."

"I'm very flattered. You're a very handsome man. Everyone looks at you."

"I guess I know that. Not very helpful. François never know when some serious or when some just want like prize. Like I say the other day. Not see real François. See manicman can, how you say?"

"You mean mannequin, I think."

"So, I mean. Having friends difficult. Takes work. Only friend see past handsome. Friend in Paris but never on tour. Even the friend might collect the trophy. Take time to see real person. Not on short tour. I think you different. I think you appreciate real François. We talk like people, not like how you say trick. The one-night stand? Okay?"

"I think you give me too much credit, François. I'm about as shallow as the next guy when it comes to physical attraction. Let's go for a walk."

François and Carl remained relatively quiet as François led Carl by the hand through a part of the small town unlikely to have any tourists. They bought sandwiches and headed toward a dock where locals kept small sailboats and a few fishing boats.

After eating, François reclined with his head in Carl's lap. "See, no matter how the trouble, how the worry, so beautiful a place. You forget the trouble and the worry and just enjoy this minute, this place."

"Sometimes it's like I have a recording running in my mind, of all the things that just went wrong, and when that tape stops there's another recording that predicts all the things that might go wrong in the future. I guess I have anxiety."

"You sure anxious fellow. Need to stop. To say in this minute there beauty. This minute perfect. This minute let mind rest. No other time matter." François seemed to drift off to sleep momentarily while he rested his head in Carl's lap.

François jerked awake. "We now go back to ferry. Do not miss ferry."

· · · ·

At five minutes to four, as they boarded the ferry, Sophia came along with yet another shopping bag full of stuff.

"Is that the same shopping bag full of stuff you had yesterday? The same stuff? Are you carrying it around?" Carl joked.

"Noooo, it's noooooottttt. It's the same shopping bag but it's new stuff. I bought me a new suitcase yesterday in that there shop near the hotel, so I have plenty of room to take it all home."

"Oh, that's fortunate," Carl said.

Helen approached. "So, I guess you couldn't find the police. I thought maybe you were kidnapped."

"No, I didn't find any police. I looked all over."

"But I saw him, and I went after him and told him what happened."

"What did he say?"

"He pretended he couldn't understand a word of English. I know he was lying but what could I do? The more I said, the more confused he looked, but he kept nodding his head like he understood, and then in the end when I asked him what he was going to do, he stopped nodding his head and started shaking his head and put his hands up like surrender, like they all do. I said, you're useless, but thank God he didn't understand that because I think if you insult a policeman in this kind of place, they can lock you up for the rest of your life."

"I doubt it, but it might be good idea," Carl said, his eyes wandering, looking for a distraction.

"You don't know—" Helen was rudely interrupted by Sally's sudden appearance.

Sally asked, "Where's what's his name?"

Chapter Thirty-One

Missing The Boat

"Not Owen!" Carl sounded alarmed.

"No, there's Owen next to Victor there. The other one. The Australian guy or Canadian or whatever he is. That almost English guy. The one that speaks the almost English." Sally sounded annoyed that Carl couldn't read her mind.

The crew members untied the ferry, lifted the short boarding bridge, and the horn sounded. Carl stood precariously on the gunwale, where the boarding bridge used to be, and looked out across the square. There, at the far end of the square, Allen ran toward them.

"Wait," Carl shouted to the captain, who, in the wheelhouse, couldn't hear him. He shouted to the mate with the rope in his hand, "Wait!"

The mate shrugged his shoulders. Carl put one foot on the dock, the other on the gunwale of the ferry, balanced with several inches or so of water already widening beneath him.

Shouts in Italian. The mate's shrugged shoulders became wild gesticulations with whole arms. Other crew joined him, all shouting for Carl to get into the ferry. But no one tried to pull Carl onto the boat. By their hand gestures it seemed as if some wanted to push him onto the dock, others wanted to pull him into the ferry. Allen ran toward them, within one hundred yards, but the ferry had drifted a foot from the dock. Carl was starting to stand splay-legged between the ferry and the dock. François came out of the cabin and offered Carl his hand. "Jump. Come off there. Too late for Allen."

The first mate tried to reach and retie the boat, to pull it closer. Two crew members pushed the first mate's hands away. "Too late," they imitated François's English, laughing, as if hoping to see the stupid American fall in the drink. The passengers murmured and a few of the women screamed, as if witness to a calamity, as if Carl had already drowned. Allen reached the pier and jumped onto the ferry, caught by two crew members. Carl relinquished his foot from the dock, and unsteadily shifted his weight onto the moving ferry, caught by François, who's normal lovely olive complexion had turned white.

"Whew…" Carl said, wiping the perspiration from his forehead and bowing to the few passengers whose attention he still held.

"Thank ye, mate," Allen said and took a seat.

After landing and disembarking, François pointed the crowd toward the mainland ferry and started walking toward it with Carl. "You go opera tonight?" François asked, more enthusiastically than Carl expected.

"I'm not so sure. I'm a little tired and it is three more hours until the performance begins."

"You come home right after opera. It not be too late. I wait up for you." François sounded endearing and paternal, squeezing Carl's upper arm the way he always did.

"I guess it's a once in a lifetime opportunity, and I haven't seen Hank in years." Carl sounded less than enthusiastic.

"Right. You hear great music. Visit with great old friend, new friend Violeta Herrena, very famous. Both famous."

"Okay, you're all right to take the kids to dinner tonight? Tonight is the villa for dinner?"

"I okay to take to villa. Easy to go to villa. Villa out in nowhere. Nobody get lost out there. Nothing can go wrong at villa dinner."

"Okay. I'll stay in town and go to the opera." Carl touched François's shoulder, sounding more resigned than enthusiastic.

Chapter Thirty-Two

Déjà Vu Again

Carl wandered in and out of shops, explored the Lido, stopped for a snack and finally found his way to *Teatro La Fenice* for the performance of *Norma*.

Carl waited in a short box office line, but considering the weekday performance, it looked like a decent crowd. The opera house was not as large as La Scala or Palermo, or even Rome, but still a major Italian house. To Italians, weeknights didn't make much of a difference as far as opera attendance went, especially with talent such as Violeta Herrena and even Hank Thallman, whose star had risen, particularly in the European houses.

The box office clerk handed Carl two tickets, but he immediately turned in the second ticket for resale. The box office treated him like a dignitary and called an usher to personally escort him to his box. The usher showed him to a prestigious seat, in the box next to the center box on the parterre, probably among the most expensive seats in the house.

The performance was glorious. Regional opera performances emphasized the music and the voice rather than dramatic acting effects or elaborate staging. Singers often walked to the center of the stage and sang an aria directly to the audience, as if in recital, although a modicum of acting had become customary in recent years. Singers occasionally disrupted the action and sang the aria a second time if the audience called for it with long applause.

Violeta, Hank, and the whole cast sang in top form. All the issues from the rehearsal, two days before, had been resolved. Even the chorus line of Druids came off with a random dignity.

Carl stayed in the house after the performance and then slowly made his way backstage. The house was amazingly unguarded. In New York or San Francisco, it was impossible to get past multiple armed security guards. Hank waited for Carl in the hall outside the dressing rooms as it took Violeta a little longer to change out of her Druid priestess costume. Even in street clothes, Violeta looked larger than life, with a dark purple cape surrounding a plain full-length lavender wool dress, still theatrical, and not at all understated. She wore tiers of what looked like real gold necklaces and matching bangles on each wrist. Hank wore a black sports coat with an ascot tied casually about his neck. He looked very stereotypically artistic.

"Where do you want to go, Carl? You're our guest."

"I don't know Venice well enough to choose. I was at *Alle Corone* the other day for lunch. How about that?"

"That marvelous choice," Violeta answered. "I know Ernesto there. He take care of us okay dokay, how you say? I could eat horse. Let's go. *Andiamo.*"

"I guess our collective mind's made up," Hank conceded. "I don't get to Venice that often either. This is only my third performance here."

The three walked along the canals a short distance to the palace courtyard that contained *Alle Corone.*

A very formal *maître d'*, different from the daytime one, this one presumably Ernesto, met them at the door, and instantly recognized Violeta.

"*Mio dio*, what honor. *Diva magnifica* in my humble restaurant."

Violeta replied, "You'd hardly call me *magnifica* if you'd heard my shrill high C tonight."

"Nonsense, she was a wonder tonight like any other night," Hank asserted.

"I have very special wine special for the singing voice, I give you tonight."

"Bring two for me!" Violeta joked.

"And a horse," Carl added, remembering Violeta's earlier comment, but everyone looked at him as though he'd said something crazy.

Then Hank laughed, pointing at him. "Still that sense of humor."

Ernesto directed the three to a table by a window, away from the cluster of late-night diners, so they could have some privacy. Privacy became impossible since a few patrons recognized Violeta, and in her costume, which was not a costume, she exuded theatrical personality. As they made their way to the table, she offered her hand to a few of the patrons who wanted to pay tribute to her, which she accepted gracefully. She looked like someone important, and in Venice everyone would recognize a famous soprano. A few seemed to recognize Hank.

Finally, the three made their way to the table, led by Ernesto, patient and so proud to have celebrities in his restaurant this evening. Ernesto stood tall, shoulders back, clutching three menus, as haughty as if he'd created the party of opera singers. Violeta pushed the offered menus back toward Ernesto and whispered something, presumably in Italian, to Ernesto, and he went away.

"You have excuse my Italian and my English, fellows. I born Guadalajara, not Italy so Italian I learn for school and career, not restaurant. English, too, but we speak at home so easier English than Italian but still no good. You excuse I not talk so much tonight as voice tired and need rest."

"That'll be the day," Hank chided.

Carl and Violeta laughed.

"So, Hank, your career really took off right after we graduated from college."

"That was all due to a chance meeting, really an introduction through a friend, of Leonard Bernstein. Of course, I worked hard, and my voice really matured fast, all of a sudden really, but Leonard Bernstein launched my career."

"I don't know if you're being fair to yourself, Hank. You had a marvelous voice in college. It was a highlight of my college years to accompany you."

"If you hadn't been willing to work with me so much, and so often, I would not have advanced so soon and so far and known so much repertoire."

Violeta interrupted with a complete non sequitur. "So, Carl, I want to know about this Francis man."

"Oh, François, he's just the tour director for this group I brought to Italy."

"It look like more. I can tell the vibe he more than tour guide. He very handsome. You watch out for handsome." Violeta pointed and shook a fork at Carl.

"Don't worry, Violeta, in a few days I go home and then I forget François."

"Best you forget François right here."

"Why do you say that?"

"It just feeling I have. I have the feelings."

"I forgot to tell you, Violeta is psychic." Hank reached across the table to pat Violeta's hand.

Violeta gently slapped Hank's hand away, playfully. "Have nothing to do with psychic…although I read palm if you want. But not psychic. What do you think white on finger mean?"

"What do you mean, white on finger?" Carl looked at his fingers, feeling a little puzzled.

Violeta massaged her ring finger that bore an enormous solitaire emerald. "I notice right away white on ring finger on François. I, of course, look for ring. Always I look for ring. I want to know married or no. This one married but not want to show it. But it show. He want to play around with rich American guy."

"No. I don't think that's true."

"I noticed the ring finger, too," Hank said to Violeta, almost as if Carl were not even at the table.

"You be careful not get feelings hurt, Carl. I know the travel type. Home not so much, opportune to fool around much. Singers same way." Violeta wagged her finger looking back and forth at Carl and Hank, scolding.

"Well, so far there hasn't been any fooling around so there's nothing to worry about."

"You mark words. He married. I don't know to man or woman. Usually, I tell but in this case slick. He too slick. Maybe type not matter man or woman. Doesn't matter he married to man, woman, or poodle…"

Carl and Hank burst into laughter, Hank reached out and patted Violeta on the elbow. "Let's change the subject."

They went on talking about musicians they'd worked with, conductors all three had suffered under. Carl became subdued as his abbreviated career left him with less to talk about. As soon as they finished with one course, unprompted Ernesto brought another, and another until they were eating small pieces of cake, mostly chocolate with some sort of liqueur. Carl glanced at his watch and saw it was close to two o'clock. "My group takes off for Assisi first thing in the morning. Jesus, I'd better run. I've got to get up really early."

"Ernesto call you water taxi. He call two taxi and we go back to our hotel and you go to your hotel and I see you at next opera." Just then Ernesto walked up to the table with what looked like the bill and dramatically tore it up in plain view.

"You come to Ernesto any time. Diva is Ernesto guest always."

Violeta grabbed both Ernesto's hands and shook them, "Thank you, Ernesto. You such dear. Violeta get rich and fat if she stay in Venice and not pay Ernesto. I be back October *Aida. Fenice* open with *Aida* next season."

Ernesto pulled his hands away from Violeta and clutched his heart, raised his face toward heaven and uttered, "*Aida*, celeste *Aida*."

"You got it, bub," Violeta practiced her slang and poked Ernesto in his ample gut.

Chapter Thirty-Three

Too Late

Carl took the first water taxi to Marghera then walked the remaining five minutes to his hotel. He found the lobby dead quiet at this late hour and took the elevator up to the suite. A light shone in the living room, but the bedroom appeared dark. Carl entered the bedroom gingerly, not wanting to wake François. François slept soundly, taking up less than half the bed, and turned on his side, faced away from Carl. Carl walked to the side of the bed where one of François's hands dangled off the mattress. He bent down, then kneeled to get a better look at the fingers. François withdrew the hand and turned onto his other side without waking up. Carl looked, but the other hand remained out of sight. Carl slipped out of his clothes and got under the covers, eventually drifting off to an uneasy sleep.

Carl awoke around six o'clock to the sound of François in the shower. The room felt cold. Carl got up slowly, gathered his clothes, and packed his suitcase. François's open suitcase and a backpack already sat next to the door.

François came out of the bathroom fully dressed. "I not want to wake you, so you sleep extra minutes. I go get fast breakfast, check off luggage. You take time." He threw the clothes he carried into the suitcase, squatted on the floor to close it, then stood and kissed Carl on the cheek as if they were some old married couple. "You take time and I see you on bus. Don't worry about kids this morning. You have good opera last night?" he asked as he moved through the living room toward the door.

"Terrific. It was terrific. And what nice people. Did you enjoy dinner at the villa?"

"Villa fine."

An unusually curt answer for the usually verbose François. "No incidents?" Carl asked.

"Only small incident. Really nothing. Helen think she leave cell phone at villa. We almost back to Venice when she think she left cell phone there. So, what we do? We turn around and drive back to villa. Everybody tired and mad at Helen."

"I know where this is going."

"Just as we getting to villa, she find cell phone between seat. It fall her pocket, or she drop it and it go between seat. How you like that? An hour waste for everybody. If I could slap, I would."

"I've felt the same way many times."

"I got to go watch suitcases get on bus. I see you later. You bring suitcase François?" Without waiting for an answer, François opened the door, and with a brief wave to Carl, disappeared.

Out of curiosity Carl walked to François's suitcase and flipped the luggage tag over. 42 Jules Massenet Blvd. 35104 Nuille, France. Carl wrote down the address in his tour book but ignored the suitcase when he left for breakfast.

Carl left the restaurant after most of his clients had finished breakfast with only about ten minutes before the departure time. He went upstairs to use the bathroom one last time and to have a last look for anything left behind. François had apparently come up for his suitcase or else the porters checked the room and took it. The driver finished loading suitcases and they waited for a few stragglers to board the bus. As Carl approached the revolving doors, the manager came running to him clutching an envelope.

"*Dottore*. Before leave you take care this?"

Chapter Thirty-Four

Breakdowns, Nervous And Otherwise

"What's this?" Carl turned to the manager and reluctantly took the envelope.

The label read, Invoice. The envelope contained two copies of an invoice, one requiring a signature and a credit card. The invoice read:

>Room upgrade to Suite (2 nights) Euro 400
>Room service: Euro 120
>Room service (bar): Euro 60
>Room service (bar): Euro 60
>Laundry service: Euro 90
>Total Due upon Departure: Euro 730

"Holy shit! You expect me to pay this?" Without waiting for an answer, Carl looked at the manager. "Wait here a moment, please."

Carl stormed out to the bus where François started climbing aboard after the last of the passengers.

"François. What is this all about?" He handed François a copy of the invoice.

"Oh. You not supposed to see. That mistake. I take care of. Just minute. You get on bus ready to go."

François left the bus while Carl went to his seat and settled down. In a suspiciously short amount of time, not the amount of time it would take to process a credit card at the reception desk, François came back to the bus, instructing the bus driver to step on the gas.

"*Andiamo, Andiamo!*" François said as he prodded the driver in his right shoulder. The driver pulled away as if driving a sports car and the force threw most passengers' heads back into the headrests. Carl looked out his window and saw that the hotel manager, another piece of paper in hand, had come through the revolving door and shook the piece of paper at the retreating bus.

"I think François pulled a fast one," Sally said, sitting across the aisle from Carl because of the day's seat rotation. Carl shrugged his shoulders.

About a half-hour out of Venice, Helen worked her wobbly way up the aisle and stood beside Carl's seat. She stood there as if she couldn't come up with the words to what she had to say. Carl decided to wait.

"I have a problem."

"Yes, Helen?"

"Remember how François said we had to check the safe?"

"Yes, I do…don't tell me."

"My passport. I put my passport in the safe in Venice. But I forgot to check. I left it there."

"Jesus Christ."

"I know. I know. But you know how upset I've been. Getting robbed twice. That's more than anyone should have to take. I'm just not myself. Now what am I going to do? Is there time for the mail to get it to Rome?"

"I don't think we can rely on mail. Let me ask François to turn around. Go back to your seat. We'll deal with it. You're sure it's in the safe? It's not like your cell phone last night?"

"No. I put it in the safe. Olivia saw me do it. You can ask her. We argued about it, and she wouldn't put hers in there."

"Smart girl."

Carl got up and went to François's seat in the front of the bus. He told François the story and François remained entirely stone-faced. Barely grunted in response. No friendly pat on the knee or shoulder. In Italian, François told the driver to take the next exit and turn around.

A quick phone call from François confirmed that a maid had found the passport already and turned it in at the desk. Both François and Carl understandably hesitated to go into the lobby to retrieve it. Luckily,

Olivia volunteered. "I'll go get it," she said and moved toward the door. No one stopped her. She came back out momentarily as the manager did not try to accost a random passenger about the unpaid invoice.

The second attempt to drive to Assisi started smoothly. When it became office hours back at World Tours headquarters in London, Carl called his representative.

"Hey, Shelley."

"Greetings Carl. How is Italy?"

"My people are a pain in the ass, as usual, but the scenery is terrific. Hey, this has never happened to me before, but François, our tour director, upgraded the Venice hotel to a suite for me and him. That's never happened to me before. I thought maybe he knew the management so well he could pull strings, but as I was leaving the hotel this morning, they handed me a bill for more than seven hundred euros."

"Seven hundred euros? Jesus!"

"That's what I said. I called on Jesus, too. I think they charged four hundred for the room for two nights and then all sorts of room service… only some that I knew anything about, but like laundry? I'd never have a hotel do laundry…but I was out a lot…ran into some old friends while François stayed at the hotel."

"Let me see if I can make a few phone calls to our operator in Italy. See if anything showed up. So, you didn't ask for the room, he did?"

"Correct. I had no contact with the management, didn't even order room service. We had the room for three nights and they charged us for two. Maybe the management offered it the first night free? I really don't know. François had to have arranged all of it."

"Well, don't worry about it. Our operator in Italy knows the tour directors and if this François guy's got to pay a bill, he's got to pay it. Just lay low."

"One other thing, Shelley, can you find out about this François guy?"

"What sort of things do you want to find out?"

"Where he lives. No. I know that already, I think. If he's married and to whom. Tours he normally does."

"Why do you want to know things like that, Carl?"

"Well, he's been a little, how would you say, friendly? And I'm trying to figure out if he's on the up and up."

"I understand. That's a no-no. He should know better. I'll see what I can find out. Call you right back."

Maybe fifty or so kilometers later Carl's cell phone rang and it was Shelley.

"Greetings, Carl. Shelley here. I did not find much about François, although he's worked for us on and off for at least three years, steady for a tour director. Anyway, he's got a wife, Lisell Wolf, and they live outside Paris and she also works for us. Cruise director on one of our Rhine River cruises. She's on the *Neptune* right now. Steady work. She just gets home off-season when they're both off during mid-winter."

"That's interesting, Shelley. It was a little hard to figure him out, but I think I got it now. Is his last name Wolf, too? That would be appropriate."

"No. He goes by the last name Duperie. But don't worry about the seven hundred euros. Either the hotel will eat it, or they will get François's information from us if they ask. They won't get any information on you from our Italian operator, and if they call here, we'll deny that you had any responsibility for any extras and refer it all back to the tour director. The volume of business we give that hotel, they shouldn't bother us with nonsense like that."

"You're a lifesaver, Shelley. Thank you."

"You're welcome. Thanks for all you do, Carl. Everyone knows you have tough groups to deal with. Famous throughout the industry."

"Gee. Thanks. What a thing to be known for."

A jolting motion disrupted Carl's call, and a mechanical groan sounded as the bus came to a stop on the side of the road.

"Gotta go, Shelley. Something just happened to the bus."

Carl made his way to the front of the bus. Most passengers were sleeping and only a few were aware and concerned about the bus.

"What's going on, François?"

"The bus make problem. Not know until driver check out." In the background came the sound of an engine compartment opening, some clanging, then the compartment slamming shut.

The driver came to the door, ending a conversation on his cell phone, and spoke in rapid fire Italian at both François and Carl. When the driver finished, François turned to Carl. "Vacuum hose bust. It old. New one take two hours from Arezzo. What we want to do?"

"Two hours! That's a long time, especially in the sun like this without the bus running and no air conditioning. It looks like we're within a mile of Assisi...a kilometer? What if we walk the rest of the way? The bus can come get us when it's fixed."

François nodded. "Okay for me. Some have trouble walk. They can stay if want. I give walk tour of Assisi."

"That should work. Look, it seems flat the rest of the way. It shouldn't be too much effort," Carl said.

François got on the microphone and announced the plan. Surprisingly, no one in the group protested. Contrarily, they seemed to be treating it as some sort of adventure.

"*Andiamo*!" François said and they cheerily started leaving the bus.

As the first group of four or five headed out of the bus and up the dusty street, a minivan pulled to the side of the road ahead of the group. The driver popped out, a stringy little wizened, bowlegged man, a farmer, but cleanly dressed, and he motioned for the five to get in his van. He opened the back door and then went around to the other side and opened the front passenger door. A crate containing a few live chickens filled the doorless luggage compartment at the back. The five looked at one another and then back toward Carl. "Go ahead. Take the ride," he said.

"Ask him to leave you right on the other side of bridge," François said, pointing ahead. They no longer hesitated, loaded up the minivan and sped away, leaving a trail of dust.

Another group, including François, started out and only got a hundred yards or so from the bus when a car, a late model upscale Audi, pulled in front of them. A well-dressed woman got out and motioned for them to get in the car. In this case, the group didn't hesitate. Another minivan followed that. Then the original minivan with the chickens came back for more, as did the Audi.

Carl raised his arms to heaven. "There is a God," He looked out on the magnificent green valley, dotted with tall, thin cypress, that spread out to the west of Assisi.

Carl watched as volunteer vehicles picked up each small group until he stood alone at the bus. Only three passengers decided to wait on the bus, Helen, Cory, and Sophia. "You don't have to stay with us. We'll get to see a little of the town when we pick you up," Cory said.

Carl had left the bus, by himself, and had started walking toward Assisi. It was not a flat road, but a gradual incline, really a hill. And it was getting warmer. The sun was at its height in the sky, really the warmest part of the day. No one stopped to pick him up. He shook with anger. He picked up a baseball-sized stone that appeared loose on the low stone wall beside the road and threw it out into the nothingness as hard as he could, letting out a scream, a howl, an animal yelp.

Then he looked out beyond the stone wall. He sat on the stone wall as if overtaken by sudden calm. Italy appeared intensely green this time of year, the hills opening one into another. The air so clean and dry. Below Carl, in the distance, stood beautiful stone farmhouses with their tall, pencil-thin cypress trees. Carl remained for a few minutes enjoying the uninterrupted magnificence. Soon, at a quicker, more energetic pace, Carl began his ascent to Assisi. Huffing and puffing, he finally found the group gathered in the main square in front of the cathedral.

"What took you so long?" Sally asked. "Wasn't so flat, was it?"

"It wasn't so bad," Carl huffed and squinted as a bead of sweat found its way into his eye. François, looking totally at ease, had already dismissed the group.

"We rode in the Audi with that nice lady, I think she was a doctor from what I could understand. I had no idea an Audi could be that nice."

"Rub it in, Sally, rub it in."

Sally and Carl were interrupted by shouts. "He hit me! He hit me!"

Chapter Thirty-Five

Things As They Appear

As Mary lumbered off the square and onto the narrow roadway, a motorist began backing out of a parking space. Wide and short, Mary did not enter the driver's rear view. Oblivious, she walked behind the reversing car. The fender touched her hip, however, in slow motion. The contact startled Mary and she shrieked, or roared, more like a tornado siren back home, so that the whole town came to attention. Mary held her hip and shouted, "He hit me. He hit me." As she realized a crowd gathered, she got even louder. *"He hit me!"*

The motorist, horrified, immediately ceased his backward motion and jumped out of the car. Hands clasped about his head, looking up to heaven, he practically kneeled in front of Mary, moving around her to see where she might be hurt.

Carl arrived just as Mary continued her amplified mantra, "He hit me."

Carl got in her face, shouting so that she could hear him above her own din. "Are you hurt?"

Mary looked in all directions except at Carl. When Carl finally grabbed her shoulders, Mary suddenly became silent, and gave a moment's thought. Her right hand went to her right hip, where apparently, she had been struck. "No…but he did hit me," she said, quietly.

"I think we ought to move out of the street, Mary," Carl cautioned her. He took her by the elbow, like trying to lead a mule, back onto the sidewalk. Mary now walked with an exaggerated and gruesome limp. "Do you think we should try to see a doctor?"

"No. I'm not hurt. I was just scared," Mary offered, a little apologetically, suddenly calmer.

"Maybe you should just sit there." Carl indicated a table at an outdoor café. "I'll buy you a drink."

"Oh, that would be so nice. Can Ida Sue come with me?"

"Sure, you and Ida Sue get whatever you want." Carl left ten euros on Mary's table and headed for a walk on his own around Assisi, not joining François.

The bus, repaired and running quietly, pulled up to the town square exactly on time, when everyone was tired and ready to leave. The passengers loaded aboard, new shopping bags in hand. Sally stopped to put hers in the overhead compartment. Eugenia, the quiet sister, followed her and placed hers behind Sally's.

"I told you not to mess with my things," Sally said.

Everyone seemed tired and on-edge, including Eugenia. The seat rotation ensured that Eugenia always sat behind Sally. Sally and Eugenia exchanged some angry but quiet words before both settled down. The drive down the mountain, toward Rome, occurred without further incident, passing through gorgeous scenery, but most of the passengers slept through it.

At a rest stop, Sally approached Carl. "You know you have some big trouble on this bus."

"Big trouble?" Carl sounded more skeptical than curious. François came and stood beside Carl, sensing a complaint stirring, like a kettle coming to a boil.

"What so the matter?" François asked Sally.

"There is a gun on the bus."

"*Impossibile.*" François intoned exaggeratedly, his arms flung wide in disbelief.

"No. Eugenia told me she had a gun. When I told her not to touch my things because I bought some valuable jewelry I didn't want her to mess with, she said that she bought a gun and that she would shoot me if I didn't shut up. I swear, she told me to shut up."

"Impossibile to buy gun in Italy. Impossibile to bring gun through security in airport."

Carl suppressed a smile.

"I don't think impossible. Suppose she found one of those mafia people and bought it. I'm sure you could if you wanted to. What about that there gun factory? Don't tell me you don't have guns!" Sally insisted.

"No. No mafia. Mafia in movies. Guns in movies. American movies. Not Italy."

Carl cut in. "Listen, folks. I'll go have a talk with Eugenia and resolve this." He went into the rest stop market while François stood with Sally outside. He found Eugenia looking at some leather wallets.

"I knew you'd be looking for me," Eugenia chuckled quietly, without even turning to look at Carl, her two sisters standing by, minding their own business, but listening.

"I just have to ask, that's all."

"No. I don't have a gun. Of course, I don't have a gun. I was just fed up with that bitch. Every time I walk past her seat, it's 'Don't touch my things,' and 'Don't touch the back of my seat, it hurts my back.' I think it's a racial thing. Other people grab the seats when they walk. And she gives them dirty looks, but I'm the only one she says anything to. You can tell she's just a ball of hate. She's like a cat got tar in her fur. And you know how you sometimes grab that edge of the seat to keep your balance when you walk down the aisle? That's all it was. I try real hard not to do it. I didn't even put my stuff near hers in the overhead and she still says, 'Don't go near my stuff.' I've had it. I thought I'd get her to keep her big trap shut if I scared her a little. Make her think I was about to shoot her. I had no idea she'd take it that seriously."

"You know these people, Eugenia. They are very literal. I'm not trying to claim she's not a bigot. There's a limit to what I can do about that. The other problem is there's not much sense of humor around here. She had no idea you were yanking her chain. She's entirely unaware she has a chain. I'm just going to let it go. Maybe she'll be on edge the rest of the trip and leave everybody alone. One can always hope for peace."

"And some just needs their asses kicked," Mahalia, nearby, added.

Chapter Thirty-Six

Getting Over Oneself

Back at the Cielo Borgia Hotel in Rome, it felt like coming home for the last night of the tour. The homestretch. Carl took up his usual position to observe the check-in process and after handing out all the keys, François came to Carl, not with his usual smile, but more matter-of-factly.

"You have room to yourself tonight. I have new group arrived today. I have to meet at their hotel to orient. I stay there tonight so I not see you after dinner."

Carl's smile dimmed. He kept eye contact with François, but eventually looked away, tears welling up in his eyes. Carl took a deep breath and let it out slowly.

"I take you to dinner then leave. I leave you in charge." François sounded cold, not applying his usual seduction.

Before Carl could react, Ruth Ann pushed her way between Carl and François and waved an envelope and a credit card in front of Carl's face, practically brushing his nose with it. Carl stretched his neck back, like a stork, to prevent getting his eyes poked out. "I got it! I got it! I knew it would show up."

As Ruth Ann calmed down and stopped flailing her hands, Carl noticed something strange about the envelope. He caught it in her hands and turned it so that he could read it.

"Ruth Ann. This wasn't forwarded from Venice."

"What do you mean?" She looked annoyed and pulled the envelope back.

"It has a return address from back home, and the address hasn't been forwarded. It was sent to Rome all along. I thought we agreed that you would have it sent to the Venice hotel?"

"Venice. Rome. What's the difference? I got confused. No. I told them this address." She pointed to the Rome address on the envelope.

"And you drove us crazy for days looking for this thing in every other city?"

"'Cause I couldn't remember what hotel I had it sent to. It doesn't matter. I got it now. I still have a few hours for shopping."

Carl turned to François, who watched the exchange, looking relieved to have had a momentary distraction from an encounter with Carl, and also looking relieved that this group was coming to an end. "That's fine about tonight, François. I understand that you've got to get with the new group. Thank you for all you did."

François put his arm around Carl and walked him to a quiet corner of the lobby. "You think, Carl, sometimes the expectation better than the reality?"

Carl looked at him a little watery-eyed and didn't say anything.

"I no say so good. I mean anticipation better than the real. You look forward to love François and François look to love Carl but think about. Where it go? It be less dear if happened. Now, memory of time together, walk and sit together, lovely lunches. Best thing we do."

"I guess so. It was the best we could do. Circumstances and all."

"So, we have what we have and it lovely, no?"

"Yes," Carl said, choking back a sob, like a child, with no control of his disappointment. "I think I'm coming down with a cold."

François reached in his pocket and handed Carl a tissue. "Problem for everybody want more. Sometimes is no more. But if believe little be enough then everyone happy. Can you be happy?" François reached for Carl's elbow.

Carl remained silent for what must have been a whole minute, taking the tissue he got from François to dry his eyes. "Maybe I can be happy. I'll have to think about it." He looked anything but happy.

"I think part of you problem you think too much. You think about everything like everything have future. Then no time for now. Reality there no future for Carl with François. There only now. Now become past very soon. Then a memory. Take good memory. I enjoy you. I hope you enjoy François."

"Yes, François. I understand. I fell for you. I have to reframe my feelings toward you."

"You call whatever, but you make into another thinking instead of a feeling."

"You're right, François. I'll try."

"You no try. That problem. You just be."

"Okay. I need some time to myself." Carl wandered off toward the elevator.

Carl went to his room and paced back and forth. He stopped pacing. He rummaged through his suitcase and pulled out the World Tours directory. "What was it…Greek god? Pluto…no Neptune…something watery. Here it is. Rhine River cruises, that's correct." He continued reading. "For all mail and packages use land address: World Tours – *Neptune*, Ringstrasse 11, 66957 Schweix, Germany." He continued talking to himself. "And what was her name…Lisell. Different last name. Name for François. Of course. Wolf. Should have been François's last name. Lisell Wolf."

Carl slowly walked to the desk in the hotel room, opened the drawer and extracted an envelope and placed it on the writing surface. He sat down and looked at the blank envelope. He picked up a pen, hesitated, then began writing.

Lisell Wolf c/o

Then he stopped to think.

Carl completed the address and stared at the envelope:

Lisell Wolf c/o

World Tours – *Neptune*

Ringstrasse 11

66957 Schweix, Germany

He took the invoice out of his pocket and wrote across the top, "François: Thanks for a lovely, romantic time in Venice. But I'd get checked for a social disease if I were you. You're the best! XXX"

He folded the invoice and shoved it into the envelope. He went to the registration desk to buy a stamp. The registration clerk put out his hand to accept the envelope for the mail. Carl looked at it, shook his head. "Do you have any medicine for a sore throat?"

The clerk handed him a small box of pills, probably aspirin. Carl put the box in his pocket, tore the envelope in half, and dropped it into the waste basket next to the registration desk. The clerk shrugged his shoulders and turned back to his work.

Not far from the hotel, a restaurant served the tour's final meal together. François said his goodbyes before the dinner and collected envelopes from almost all the passengers, as collecting the prescribed tip constituted the most important event of the tour for a tour director.

"I leave you now, Carl." François approached Carl with outstretched arms. Carl stiffened his shoulders and stepped back but François grabbed him in a tight hug. "You ask for me next tour? Not matter where. Mostly Italy but can do others." He whispered directly into Carl's ear. "Then we continue where we left."

Carl blushed. "Sure, François," Carl said, pushing François away.

"You feel better now? You now enjoy tour?"

"I guess you started to mean more…" Carl choked on his sore throat.

"I think *Dottore* not so happy. The friendship better than the other thing. Have affair messy, have friendship good forever. Remember to appreciate. Not expect. That's why I say come back to Italy and I show you more good time. Next time you remember you bring artist and author. They here already, I think. You just look for them. Bring big group like this and I think I give you happy time."

"Sure, François. Anyway, I better get on the bus. They're waiting. Everyone wants an early night. They have to pack for the trip home. I don't want to be the one everyone is waiting for."

When they returned from the restaurant, Carl waited in the lobby until the last of the passengers took elevators to their rooms. As the last group disappeared, Nora appeared at Carl's side.

"Ann is really sick. I'm not sure what's wrong. She seems very confused. I mean more confused than usual."

Chapter Thirty-Seven

Getting Over Everything

"It doesn't sound like the flu, does it?"

"No. I don't think she has a fever, but she's very dizzy. She could hardly get on and off the bus today. It's been getting worse all week."

"Let's go up and see what's wrong," Carl suggested.

"I just wish we could have gotten home before something like this happened," Nora Sue added.

Ann sat on her bed, staring out into space.

"Ann, I brought Carl up to see you," Nora said. "Maybe he'll know if you need a doctor."

"I don't need a doctor. I've got to figure out what pills to take," Ann said, suddenly animated.

Carl wrinkled his brow. "What do you mean, Ann? Don't you take whatever the prescription says on the bottle?"

"I didn't want to take all those bottles with me, so I just emptied all the pills into this box." She showed Carl a small plastic box full to the brim of different-colored pills. "I thought I could remember what each one was and how often I was supposed to take it, but I think I forgot. I've been doing my best all week."

"Jesus. That was not a good idea, Ann."

"Well, I know that, now that I feel sick, but for a few days I felt fine."

"Maybe the hotel's doctor could figure this out. Let me take them down to the reception desk and see if there's a doctor on call."

"Well, okay. I guess I shouldn't take any more anyway. I wish I could be sure which are my blood pressure pills."

"Let's see if a doctor can sort them."

"Okay."

Carl went down to the front desk and found that the hotel's on-call doctor was due to check in around nine o'clock. Carl left the box of pills with a note about sorting them out. He left a second note asking for some antihistamines for his growing sore throat. He came back down to the registration desk at ten o'clock and found the box entirely sorted into small envelopes with names and instructions on each. Like a miracle. The clerk also handed him a vial of pink antihistamines for his worsening sore throat. He brought the pills back to Ann. "Please leave them in the envelopes and take them only as the doctor instructed." Carl went up to his room, hoping to get at least a few hours' sleep before leaving for the airport.

• • • •

A different bus and driver waited for the group at four o'clock the next morning. The cheapest flights, those normally purchased by World Tours, were the early morning flights. To get to the airport three hours in advance, which made no sense at all, World Tours insisted on a four o'clock departure from the hotel. The hotel restaurant did not open until six o'clock, so these early morning travelers went to the airport without their customary barn-buster breakfasts with bacon. Instead, boxed breakfasts awaited the departing, including a sandwich, fruit, yogurt, and orange juice. The passengers carried their boxes onto the bus, one more package to carry. Sophia arrived with her extra suitcase, probably full of junk, and the hold of the bus had to be reopened and reshuffled to accommodate it.

When Carl saw the luggage compartment already loaded, he panicked. He didn't recognize the driver.

He approached the driver. "Did someone check off the suitcases against the passenger list?"

The driver shrugged his shoulders and Carl walked away, shaking his head.

They arrived at the airport at four thirty with all the ticketing and baggage counters still closed. Even the snack bars didn't open until five thirty.

Sally used the opportunity to complain. "World Tours shouldn't have made us come this early. Why did you make us come this early? Check-in doesn't start until five thirty. Even the entry doors don't open until five o'clock, and no place to sit outside, in front of the terminal."

"They're not my rules. At least it's not cold. Not that cold anyway. And you'll be sitting for a long time today. The snack bars open at five thirty. World Tours says to arrive three hours in advance. The airlines say three hours also."

"What idiots. I can see early, but not in the middle of the night."

"There's not even any place to sit down," Helen complained, ironically seated on the perch of her walker.

When security guards came and unlocked the terminal doors, no porters appeared, and only a few luggage carriages stood on the sidewalk. A euro had to be inserted in a slot before separating a carriage from its security chain. Some of Carl's passengers paid for a carriage but others just relied on the wheels of their suitcases to cross the lobby. Mahalia, with her refrigerator suitcase, stopped halfway across the lobby, dropped the handle and the monstrosity crashed to the floor. Mahalia had tears in her eyes, but they were tears of anger. Her sisters stopped to watch.

"I am so sick of this thang. Ah never say it, forgive me Lord, but this goddamn thang. I thought we weren't going to have to carry luggage on this trip." She tore the zipper around and opened the top. "Does anybody want some books?" She lifted at least five encyclopedia-size hard-covered books from the mess. "Here. I'll just leave them here. What about shoes? Almost new shoes? Anybody want shoes? I'll leave them here, too."

"Mahalia. We're almost there. You won't have to pull it much more," Carl suggested. "Why don't you take your stuff?"

"No. I have to get through New Orleans and I'm not carrying this goddamn, Lord forgive me, stuff anymore. Who needs this shit." She threw out handfuls of clothes that included balled up underwear of questionable cleanliness, dresses, and the remaining shoes. When satisfied that she had only a few packages purchased on the tour and a cosmetic bag, she closed the suitcase and resumed her sojourn across the lobby to the check-in desk, leaving behind a pyramid of debris almost dead-center in the middle of the departure lobby. Anyone who approached the pile was deterred from picking through it by the offensive line of private garments that surrounded the pile like a minefield.

Crowds started to gather at the ticket counters, so Carl moved his group along toward the check-in area. Americans, British, and most Europeans, all have a sense of the queue. They form lines. They maintain order. Not in Italy and most Latin countries. They form crowds. They huddle. People push to the front. It's cheating but thought of here as survival of the fittest. Might makes right. Carl tried to keep his group together and stayed in front, trying to prevent outsiders from cutting ahead. Finally, he got to the counter. "Can you check my whole group? I have forty-five people going to the same place. To New Orleans."

"They wait in line like everybody else," the aged bimbo said without looking up at Carl. Carl raised his hand so everyone could see which counter he used. Some deflected to other counters, but that didn't matter at this point. It was only a matter of time before the crowd disappeared, like sludge eventually going down a clogged drain. Halfway through, Mahalia sidled up to Carl as he watched each passenger check in.

"It's Victor. You need to come and help Victor," Mahalia said, pulling Carl by the arm.

Chapter Thirty-Eight

Homeward Bound

Carl noticed that the few of his passengers who remained to check in did not include Sally so he felt safe moving on to see about Victor. By the time Carl worked his way down the line of check-in counters, only the three sisters waited where Victor had been.

"What went wrong?" Carl asked the huddling sisters.

"It's Victor. He didn't have his passport. Or the wrong passport, or something like that. We couldn't understand the I-talian and neither could Victor. They took him to some office just there," Mahalia said, pointing to a wall of offices perpendicular to the check-in lines.

"Did you see which office?"

"I think it was the one almost in the middle."

Carl broke away and started walking toward the bank of offices. Then he diverted. Carl avoided the office that may have contained Victor and headed to security. The delay at the registration desk allowed all his clients to pass through security ahead of Carl so that he had no other messes to straighten out. He coughed and cleared his throat. His nose started to run.

Carl accounted for all his passengers at the gate, except Victor. The entire check-in process, as usual, only accounted for one hour of the three-hour airline-recommended wait time. The next hour and a half of waiting seemed interminable. With just a half-hour to go before boarding, a motorized conveyance pulled up to the gate, driven by a uniformed security agent, bearing Victor, alone, like a dignitary, a potentate. A crowd of Carl's passengers, for some reason particularly women, surrounded Victor like a rock star. The crowd parted as Victor edged his way toward Carl.

"You would have left me there, wouldn't you!" Red-faced and sweaty, mouth open to reveal dark spaces of missing teeth between veritable yellow tusks, Victor growled at Carl, like a senescent wolf. Everyone became aware of an enormously foul smell emanating from Victor. Carl took a step back.

"For one thing, I didn't know where you went. And another thing, I'm not responsible for your passport. You are supposed to be an adult."

Victor advanced upon Carl who put his hand on his stomach, preventing himself from retching. "I will never travel with you again!" Victor hissed.

Carl recoiled, then shrugged his shoulders. "You aren't allowed to travel with me ever again, so we're even. You're on the blacklist. Congratulations."

Victor let out a final caustic huff and moved toward the boarding line. Most of Carl's passengers, and even others, had gathered around expecting the confrontation to become physical, a last bit of entertainment before boarding the flight. As the spectators diffused, most people headed toward the boarding line.

Carl found his aisle seat. The two passengers next to him were complete strangers who he would not have to engage in conversation except for a polite greeting. Just as he leaned his head back against the seatback, a spike settled, sharp end first, into the top of his head. He jerked forward then turned around. Briana leaned from the seat behind him and poked her bird-of-prey style talons that she had instead of fingernails into Carl's scalp. Her dubious black hair wobbled precariously on top of her head.

"Hey there! This will be fun! Imagine my luck getting to sit right behind you," Briana squealed, bouncing up and down like a child and flashing the sharpened claws toward Carl.

"Jesus," Carl whispered, but his eyes widened in fright as he ducked the potential slashing. "Imagine my luck, Briana. Try to relax and not get too excited. I just want some food and then I'm going to sleep."

Airlines serve meals on a schedule that makes no sense in the real world. About two hours after the flight took off, the crew served lunch, even at nine o'clock in the morning. Then an hour before landing, even at five o'clock in the afternoon, they served breakfast. Airline time worked like that.

Chicken, beef, or vegetarian pasta made up the choices. Sitting only halfway back in the economy section meant that all three choices should still be available when the rolling food cart approached Carl.

Carl struggled to sit still while the passengers in front of him ordered and receive their food before him. Carl had, hours ago, devoured every scrap of his box breakfast from the hotel. The flight attendant was finally only one row away.

The lady in front of him wanted to know how they cooked the beef. She acted as though she was in a three-star Michelin restaurant. The flight attendant, clearly not having any contact with the chef, stalled. She said it looked like some type of gravy, brown, she thought. Do they use onions? She thought not but couldn't swear by it. Do they use onions in the chicken? She couldn't be sure. Were there nuts on anything? She couldn't be sure but probably not as nuts have been banished from most flights, even more totally so than guns and shoe bombs. The flight attendant suggested that maybe there would be an extra vegan meal or kosher meal available. No, that wouldn't be substantial enough. "Would you check what that vegan meal is, anyway, even if I don't want it?"

"Certainly." The flight attendant disappeared toward the front of the plane. That killed another five minutes during which the serving stalled.

"The vegan is a salad with grains."

"That sounds awful, I think I'll choose the beef."

Finally, it became Carl's row's turn to order. Here the issue was the side dishes.

His neighbor asked, "Is bread served with that?"

"All the meals have a dinner roll."

"What is the vegetable?"

"Broccoli."

"I hate broccoli. What does the chicken come with?"

"Green beans."

"Could the green beans be substituted for the broccoli in the beef dish?"

"No. They are all sealed in plastic. There can't be any substitutions. So sorry. But how about a free glass of wine as compensation?"

"Oh yes. Definitely free wine. Is it red or white? Oh, either? I guess it will depend then on whether I have chicken or beef. I don't think you ever told me about the side dishes for the pasta."

"Just get any fucking thing and eat it," Carl said under his breath. "I'm dying here." He squirmed in his seat from hunger, irritation, and his sore throat. The two passengers next to him alone had taken a half hour of the flight attendant's time. Everyone except Carl seemed complacent about the delay. Carl was the only one who appeared visibly annoyed. He turned his head to see Briana, fully attentive, taking in every word of the food discussion as if she found it entertaining. Why did not a noisy riot brew? Why was Carl the only one who appeared irritated? Everyone else seemed mesmerized by their LED screen with earphones nullifying, like laughing gas, any dissonant process that might occur in their brains. The flight attendant had completed serving the passengers on the other side of the aisle and asked for the cart to move farther down. Carl's flight attendant accommodated her by pushing the cart at least five rows back. Then she came back and started with Briana. Carl turned and exploded.

"You skipped me." Carl's voice came out rasping and hoarse from his cold.

"Why didn't you say something when it was your turn?"

Carl was speechless.

"If you didn't order when you were supposed to, you'll have to wait until we're done and have what's left over."

"Lady, unless you want that cart spilled on the floor and your head stuck out a window, you'll hand me a pasta."

"We're all out of pasta, "she said, professionally ignoring Carl's hostility.

"Give me chicken, give me beef. I'll eat anything. You have taken so goddamn long that now I'm starving to death."

"Using profanity is going to get you nowhere. Don't make me call the purser."

"Please, lady. Please. Just any food. Please. I'm dying here," Carl rasped.

The flight attendant handed him a package that turned out to be pasta. "Go figure," Carl said to no one in particular.

Carl ate his tiny meal, trying to prevent the sloshing of contents onto himself when he ripped open the stubborn individual plastic wrappings on everything. The narrow plastic containers sat precariously on the miniature plastic tray and in his haste, Carl had torn off all the plastic wrappings without first excavating the flimsy plastic eating utensils from underneath the "food." The napkin was the first essential, to dry his running nose. Salad spilling onto pasta made the extraction of a napkin difficult, and an unlikely-shaped round dinner roll tried to escape the tray altogether.

Carl decided to eat one course at a time, bringing the plastic container near to his mouth before shoveling in the contents, as the distance a fork had to travel from the tray table to mouth, on an airline flight, became somehow much greater and fraught with potential mishap than a similar distance while seated on earth. The lack of gravity or some other phenomenon of advanced physics made the plastic forks and knives so brittle that they shattered if one speared food with too much gusto. Carl found it much more expeditious to slide the food off the plastic container directly into his gaping mouth, like sweeping it into a dustpan with a relatively tiny, four-inch opening. Not likely everything will go in. One had to be gentle when one wanted food so desperately.

Since Carl started his lunch late, his seatmates finished earlier and signaled they needed their restroom break. Carl started to ignore them and then tried to get up, bearing all the eating paraphernalia in both hands before realizing he remained strapped into his seat. He put down the lunch items, unbuckled, and stood again, only to the onslaught of a drinks cart approaching his seat.

"Now you've done it," his seat partner scolded. "Now the aisle will be blocked for a half hour, and I have to go now."

Carl sat back down and turned around to look toward the back of the plane. Briana stared at him. She leaned forward enthusiastically. "You need something? You want me to get something for you?"

Carl ignored her and turned to his seatmate. "You can head to the back of the plane. There's nothing blocking your way in that direction." Carl clutched his debris and once again stood up into the aisle. A few plastic containers defied the miniscule gravity that existed during a flight, left the tray, and landed on the floor. Once the two passengers left for the bathroom, he retrieved whatever had not rolled back under the seat, or who knows where, into those far mysterious recesses of aircraft.

Carl took both an antihistamine he'd gotten from the hotel doctor and a mild sleeping pill that he kept in his carry-on luggage.

Hours later, Carl woke to a smiling flight attendant waving a breakfast pizza in front of his face. He accepted it enthusiastically. After breakfast, Carl got up and looked for the purser to make sure his two wheelchairs, or some sort of assistance, was available for Cory and Helen, who always required help. As usual, the crew said his clients should wait until the plane emptied of passengers and the jetway cleared before disembarking. He decided to wait with Cory and Helen to make sure it went without a hitch.

Sure enough, at Louis Armstrong Airport, two wheelchairs waited in the jetway, but no attendants in sight. Cory and Helen took their seats in the wheelchairs.

"I'll go up to the desk and see if they can call for attendants," Carl said.

"You better hurry up. We have a bus to Jackson to catch."

"Don't worry. We can't leave without you."

The counter had a line in front, but Carl noticed a security officer standing near the edge of the gate waiting area.

"Excuse me, ma'am, I ordered two wheelchairs for two of my clients on this flight, and the wheelchairs are there but no attendant. Can you call for two attendants?"

"You can see we're busy. This is the afternoon rush hour and we're short-staffed today. I'll call, but I can't promise anything. You might have to do it yourself."

"Myself? But there's two of them!"

"The attendants handle two at a time. Some of the good, experienced attendants do three."

"Thanks. But I'd appreciate your trying to get us some help here."

Carl headed back to the jetway. One of the airline officials tending the counter reached with an arm and stopped him. "You can't enter the jetway once the aircraft has unloaded, sir. Wait until we call your flight."

"I was on that flight. I left two wheelchair clients down there. I've got to get them."

"Sorry, sir, but you'll have to wait for an attendant. I can call one for you."

"I'll need two."

"One attendant can handle two wheelchairs, sir."

As soon as she turned to pick up the phone, Carl charged into the jetway. He found Cory and Helen nodding off, apparently unconcerned about their abandonment. "I can't find an attendant. We'll have to get out of here on our own."

"Well, you should have made arrangements in advance," Cory scolded.

"I did. How do you think the wheelchairs got here?"

"I guess you forgot the other part of the instructions, about somebody to push them. I guess you can do it. It's not rocket science."

Carl roughly took the handles of Cory's wheelchair and started up the jetway. He pushed her to the top of the jetway and gave the wheelchair a great shove out into the waiting area, staying out of sight of that airline official who told him he couldn't enter the jetway. Cory looked as if she'd somehow been forcefully ejected from the jetway like a human cannonball in the circus. People jumped out of her way. She ended up beside the check-in counter and Carl quickly retreated to retrieve Helen. Once the two wheelchairs were in the waiting area, completely ignored by the airline official who supposedly called for help, Carl prepared himself for the ordeal of getting through the airport.

"The attendants push two wheelchairs at a time, I'll have to do that too, I guess," he said to Cory and Helen.

"What are you going to do with our carry-ons? You can't just leave them," Cory complained.

"Okay, Cory, yours is small so you hold it in your lap. Helen, yours has wheels so I'll drag it with my spare hand."

Carl aligned a handle of each wheelchair at the center so that he could grab them with one hand. He slipped his carry-on, a backpack, on his back. He pushed and met with tremendous resistance. He found the levers to release the brakes. Pushed again. Some movement but he felt tremendous resistance from Cory's side. He walked around to the front. "Cory, will you put your goddamn feet up on the footrests instead of dragging them on the floor."

"Don't talk to me that way."

"Okay, dear. Please put your lovely petite feet on the footrests so we can move! Is that nice enough?"

"You sure have some rough edges. Okay. What are you waiting for? Let's go."

Carl pushed the two wheelchairs out into the main aisle of the terminal, nearly broadsiding countless passengers. Two wheelchairs put together didn't steer so well. He had to go left. He stopped and separately turned each wheelchair to the left, then put them together, and started off. Suddenly he sneezed. He had to stop. No tissue. Abandoning the two wheelchairs in the center of the passage, Carl ran to the nearest restroom, covering his besnotted face with his hands. He grabbed almost an entire role of toilet paper and returned to the wheelchairs that diverted pedestrian traffic like boulders in a fast-flowing river. He started off again. He may have run across a few toes, possibly a small yapping dog, collided with a baby carriage, various unattended children, and had to correct course just before running into several more gate waiting areas. There were altogether three trajectory corrections before reaching the elevator bank with its moderately long line. When his turn came for an elevator, he pushed Cory's wheelchair in first, relieved her of her carry-on case that he set down on the floor next to her, then stepped out to get Helen. Immediately the elevator door shut behind him. "You idiot… what am I supposed—," Cory shouted. The voice faded as the elevator descended.

The elevator reappeared empty. He entered the elevator with Helen. After descending, the door opened to a hallway sans Cory. The elevator stopped on no other floors. He strained his eyes farther down the hall and saw a security guard pushing Cory.

"Cory. Cory," he yelled in what had become a hoarse, painful-sounding voice. The security guard turned to see about the disturbance. "Stop," Carl shouted as he rushed forward with Helen, dragging the carry-on, which refused to stay on its wheels at this speed and flopped around behind him, hitting him in the heel of his foot and almost tripping him. His nose ran like a faucet, but he couldn't stop to staunch it.

"Cory. Did you plan to just take off and leave me looking for you?"

"Well, this nice man asked me if I needed help, and to be completely honest, yes, I did need help, so I let him help me."

"That's terrific. Can you take us to passport control?" Carl addressed the middle-aged, uniformed security guard.

"I can take you to the entrance, but you'll have to take over in the line. I can't wait in the line. You'll have to get a wheelchair attendant for that."

"Forget it. Just get us that far and I'll take them again."

"You sure you're up to it, bud?" The security guard looked up and down at the sweating, disheveled, red-nosed, bleary-eyed Carl. "Looks like you was rid hard and put away wet."

"Thank you. Do you mind if we go now? I have forty-three passengers ahead of us in a group."

"Anything you say, pal."

Carl had a much easier time pushing only one wheelchair and pulling one suitcase. They got within distant sight of the entrance to passport control, moving alongside the entrances to restrooms, when Cory raised and waved her hand. "I have to go."

"Can't you wait until we get through passport control?"

"No. I better go now. There's probably a line at passports."

The security guard wheeled Cory to the entrance of the women's room, and Cory got up with little difficulty and walked in.

"Does she really need a wheelchair?" the security guard asked.

Carl just shrugged his shoulders.

Cory came out ten long minutes later, resettled herself, her oversized purse, and her carry-on in her lap. "Okay. Let's go. What are you waiting for?"

As they approached passport control, a line blossomed, it weaved, it wrapped all the way around a gymnasium-sized room. To the left, travelers stood in front of any one of dozens of computer kiosks, the modern passport control where a computer created a customs declaration, complete with photograph. The line moved with glacial speed. By now, all Carl's clients had cleared the declaration area and stood on the switchback line waiting to hand the declaration to a customs official.

Just as he parked Helen's wheelchair and accepted responsibility for Cory's wheelchair from the surly security officer, Carl told Cory to offer the officer a dollar tip. Cory reached for his arm, sounding panicked. "My passport. I left my passport on the counter. We have to go back."

Chapter Thirty-Nine

Inadvertance And Inexcusable Neglect

"What are you talking about?"

"My passport. I left it on the counter in the ladies' restroom. I'm sorry, but I know that's where I left it."

Carl visibly lost it. His hands shot up as if to crush his skull. He turned a deep shade of crimson. He rasped out through his sore throat. "Why, for fuck's sake, would you take your passport out in the ladies' restroom and put it on the counter? I can't imagine what in goddamn hell you were thinking!"

Cory recoiled from Carl who looked positively atomically explosive.

"I guess I wanted to look at it and make sure it was okay and then one of the stalls opened up and I had to take it in a hurry or lose my place and I just put it down."

"Jesus Christ. Helen, you'll just have to wait here." He turned to Cory. "I don't think there's any chance your passport is going to be just sitting on the counter in the ladies' room now…what…a half-hour later, but I guess we have to look. Then we'll just have to find some authority to bring you to. I can't be responsible for this. I've got to get the other forty-four people home."

"I know. I know. I'm sorry. It won't happen again…"

Carl turned Cory and her wheelchair around and started back toward the restroom with as much speed as he could muster going against the tide of new arrivals—groups, and clumps of travelers, towing unwieldy suitcases, baby strollers, dogs on long, hazardous leashes, and other wheelchaired passengers—all moving in the opposite direction. Progress was painfully slow. He reached the restroom and practically dumped Cory out.

"Go in and have a look. Quick."

Cory got up and, leaning on the walls for support, made her way awkwardly into the rest room, suddenly in touch with her mobility issues. Carl sat in the wheelchair to catch his breath. A couple of moments later she came out, chipper, not holding on to the wall, clutching the passport with both hands. "See. It was exactly where I said it would be. Nobody touched it."

"It's like a miracle, Cory. Now we're going to have to find out how to make you into a saint."

Helen waited in her wheelchair just before the kiosk area, and a few of Carl's clients still remained in the switchback customs line and final security check before they could enter the unsecured part of the airport. Carl, Cory, and Helen moved forward and upon entering the metal detector and security checkpoint, they found Victor, Owen, and a few of the ladies waiting on the line. Victor seemed to be holding up the works.

"Victor was traveling with an expired passport," Sophia said to Carl. "That there's why it took so long getting his customs declaration. They finally decided to let him through to security."

"Victor, you have to take your shoes off," Sophia instructed Victor.

Victor bent down to loosen a shoe. The smell that emanated seemed to have color and substance, like the mustard gas used in World War One, which would have smelled like roses compared to this. Like mustard gas, it could be seen coming out in a green fog. Carl saw Sophia and the other ladies involuntarily lean away and practically topple with the onslaught. Carl stepped back. Even with his stuffed-up nose, he recoiled. Worse than rotting filth. Indescribable.

The security agent slipped on a mask. They seemed to be prepared for such an event, although this case must have been extraordinary. "Your passport, sir," the muffled security agent said, as he stretched an arm full length to take the expired passport without getting any closer to Victor than necessary.

"You were traveling with an expired passport, sir. You need to wait in that room, the glass room, first door on the right. You will claim your luggage here and go through a customs inspection while we verify your nationality."

"You can't do that to me. I'm an American citizen. I'm a veteran. I fought for this country. I have freedom. You better let me go. I'm an American citizen. I have my rights."

"Welcome home, sir. You'll have your rights, right in that room there. Now, please do as you're told, or we will have to temporarily incarcerate you."

"Shit. That's what this is. It's all bullshit."

Two armed security guards came up on either side of Victor and ushered him to the glass cubicle with his backpack that bulged conspicuously. Once the guards secured Victor in the room, one guard made a hand in mouth gagging gesture to the other and both shivered. Carl passed through security, left Victor, and headed for the baggage claim area.

Since landing, several hours had passed. After collecting their luggage from a carousel, the group moved toward the terminal exit, where, presumably, the bus waited. Carl called a number for the driver who had long since gone to a parking area, as his time in front of the terminal had expired an hour ago. Drivers did not always wait this long.

Most of the group gathered around Carl. "Everyone go out through door six and our bus should be at the curb to your right. Remember Gulf Shores Transportation Company. Gulf Shores. Remember that. Don't get on the wrong bus. No matter what you do. Don't get on the wrong bus."

As the throng moved toward door six, Briana came running up to Carl. "My suitcase. It's missing. I looked everywhere. It's missing."

Chapter Forty

More Inexcusable Neglect

"Okay, Briana. I'll help you look for it and then if we have to, we'll go make a claim. They usually turn up within a day if they really are missing, and then they bring it right to your house by messenger. It's not so bad."

"But I might never see it again. That could happen. How do you think all those suitcases get to that place in Alabama where they sell lost suitcases?"

"Let's have a look. What color is it?"

"It's red. I picked red because nobody has red. Or not many, anyway, so it's easy to spot."

Carl walked around carousel number five where his group's luggage came in. A few red suitcases rode the carousel, but they were from the next flight that had arrived. All the luggage from their Rome flight had either been moved aside or taken to another area. Just to be sure, Carl looked at anything red on the carousel but saw nothing with Briana's name or a World Tours tag. He did the same for the two carousels on either side of the one they had used. Nothing.

Briana pouted as Carl called the driver.

"It's almost an hour. We got fifteen minutes to load. I'm going to have to take the bus with all these people back to the parking area. Maybe I'll have to get on the interstate and drive around the airport. You're not supposed to have passengers back there in parking. What do you want me to do?" the driver asked.

"I guess you should go to parking anyway and wait. Explain to whoever asks that the tour organizer is looking for lost luggage. If there's a fine or a charge, tell them World Tours will pay it." Carl coughed, losing his voice as his sore throat gradually turned into laryngitis.

"Okay, let's go to lost luggage claim," he croaked like a geriatric frog.

Carl located the lost luggage claims office, adjacent to the carousel area, a small room with a counter just like the ticketing counters, and found the room piled high with yet unclaimed luggage. Carl walked to the counter with Briana in tow, waited his turn behind three other bereft passengers, and then explained his situation to the attendant behind the desk.

"Before you go through the trouble of filling out one of these three-page forms, why don't you look at what's been brought in recently," the attendant counseled.

Briana already started upending suitcases, trying to get to the few red ones. "It's not here," she said, dejectedly.

Carl walked around and noticed a World Tours tag on one of them that Briana had just pushed aside. "What's this red suitcase?" He asked Briana.

The tag read, Mary Maples, Jackson, Mississippi.

"What the hell?" Carl stared, dumfounded. "Mary Maples is one of our passengers. You know her. What is her suitcase doing here?"

"I don't know. I just know it isn't mine. It looks exactly like mine, though," Briana whined.

Carl remained silent for a moment. "I bet I know what happened. You and Mary have the same red suitcases and she picked up yours without looking. That's got to be it. Let's take this and go."

"But what are we going to do about mine? We didn't even fill out the form."

"My guess is yours is already on the bus."

"But…" Briana stared blankly with non-comprehension.

Carl grabbed the suitcase, called the driver, and with almost no voice left, arranged to be met at door six. When the bus drove up, Carl called the driver down.

The corpulent driver, surprisingly nonplussed, greeted them, "You found it. Took long enough. You should have just made her wait and get it delivered if they can't take care of their stuff better than that."

"I have to ask you to do one last thing. We've got to see what name is on the other red suitcase under the bus."

"Jesus. I'm supposed to get y'all home to Jackson. That's it. Nobody said anything about loadin' and unloadin'."

"I realize it's a lot of trouble. Here…" Carl checked his pockets and came up with two twenty-dollar bills. "Here, if you'll just look, I'll give you forty dollars."

The driver opened the first compartment. No red suitcase. He opened the other compartment. No red suitcase.

"I can't open the side facing traffic."

"Just shuffle them around a little. I know one other passenger had a red suitcase. There were two of them."

The driver removed a row of suitcases and exposed, at the end of the second row, a red suitcase with a World Tours tag bearing a passenger name. Carl crawled into the hold and looked.

Briana Deal

"I knew it. It was on the bus all the time. Sorry. Just add this one to it and let's get going." Carl handed the driver Mary's suitcase, the forty dollars, and boarded the bus, heading straight to Mary's seat.

"Mary, hello, I hate to interrupt your conversation."

"What, what's so important? We should be home by now."

"Did you pick up your suitcase from the carousel and bring it to the bus?"

"Of course, I did. What, do you think I want to leave my stuff here? I bought a lot of good stuff in Italy and no thanks to you I almost got run over by that car in A Sissy or wherever that town was."

"Mary. Did you check the luggage tag to make sure it was your suitcase?"

"I don't have to. I have the only red one."

"You should have checked. Briana has a red one, too, and that's the one you brought to the bus. I just spent the last two hours looking for Briana's suitcase and it was already on the bus. Yours was the missing one. You left it at the luggage carousel. We kept everyone waiting all that time because of that mistake."

"Well, tell her she doesn't have to thank me for carrying it for her." Mary turned back to her conversation, and Carl, exhausted, turned to look for an empty seat.

As the bus pulled away from the curb, Carl, looking very unsteady, held onto a seatback. Everyone either slumped, asleep across two seats, or had their packages and carry-on in the seat next to them, as if no one had the energy to use the overhead bin. Not a single spare seat. Even the front, usually reserved for him, was taken by Owen with his backpack. He passed Ruth Ann who, awake, sitting up, lounged, with her left leg across the empty seat next to her.

"Ruth Ann, do you mind if I sit here. There are no free seats on the bus."

"Oh, No. No…my foot is much too sore from all that walking. I've got to keep it elevated."

Chapter Forty-One

Be It Ever So Humble, There's No Place

Carl took a deep breath and held on. He looked about ready to do something violent but moved on. He removed the backpack on the seat next to Owen, looked momentarily at the little room left beside his mule-sized butt, shoved his backpack into the overhead rack, and sat down, all without disturbing Owen's sleep.

The ride to Jackson seemed interminable. He asked the driver to stop at a rest stop about thirty miles from Jackson because for most passengers, the drop-off point in Jackson could still be as far as a half-hour from their homes. Some passengers didn't wake up, some complained vocally about stopping and delaying their return, and a few expressed gratitude because they couldn't have held it much longer.

About fifteen minutes before reaching Jackson, Carl picked up the microphone, which he had to turn to full volume because his voice was essentially, and from the way he held his throat, painfully gone.

"Good evening, folks. I hate to wake you up, but we're about to arrive home and I don't want you to miss it." Not as much as a single chuckle. He crossed his fingers behind his back before continuing. "I really enjoyed having you all along on this tour. We saw some fantastic sights together. A real once-in-a-lifetime experience. Many of you bought a lot of stuff and you have a lot of stuff on this bus. Please make sure, before you get off the bus, that you have everything that belongs to you. Check the overhead. Check under the seats, in the seats, everywhere.

You can't imagine the pile of junk, I mean treasures, that I have at home that no one's claimed. Someday I'm going to bring the stuff on a trip and auction it off for charity. Anyway, check really well, and be careful, and I hope to see you again on the next tour." He uncrossed his fingers.

Carl remained behind to ensure that all passengers collected their luggage, and then made his rounds with the driver, collecting debris left on the bus, which consisted of various sweaters, jackets, umbrellas, a wallet, a cell phone, some sort of listening device, and two shopping bags loaded with what looked like souvenirs. The driver helped Carl carry the stuff out and made a pile next to his suitcase. He thanked the driver and just as he picked up his cell phone to call a cab, his gleaming silver Bentley Arnage, old but venerable, entered the parking lot, circled around, and stopped between Carl, the pile of debris, and the idling bus. Chuck emerged from the driver's door.

"Just thought you should come home in the style you're used to!"

"Oh, Chuck. Did I ever tell you that I love you?" Carl croaked.

"Don't start now. It wouldn't seem genuine under the circumstances." Chuck helped load the crap into the spacious trunk. Carl luxuriated in the soft leather passenger seat, and as Chuck drove off, they heard the news airing through the eight strategically placed speakers of the Bentley's deluxe sound system.

"This in from the New Orleans airport. Five o'clock this evening a Jackson man was arrested at the Louis Armstrong International Airport traveling with an expired passport. He was carrying what is estimated to be more than twelve thousand dollars of stolen gold and jewelry, thirty unopened packages of potato chips and snack foods, an assortment of boxed restaurant food in various states of decay, necessitating calling a biohazard team to remove this Jackson resident and his debris from the airport facility to a Louisiana correctional facility. Authorities are trying to determine how this man, apparently a vagrant, was able to rob so many stores, apparently all across Italy. Bail was set at thirty thousand dollars…" Carl reached and turned off the radio.

"Can you imagine that?" Chuck asked.

"No. It is truly beyond my imagination."

"So, how was the trip? Sounds like you lost your voice?" Chuck reached and affectionately rubbed his knuckles against Carl's cheek. "Don't worry, I have some hot homemade chicken soup waiting for you, fresh sheets on the bed, a warm puppy named Ponce, who, like you, also has a wet nose. So how was the trip, anyway?"

"Oh, you know. The same old thing."

"Oh, come on! You were in Italy for seven days. For sure something exciting must have happened."

"Well, you know, the same old thing. I met this hot Italian, or was he a Frenchman? And had a torrid affair the entire time. He wore me out."

"Carl, you are the best storyteller I know. I can't wait to hear all about it…that's after you kiss Ponce on the dry part of his nose."

ACKNOWLEDGMENTS

Books are collaborative processes. Not only do authors require proofreaders and editors, they require encouragement, inspiration, and the faith of others in their writing.

I could not have had better editing and proofreading than that offered by Flashpoint Publications. My gratitude extends to publisher, Patty Schramm, for having faith in and enthusiasm for my writing, and to Micheala Lynn for her insightful editing and patience with my manuscript.

I offer special thanks to my former grade school classmate and proofreader, Michael Wulff, for his professional scrutiny of my manuscripts and limitless encouragement that keeps me writing.

I feel gratitude toward every Italian tour guide I experienced and the Italian Ministry of tourism for information and the setting of this book.

Going back further, I thank my fifth-grade teacher, for whom no political borders existed and no international animosities discouraged. She saw only delightful diversity in every region of the world and instilled in me a love of geography and travel. Likewise, somewhat later in life, I received encouragement from a graduate school professor who told me I should be going to Hollywood as a writer rather than where I was destined, to the classroom as a teacher.

I am grateful to National Endowment for the Humanities for giving me opportunities to see the world at close range.

My friends, my family, George.

My thanks.

ABOUT THE AUTHOR

Martin P Mayer believes in turning failure into advantage. Thus, he reinvented himself more than any other human being, employed as a musician, teacher, librarian, paralegal, school administrator, house painter, psychologist, chief financial officer, travel consultant, most recently a boulevardier, and always a writer. Having earned doctorates in counseling psychology and school administration from The University of San Francisco, he received two grants from the National Endowment for the Humanities, the second including music studies in East Germany. His humorous travelogues have been published in numerous motoring magazines. Mayer's fiction contains humor mixed with historical research, social conscience, psychological and philosophical insight. Martin P Mayer currently resides, against his will and better judgment, in Montgomery, Alabama.

Bringing rainbow stories to life.

Flashpoint Publications welcomes submissions from writers
of every color and books featuring characters of every color.
In addition, Flashpoint Publications encourages job applicants
of every color whenever a staff position becomes available.
We believe that EVERYONE is entitled to a seat at our table.

www.flashpointpublications.com

www.ingramcontent.com/pod-product-compliance
Lightning Source LLC
Chambersburg PA
CBHW070642100726
47907CB00007B/2075